Ellery Queen Presents
Great Mystery Novellas

Ellery Queen Presents Great Mystery Novellas

Edited by Janet Hutchings

Five Star • Waterville, Maine

First Edition
First Printing: August 2004

Published in 2004 in conjunction with Tekno Books and Ed Gorman.

Set in 11 pt. Plantin.

Printed in the United States on permanent paper.

Library of Congress Cataloging-in-Publication Data

Ellery Queen presents great mystery novellas / edited by Janet Hutchings.—1st ed.
    p. cm.
    "Five Star first edition titles"—T.p. verso.
    Contents: Tell me you forgive me / by Joyce Carol Oates —Blood paths / by Clark Howard—Piranha to Scurfy / by Ruth Rendell—The lost boy / by Robert Barnard—Out there in the darkness / by Ed Gorman.
    ISBN 1-59414-067-7 (hc : alk. paper)
    1. Detective and mystery stories, American. 2. Detective and mystery stories, English. I. Title: Great mystery novellas. II. Queen, Ellery. III. Hutchings, Janet.
PS648.D4E374 2004
813´.087208—dc22   2004046974

Ellery Queen Presents
Great Mystery Novellas

Additional Copyright Information

Table of Contents

Introduction

The so-called "father of the mystery," Edgar Allan Poe, most often wrote to a length modern publishers would call a "novella" or "novelette." Today these long stories—or short novels—have virtually disappeared from the genre. Their scarcity is partly due, of course, to a lack of markets. Hundreds of original mystery short stories are published each year in book form—most in multiple-author anthologies—but few of these collections accept works over 10,000 words. Only the two remaining mystery magazines, *Ellery Queen's Mystery Magazine* and *Alfred Hitchcock's Mystery Magazine*, regularly accept stories in the 10,000- to 20,000-word range.

In other fields, most notably science fiction, the novella and novelette have fared better. Formally defined by the science fiction community in terms of word-length, the novelette, at 7,500 to 17,500 words, and the novella, at 17,500 to 40,000 words, still have many distinguished practitioners: Awards are given yearly in each category at the several science fiction conventions. Mystery fandom's omission of these classifications from its awards is curious, for mystery and crime fiction is ideally suited to this middle length: A mystery, after all, must be short enough to maintain taut suspense but long enough to develop complex and potentially deceptive motivation.

For this rare book of novellas—a term we'll apply to stories of more than 10,000 words—we've selected not miniature whodunits like Poe's first mystery, "The Murders in the Rue Morgue," but tales of dark psychological suspense. There is a haunting quality to all five of our choices, and it derives from the primal relationships each story explores: of parent to child, or of friends and associates bound in the closest fraternity.

The authors of these novellas are virtuosos at any length, but to find them between the covers of a single volume with works complex enough to display the keen insight and deft characterization for which they all are known will, we hope, be a treat for readers.

Janet Hutchings
Ellery Queen's Mystery Magazine

Tell Me You Forgive Me?

Joyce Carol Oates

1.

The Elms ElderCare Center, Yewville, NY. October 16, 2000.

To my Dear Daughter Mary Lynda who I hope will forgive me.

I am writting this because it has been 40 yrs. ago this day, I saw by the calendar, that I sent you down into that place of horror & ugliness. I did not mean to injure you, Darling. I could not foresee. I was an ignorant & blind woman then, a drinker. I know you are well now & recovered for yrs. but I am writting to ask for your forgiveness?

Darling, I know you are smiling & shaking your head as you do. When your Mother worries too much. I know you're saying there is nothing to forgive, Mother!

Maybe that is not so, Darling.

Tho' I am fearful of explaining. & maybe cant find the words to explain, what was so clear 40 yrs. ago & had to be done.

Its strange for me to write this, & to know that when you read it, these words one by one that take me so long to

11

write, I will be "gone." I am asking Billy (the big Jamaican girl with "cornrow" hair) to abide by my wishes & save this letter for you & I believe she will, Billy is one of the few to be trusted here.

If you wanted to speak to me after reading this, tho', you could not. This seems wrong.

You have forgiven me for that terrible time, Mary Lynda, I suppose. You have never blamed me as another daughter might.

No one ever accused me, I think. Not to my face?

(Except your father of course. & all the Donaldsons. I'm sorry, Mary Lynda, you bear that name yourself, I know! But you are more your Mother's daughter than his, everybody has always said how "Mary Lynda" takes after "Elsie." Our eyes & hair & our way of speaking.)

(I think of your father sometimes. Its strange, I did injury to "Dr. Donaldson" also, yet it never worried me. I thought—He is a man, he can take care of himself. I'm not proud that when I was young if I ceased loving a man, or caring for a woman friend, I seemed almost to "forget" them overnight. I'm not proud of this, Darling, but its your Mother's way.)

So many times this past year, since I have been moved to this wing of the Center, tho' its only across the lawn from the other place—I wanted to take your hand, Darling, and tell you the truth in my heart. Not what you have forgiven me for but something more. Something nobody has guessed at, all these years! But I did not, for I feared you would not love me then. That was why I was so quiet sometimes, after the chemo especially. When I was sick, & so tired. Yet to be forgiven, I must confess to you. So I am writting in this way. A coward's way I know, after I am "gone."

There are things you say in quiet you cant say face to

12

face. I am not going to live much longer, and so <u>it is time</u>.

Last year I think it was April, when the Eagle House was razed, & you came to visit & were "not yourself"—upset & crying—I wanted to tell you then, Darling. & explain about Hiram Jones. (Is that a name you remember?) But I saw you needed comfort from your Mother, not "truth." Not just then.

After 40 yrs.! I have not been downtown to see South Main Street since coming to this place. Since my surgery etc. That part of old Yewville was meant to be "renewed"— but the state money gave out, I heard. So there's vacant lots & weeds between buildings, rubble & dust. The Lafayette Hotel & Midland Trust & the library & post office are still there, but the Eagle House is gone, & the rest of that block.

So I try to picture it in my head. Its only 3 miles from here, but I will never see it, I think.

I know its a childish way to think, he is buried beneath rubble. & <u>his bones</u> are in that debris.

"The Elms" is a good place for me, I think. I'm grateful to you, Darling, for helping me to live here. God knows where I would be living with just Medicare & Social Security! I don't complain like the other "oldsters." Tho' I am only 72, the youngest in this cottage. The oldest is that poor thing Mrs. N. you've seen, blind & with no teeth, "deaf & can't hear" etc. Lately they haven't brought Mrs. N. into the sun room even, which is a pity for her, but a relief to us. She is 99 yrs. old & everybody is hoping she will live to 100—except Mrs. N., she has no idea how old she is or even her name. There are 3 or 4 of us who are "progressing" (as the doctors call it, but this means <u>the disease</u> not us!) & those of us who are "just plain old." I am out of my time element here, because I am still young (in my mind) but the body has worn out, I know Darling its sad for you to see me, your Mother who used to be "beautiful" & vain of it.

Now I am vain of you, Darling. My "M.D." daughter I can boast of to these other old women, the ones who are my friends.

I love the pretty straw hat you brought for me to cover my head, & the bluebird scarf.

Are dead people "lonely" I wonder?

I have been writting—writing?—this damn letter for a week & it gets harder. Like trying to see into the darkness when you are in the light. The future when I will be "gone" is strange to me tho' I know its coming. When some other sick woman will have my room here & my bed.

You'd be surprised, we dont talk much of God here. You'd think so, but no. Its hard to believe in a "universe" inside these walls & lasting beyond a few days' time. Do I have a fear of God's judgement for my sins, somebody might ask. No Darling, I do not. Remember your Grandaddy Kenelly who laughed when "God" was spoken of. It was all just b.s. invented to keep weak people in line, Daddy believed.

Hell, God better believe in <u>me</u>. I'm a <u>man</u>, he'd say.

By that Daddy meant that "man" is more important than "God" because it was "man" who invented God, not the other way around.

Only just I wish I had more courage.

Daddy has been dead a long time but to me he's more real than the people in this place. I talk to him & hear his voice in my head. Since 1959! Thank God, Daddy never lived to be an old man here in "The Elms." Imagine your Grandaddy 100 yrs. old, deaf & blind & not knowing his own name or where the hell he is. He was only 55 <u>when</u> he died—thats <u>young</u>. How Time plays tricks on us. My handsome Daddy always older than me, now he'd be younger. When he died, I mean. I don't think of these things if I can.

Billy says I should not pass away with secrets in my heart. So I am trying, Darling.

Is "Hiram Jones" a name you remember, Darling? Maybe I have asked you this already.

However you were told your Grandaddy died, its best to think it was an accident like a roll of the dice. Nothing more.

Wish I could undo the bad thing that happened to you, Darling.

You were only 10 yrs. old. I cant think why I would send you into that terrible place like I did, to see where that terrible man had got to. I was drinking in those days & missing my father & that caused me to forget my duties as a Mother.

Now its a later time. You are a M.D. like "Dr. Donaldson" & so you know about my case, more than I would know myself. Tho' "oncology" is not your field. (I hate that word, its ugly!) But this is why I am not afraid of dying: when I had my surgery & my mind went out, it was OUT. Like a light bulb switched OFF. When I had you, Darling, I was very young & ignorant & believed I was healthy & went into labor not guessing what it would be, 18 hrs. of it, but afterward I "forgot" as they say but I knew what true pain was & would not wish to relive it. But this, when you're OUT, is different. The 3 times I was operated on, each time it was like "Elsie Kenelly" ceased to exist.

So if you're dead and theres no pain you cease to exist. If theres no pain theres nothing to fear.

Darling, I am a coward I guess. Too fearful of telling you what I have wished to, to beg your forgiveness. I'm sorry.

But in this envelope I am leaving a surprise for you. These ivory dice, remember? From your Grandaddy you didn't know too well. These dice he'd keep in his pocket & take out & roll "to see what they have to tell me"—he'd say. They were Daddy's Good Luck Dice he'd got in Okinowa— Okinawa?—that island in the Pacific where the U. S. soldiers were waiting to be shipped to Japan to fight & a lot of them would have died (Daddy always said) except the war ended with the A-bomb. So Daddy said these were Good Luck Dice for him. He'd toss away his medals but not these. At the Eagle House he'd roll his friends for drinks. 7 times out of 10 he'd win, I swear. The other men didnt know how the hell Willie Kenelly did it but the dice werent fixed, as you will see. Yet Daddy would snap his fingers & sometimes it seemed the dice would obey him, who knows why.

After my mother died we had some happy years, your Grandaddy & me. Maybe Daddy had a drinking problem but thats not the only thing in life, believe me.

Theres something about dice being tossed, if they're classy dice, it makes my backbone shiver even now. As soon as the dice fly out of your hand. & its an important bet, & everybody watching. I hope you will put away these dice for safekeeping, Mary Lynda. They're pure ivory which is why they've changed color. Daddy & I would roll them for fun, & one night he pressed them in my hand (in June 1959, I will always remember) & I knew this must be a sign of something but could not have guessed that Daddy would be dead in 5 weeks.

& Bud Beechum would be dead in about a year.

& Hiram Jones (maybe this is a name you don't remember) would be dead in a few years.

Well! Its too late now, Darling. For any of this, I guess.

Even for feeling sorry. Like your Grandaddy said theres
nothing to do with dice except "toss 'em."

Your loving Mother "Elsie Kenelly"

2.

Yewville, NY. April 11, 1999.

A fire. It looked like a fire: not flames but smoke.

Clouds of pale dust-colored smoke drifting skyward in
erratic surges, like expelled breaths. In the downtown area
of Yewville, just across the river, it looked like.

She was driving to visit her mother in the nursing home.
She'd delayed the visit for weeks. Poor Elsie: who'd once
been a beautiful, vain woman, with that wavy shoulder-
length dark-blond hair, now she was a chemo patient, the
hair gone, and what sprouted from her scalp was fuzzy gray
like down or mold you had an instinct to wipe off with a
damp cloth.

Mary Lynda, no: I don't mind.

I'm lucky to be alive, see?

Mary Lynda, the daughter, wasn't so sure. She was a
doctor, and she knew what was in store for her mother, and
she wasn't so sure.

She'd had a driver's license for more than thirty years
but the fact was, which she could never have explained to
anyone: in all those years she'd never once driven in downtown Yewville. She'd managed to avoid South Main
Street—the "historic" district—on the western bank of the
Yewville River. Not that it was a phobia, it was a conscious
choice. (Or maybe, yes, it was a phobia. And it soothed her
vanity to tell herself it was a conscious choice.) There were

circuitous routes to bring her to other parts of Yewville and its suburbs without any need to navigate the blocks closest to the river; though, from childhood, with the vividness of impressions formed in childhood, she could instantly recall the look of South Main Street: the grandiose Lafayette Hotel with its sandstone facade and many gleaming windows; Franklin Brothers, once Yewville's premiere department store, with its brass flagpole and fluttering American flag; the old stone City Hall, for decades the downtown branch of the Yewville Public Library; Mohawk Smoke Shop, King's Cafe, Ella's Ladies' Apparel, Midland Trust, Yewville Savings & Loan with its luminous clock tower; the Old Eagle House Tavern, gray stone, cavelike inside, with its faded sign in the shape of a bald eagle in flight, wings outspread, talons ready to grip prey. . . . She hadn't seen this sign in forty years but could see it now, swift as a headache. She could hear the sign creaking in the wind.

Old Eagle House Tavern est. 1819.

For some reason, she was going to drive through the downtown today. The "historic" district. Why not? She was curious about the smoke, and what South Main Street looked like after so many years. She'd been there last in 1960. Now, it was 1999. The bridge over the river had been totally changed, of course. Now four lanes, reasonably modern. Her car's tires hummed on the wire-mesh surface. There didn't seem to be any fire, though. No fire trucks or sirens. Main Street traffic was being diverted into a single slow-moving lane overseen by burly men shouting through megaphones. CONSTRUCTION AHEAD. DEMOLITION WARNING. She smelled a powdery-gritty dust, her eyes smarted. Damn: jackhammers. She hated jackhammers. Her heartbeat began to quicken in panic, such loud noises upset her. What was she trying to prove, driving

18

here, when there was no one to prove it to, no witness? She vowed she wasn't going to mention this to Elsie.

I'm not that girl. She was someone else.

The girl had been ten at the time. When she'd gone down into the cellar of the Eagle House that smelled of beer, mildew, dirt. The stink of urine from the men's room. She'd been sent by Momma to see where the proprietor Bud Beechum "had got to."

Now, she was forty-nine years old. She hadn't lived in Yewville for decades. She'd graduated, valedictorian of her high school class, in 1968. She'd gone to college in Rochester and medical school in New York City. She was "Dr. Donaldson"—she had a general practice in Montclair, New Jersey. She was fully an adult, it was ridiculous that Yewville should reduce her to trembling like a child.

In her life away from Yewville, "Mary Lynda" was a name she rarely heard. Among friends and colleagues she was simply "Mary." An old-fashioned name, a name so classic it was almost impersonal, like a title. She liked the formality of "Dr. Donaldson" though it was her (deceased) father's name, too. Both her parents had called her "Mary Lynda" while she was growing up. Never had she had the courage to tell them how much she hated it.

Mary Lynda! Born in 1950, you could guess by the name. Sweet and simpering in gingham, like June Allyson. Crinkly crinoline skirts and pin-curls, weirdly dark lipstick. Don't hurt me, please just love me, I am so good.

Mary Donaldson visited her mother in Yewville two or three times a year. They spoke often on the phone. Or fairly often. Until just recently Elsie had lived by herself but she'd had a run of bad luck in her mid sixties, health problems, financial problems, so she'd allowed Mary to persuade her to move into The Elms Retirement Village, which was a condominium complex for senior citizens in a semirural suburb of Yewville; when Elsie's health began to deteriorate, she moved into a nursing home on the premises. ("Next move," Elsie quipped, "is out the door, feet first." Mary winced, pretending not to hear.) When Elsie had been younger and in better health, Mary bought her a plane ticket once or twice a year so that she could come visit her in Montclair; they went to matinees and museums in New York; they were judged to be "more like sisters than mother and daughter," as Mary's friends liked to say, as if this remark might be flattering to Mary. Of course it wasn't true: Mary looked nothing like Elsie, who was an intensely feminine woman with a full, shapely body carried upright as a candle, dark blond hair that bobbed enticingly, flirty eyes, and a throaty voice. ("Don't be deceived by Mother's 'personality,' " Mary said. "Mother is a dominatrix." Her friends laughed, no one believed her for an instant.) Well into her mid sixties Elsie could pass for a youthful fifty. Though she'd been a heavy smoker and drinker, her skin was relatively unlined. She'd had only two husbands—Mary's father was the first—but numerous lovers who'd treated her, on the whole, as Elsie said, not too badly. But now, at last, life was catching up with her. Her girlfriends from childhood were white-haired, wrinkled grandmothers, the boys elderly-shrunken, or dead. In her late sixties things began to go wrong with Elsie. She had varicose-vein surgery on her legs. She had surgery to remove ovarian cysts. Arthritis in her lower spine, bronchitis that lasted for weeks in the cold damply windy climate of upstate New York. For much of her adult life she'd been a drinker, joined Alcoholics Anonymous in her early thirties, and quit smoking at about the same time. ("I must have thought I'd live forever," Elsie said ruefully. "Now look!") In fact, Mary was in awe that her mother, who'd taken such indifferent care of herself, who'd avoided doctors for decades, was in such relatively good health for a woman of her generation, and had managed even to keep her bright "upbeat" temperament. *Not a dominatrix, a seductress. Her power is more insidious.*

Driving with maddening slowness on Main Street, Mary thought of these things. And of the past, coiled snaky and waiting (for her? that wasn't likely) beyond the facades of these old, now shabby buildings. The Lafayette Hotel; the ugly discount store that had once been classy Franklin Brothers; the old City Hall which hadn't changed much, at least on the outside; the Mohawk Smoke Shop, still in business, though with a sign in its window ADULT X-RATED VIDEOS; the old Yewville Savings & Loan with the clock tower that had always seemed gigantic, a proud glowing clock face to be seen for miles, though in fact, as Mary now saw, to her surprise, the granite tower was no higher than the second floor of the bank building.

But where was Ella's, and where was King's Cafe, and where was . . . the Eagle House Tavern?

Mary stared, confused. Half the block was being razed. Only the shells of some buildings remained. Stone, and brick. Rubble in heaps. Like an earthquake. A bombing. She was tasting dust, swallowing dust; she steeled herself against the noise of jackhammers, that made her heartbeat race as if with amphetamine. There came a wrecking ball swinging in air like a deranged pendulum, and at once a wall of weatherworn stone collapsed in an explosion of dust.

Go look for him, honey. I'll wait out here.

Mommy, why? I don't want to.

Because I'm asking you, Mary Lynda.

I don't want to, Mommy. I'm afraid . . .

21

Go on, I said! Damn you! Just see where that bastard has got to.

Mommy's face was bright and hard and her mouth twisted in that way Mary Lynda knew. Her mother had been drinking, it was like fire inside her that could leap out at you, and burn.

Mommy wanted to know where Bud Beechum was, exactly. For he wasn't in the tavern when they came inside. When Mommy pushed Mary Lynda inside. Bud Beechum owned the Eagle House. He'd been a friend of Grandaddy Kenelly when Grandaddy was alive and he was a friend of Mary Lynda's mother, too. Somehow, the families were friendly. Beechums, Kenellys. Bud Beechum's wife was Elsie's cousin. They'd all been "wild" together in high school. Just to remember those times, they'd start laughing, shaking their heads. The child Mary Lynda was uneasy around Beechum. He had a way of looking at you, smirking and rubbing at his teeth with the tip of his tongue.

Mary Lynda was uneasy around most adult men, except her father and the Donaldsons: They were "different" kinds of people. They were soft-spoken, "nice." When Elsie divorced Timothy Donaldson, she was given custody of Mary Lynda and so Mary Lynda saw her father only on weekends.

Bud Beechum had been dead now for almost forty years. Yet you could imagine his big, chunky bones in the cellar of that old building. His broken-in skull the size of a bucket amid the rubble and suffocating dust.

Mommy, no. Mommy, don't make me.

Mary Lynda, do as you're told.

Mommy's voice was scared, too. And Mommy's fingers gripping Mary Lynda's narrow shoulders, pushing her forward.

It was now that Mary did the unexpected thing: As soon as she was safely past the traffic congestion on South Main, she turned left on a street called Post, and drove back toward the river, and, with an air of adventure, a sense of recklessness, parked in the lot, now mostly deserted and weedy, behind the old Franklin Brothers store.

Dr. Donaldson, why? This is crazy.

She wasn't a woman of impulse, usually. She was a woman who guarded her actions as she guarded her emotions. Not for Mary Donaldson the dice-tossing habits of her charming old drunk of a grandfather Kenelly.

And so it was strange that in her good Italian shoes, in her taupe linen pants suit (Ann Taylor), her hair stylishly scissor-cut, she was parking in downtown Yewville, and hurrying to join a small crowd of people gathered to stare at the destruction of a few old, ugly buildings. Coughing from the dust, and maybe there was asbestos in that dust. Yet she was compelled by curiosity, like the others, most of whom were elderly, retired men, with here and there some woman shoppers, some teenagers and children. (Thank God, no one who seemed to recognize Mary Lynda Donaldson.)

His bones in that rubble. Ashes.

Toxic to inhale!

Of course this was ridiculous. Bud Beechum had been properly buried. Forty years ago.

The Eagle House was being razed, spectacularly. The very earth shook as the wrecking ball struck. "Wow! Fantas-tic." A teenaged boy with spiky hair spoke approvingly. His girl snuggled against him, wriggling her taut little bottom as if the demolition of the Eagle House had a private, salacious meaning. Mary saw that the girl was hardly more than fourteen, her brown hair streaked in maroon and green, one nostril and one eyebrow pierced. She was pale, wanly pretty, though looking like a pincushion. Very thin. One of her tiny breasts, the size and color of an oyster, was virtually exposed, her tank top hung so slack on her skinny torso. She wore faded jeans, and in this place of litter and broken glass was barefoot.

That afternoon, Elsie had picked up Mary Lynda from school. She'd driven here. She'd parked her car, the yellow Chevy, in this lot, though closer to the rear of the Eagle House. *Why are we here, Mommy?* Mary Lynda asked. *Because that bastard owes me. He owed your Grandaddy, he's got to pay.* Mary Lynda knew the symptoms: Her mother's eyes were dilated, her hair hung lank in her face. When she hiccupped, Mary Lynda could smell her sweetish-sour breath.

"What's happening here?" Mary asked in the bright, friendly voice of a visitor to Yewville who'd just wandered over from the Lafayette Hotel. The boy with the spiky hair said, with an air of civic pride, "They're tearing these old dumps down. They're gonna build something new." His girl said, smirking, "About time, huh?" Mary had to press her fingers against her ears, the jackhammer was so loud. Such noises enter the soul, and may do permanent damage. She saw that beyond the adjacent lot was an unpaved alley that led toward the river. This was the lot in which her mother had parked that day. Debris was piled on both sides of the alley, some of it Styrofoam of the white-glaring hue of exposed bone. Mary was smiling, or trying to smile, but something was wrong with her mouth. "Ma'am? You okay?" The teenagers were suddenly alert, responsible. You could guess they had mothers for whom they were sometimes concerned. They helped Mary sit down—for suddenly Mary's knees were weak, her strength was gone like water rapidly draining away—on a twisted guardrail. Amid the deafening jackhammer that made her bones vibrate she sat dazed, confused, breathing through her mouth. Her legs were clumsily spread, thank God for the trousers. She was wiping her nose with her fingers. Was she crying? Saying earnestly, "A man was found dead in that building, a long time ago. A little girl found him. Now I can tell her the cellar is gone."

3.

Rochester, NY 1968–Barnegat, NJ 1974.

For years she would see a male figure, not fallen but "resting"—prone on the floor, for instance, inside a room she was passing; in the blurry corner of her eye she saw this figure, but had no sense that the figure meant death. Because when she looked, there was no figure, of course. One night, in Rochester, working late in the university library, she was swiftly passing a dim-lit lounge and though it had been eight years since she'd seen Beechum's body in that cellar, and rarely thought of it, now suddenly she was seeing it again, in terrifying detail, more clearly than she'd seen the body at the time. *He's here. How'd he come to be here?* Always a logical young woman, even in her panic she reasoned that if Bud Beechum's body was actually here in the University of Rochester library, so long as there was no linkage between the body and Mary Lynda Donaldson, a pre-med student, she was blameless, and could not be blamed.

Her instinct was to stop dead in her tracks and stare into the room, yet since she knew (she knew perfectly well) that no one was lying there on the carpet, she averted her eyes and flew past.

No. Don't look. Nothing!

She believed it was an act of simple discipline, fighting off madness. As an adult you took responsibility for your life, you were no-nonsense. High grades at the university, always high grades. She was pre-med after all. Ignore the politics of the era. Assassinations, the Vietnam War, the despairing effort of her generation to "bring the war home." For always in history there have been wars, and destruction, and people dying to no purpose, if not here then elsewhere, if not elsewhere then (possibly) here, count your blessings, Mary Lynda, her mother often consoled her; or maybe it was a mother's simple command, and it made sense. (Elsie had joined AA, Elsie hadn't had a drink stronger than sweet apple cider in years, laughing, *Can you believe it?*) So private madness seemed to Mary Lynda the worst nonsense. Stupid and self-hurtful as "dropping acid," or laughing like a hyena (that belly laugh of Bud Beechum's, how she'd hated it) at someone's funeral, or tearing off your clothes and running in the street when you didn't even look good, small breasts and soft hips and tummy, naked. Fighting off madness seemed to Mary Lynda like beating out a fire with a heavy blanket or canvas—"Something anybody could do if they tried."

It was her opinion that both Kennedys could have prevented being assassinated if they'd been more prudent in their behavior. Martin Luther King, too. But she kept this opinion to herself.

One of the men she'd loved, and would live with intermittently for several years in her late twenties, she'd seen lying in the sun in khaki shorts, bare-chested, amid sand and scrub grass at the Jersey shore. She was an intern at Columbia Presbyterian and lived a life far from Yewville and from her mother. Seeing the boy sleeping in the sun, sprawled on the sand, she stared, like one under a spell. She went to him, knelt over him, stroked his hair. The boy was in fact a young man, her age; with long pale lashes and long lank hair women called moon-colored. At Mary's touch he opened his eyes that were sleepy but sharpened immediately when he saw who she was: another man's girl. And when he realized what Mary was doing in her trancelike state, where her hand crept, he came fully awake and pulled her down on top of him, his hands gripping her head. His kisses were hard, hungry. Mary shut her eyes that hurt from the sun, she would see what came of this.

4.

Yewville, NY. 1960–1963.

Those years of Elsie chiding, frightened. *Mary Lynda, talk to me! This is just some sort of game you're playing, isn't it!*

At first they believed her inability to speak might have something to do with her breathing patterns. She breathed rapidly, and usually through her mouth. This precipitated hyperventilation. (Elsie learned to enunciate this carefully: "Hy-per-ven-ti-lation.")

Mary felt dizzy, her eyes "sparked." Her throat shut up tight. If she managed to choke out words they were only a sound, a shuddering stammer like drowning. "Is your daughter a little deaf-mute girl?" a woman dared ask Elsie at the clinic.

For approximately ten months after October 16, 1960 she was mute. And what relief when finally she wasn't expected to speak. They let you alone if you don't talk, they seem to think you're deaf, too. Except for some of the kids teasing her at school it was a time of peace. She'd never been very afraid of children, even of the loud-yelling older boys, only just adults frightened her. Their size, their sudden voices. The mystery of their moods, and their motives. The grip of their fingers on your shoulders even in love. *Mary Lynda, I love you, honey! Say something. I know you can talk if you want to.*

But mostly this was a time of peace. No one would question her words as the police had questioned her, for she had no words. Because she'd ceased speaking, she was surrounded by quiet. Like inside a glass bubble. She carried it with her everywhere, inviolable.

In school, where she was *Mary Lynda Donaldson* she occupied her own space. Her teacher Miss Doehler with the watery eyes was very kind to her, always Mary Lynda's desk was just in front of Miss Doehler's desk in fifth and sixth grades. She was *the little girl who'd found the dead man. The dead man!* The man who'd owned the Eagle House Tavern by the river. With the soaring eagle sign that creaked in the wind. When Bud Beechum was killed, his picture was printed in the Yewville paper: the first time in Bud's life, people said. Poor bastard, he'd have liked the attention.

Tavern Owner, 35, Killed in Robbery.

Strange that, in Bud Beechum's picture, he was young-looking, without his whiskers, and smiling. Like he had no idea what would happen to him.

Strange that, when Mary Lynda's throat shut up the way it did, she felt safe. Like somebody was hugging her so tight she couldn't move. Sometimes in the night her throat came open, like ice melting, and then she began to groan, and whimper like a baby, and call "Momma! Mom-ma!" in her sleep. If Elsie was home, and if Elsie heard, she might come staggering into Mary Lynda's room, groggy and scolding. "Oh Mary Lynda, what? What is it *now?*" If Elsie wasn't home, or wasn't wakened, Mary Lynda woke herself up, and tried to sleep sitting up, which was a safe way, generally. Not to put your head down on a pillow. Not to be so unprotected. She stared at the walls of her room (which was a small room, hardly more than a closet) to keep them from closing in.

Always in one of the walls there was a door. As long as the door was shut, she was safe. But the door might open. It might be pushed open. It might glide open. On the other side of the door there might be steep steps leading down, and she had no choice but to approach these steps, for something was pressing her forward, like a hand against her back. A gentle hand, but it could turn hard. A hard firm adult hand on her back. And she would see her own hand switching on a light, and she would see suddenly down into the cellar into the dark. That was her mistake.

5.

Yewville, NY. October 1960–March 1965.

The boy was a Negro, as blacks were then called, with an I.Q. of 84. This was not "severe retardation" (it would be argued by prosecutors), this was not a case of "not knowing right from wrong." Though the boy was seventeen, he'd dropped out of school in fifth grade and could not read, still less write, except to shakily sign his name to a confession later to be recanted, with a protestation of his court-appointed attorney of "extreme police coercion." The case would receive the most publicity any murder case had ever received in Eden County. In some quarters it was believed to be a "race murder"—the boy, Hiram Jones, had brutally killed and robbed Bud Beechum because Beechum was a white man. In other quarters, the case was believed to be a "race issue"—Hiram Jones was being prosecuted because he was a Negro. Because his I.Q. was 84. Because he lived in that part of Yewville known as Lowertown, a place of makeshift wood-frame shanties with tin roofs. Because the testimony of his family that Hiram had been home at the probable time of the murder was dismissed as lies. Because when he'd been arrested by police he had in his possession Bud Beechum's wallet, containing twenty-eight dollars; he was wearing Bud Beechum's favorite leather belt with the silver medallion buckle; Bud Beechum's shoes were hidden in a shed behind the Jones's house. These items, Hiram claimed he'd found while fishing on the riverbank, less than a mile from the Eagle House. Yet when police came into Lowertown to arrest him, having been tipped off by a (Negro) informant, Hiram Jones had "acted guilty" by trying to run. He'd made things worse by "resisting arrest." Police had had to overpower him, and he'd been hurt and hospitalized, his nose and eye sockets broken, ribs cracked, windpipe crushed from someone's boot. He would speak in a hoarse, cracked whisper like wind rattling newspaper for the remainder of his life.

Always Hiram Jones would deny he'd killed the white man. He would not remember the white man's name, or how exactly he'd been charged with killing him, but he would deny it. He would deny he'd ever been in the Eagle House. No Negroes in Yewville patronized the Eagle House. He would be tried as an adult and found guilty of second-degree murder and robbery, he would be incarcerated while his case was appealed to the state supreme court where a new trial would be ordered, but by this time Hiram Jones was diagnosed as "mentally deficient"—"unable to participate in his own trial"—so he was transferred to a state mental hospital in Port Oriskany where, in March 1965, he would die after a severe beating by fellow inmates.

6.

The Eagle House Tavern, Yewville, NY. October 16, 1960.

At the bottom of the wooden steps there was a man lying on his side. Like he was floating in the dark. Like he was sleeping, and floating. His arms sprawled. Maybe it was a joke, or a trick? Bud Beechum was always joking. *Hey, I'm kidding, kid,* Bud Beechum would say, in reproach. *Where's your sense of humor?* If he saw you were frightened of him, he'd press in closer. He smelled of beer, and cigarette smoke, and his own body. His stomach rode his big-buckled belt like a pumpkin. He had hot moist smiling eyes and the skin beside those eyes crinkled. He'd been in the Korean War. He boasted of things he'd done there with his "bayonet." He refused to serve Negroes in the Eagle House because, as he said, he owed it to his white customers who didn't want to drink out of glasses that Negroes drank out of, or use the men's room if a Negro had used it. His wife was Momma's cousin Joanie who smelled of talcum. Once at the Beechums' in the old hay barn where kids were leaping into hay and screaming like crazy, bare arms and legs, Bud Beechum laughed at Mary Lynda for being so shy and fearful—"Not like your Momma who's *hot*." Because Mary Lynda didn't want to run and jump with the others into the hay loft. Bud Beechum teased her pretending to grab at her between the legs with his big thumb and forefinger. *Uh-oh! Watch out, the crab's gonna getcha!* It was just a joke though. Bud Beechum's face was flushed and happy-seeming. So maybe now, lying at the foot of the steps, in this nasty-smelling place with the bare light bulb that hurt her eyes, maybe this was a joke, too. Bud Beechum's head that was big as a bucket twisted to one side like he was trying to look over his shoulder. Something glistened on his head, was it blood?

Mary Lynda was fearful of blood. She began to breathe in a quick light funny way like the breath couldn't get past her mouth. Was Mr. Beechum breathing? Or holding his breath? His mouth was gaping in surprise and something glistened there, too. There was a smell—Mary Lynda's nostrils pinched—like he'd soiled his pants. A grown man! Mary Lynda wanted to run away, but could not move. Nor had she any words to utter. Never had she spoken to Momma's man friend Bud Beechum except shyly in response to a teasing query and that only sidelong, out of the corner of her mouth, eyes averted. You could not. You did not. She stood paralyzed, unable to breathe. She could not have said why she was in this place. Or where exactly this place was. A dungeon? Like in a movie? A cave? It made her think of bats: She was terrified of bats, that got into little girls' hair.

Of the Yewville taverns where Momma went when she was feeling lonely her favorite was the Eagle House because that had been Grandaddy Kenelly's favorite, too. There, Mary Lynda was allowed to play the jukebox. Nickel after nickel. Sometimes men at the bar gave her nickels. Like they bought drinks for Momma. Bud Beechum, too—"This one's on the house." Mary Lynda drank sugary Cokes until her tummy bloated and she had to pee so bad it hurt. If Momma stayed late she slept in one of the sticky black vinyl booths. All the men liked Momma, you could tell. Momma so pretty with her long wavy dark-blond hair and her way of dancing alone, turning and lifting her arms like a woman in a dream.

Mary Lynda had overheard her parents quarreling. Her father's voice, and her mother's voice rising to a scream. *Because you bore the shit out of me, that's why.*

Such words, Mary Lynda wasn't allowed to hear.

Why was this afternoon special? Mary Lynda didn't know. Momma had come to pick her up at school which wasn't Momma's custom. Saying she didn't have to take the damned school bus. They'd come here, and parked in the next-door lot. It would turn out—it would say so in the newspaper—that the front door of the Eagle House was locked, only the back door was open. There were no customers in the bar because it was early: not yet four o'clock. Momma talked excitedly explaining (to Mary Lynda?) that she was in no mood to see Bud Beechum's face. "Just tell him I'm out here, and waiting." Momma repeated this several times. It wasn't clear why Momma didn't want to see Bud Beechum's face yet wanted Mary Lynda to find him, to ask him to come outside so that Momma could talk to him. For wouldn't she have to see his face, then? But this was Momma's way when she'd been drinking. One minute she'd grab Mary Lynda's head and kiss her wetly on the mouth calling her "my beautiful baby daughter," the next minute she'd be scolding. Only fragments of the afternoon of October 16, 1960 would be clear in Mary Lynda's memory. For possibly much of it had been dreamt, or would be dreamt. Her throat began to shut up tight as soon as she'd entered the barroom looking for Bud Beechum who was always behind the bar except now he wasn't. She'd have to look back in the kitchen, Momma said. She wanted to leave but Momma said no. *See where that bastard has got to. I know he's here somewhere.* Mary Lynda saw Bud Beechum, and the thought came to her, *He's dead.* She giggled, and pressed her knuckles against her mouth. The day before, Momma had kept her home from school with an "ear infection"—a "fever." When you have a fever, Momma said, you might become "delirious." You might have wild, bad dreams when you weren't even asleep and you couldn't trust what you saw, or thought you saw. So she'd called Mary Lynda's school and made her excuse. Yet, yesterday, it had seemed to Mary Lynda that Momma kept her home because she was nervous about something. She was edgy, and distracted. When the telephone rang, she wouldn't answer it. She wouldn't let Mary Lynda answer it. After a while, she left the receiver off the hook. She made sure every blind in the house was drawn, and lights were out in most of the rooms except upstairs. When Mary Lynda asked what was wrong, Momma told her to hush.

Already, yesterday was a long time ago.

Mary Lynda was crouched at the top of the steps staring down to where Bud Beechum was lying. Looking like he was asleep. *No: He's dead.* Still, Bud Beechum was tricky, he might wake up at any moment. Maybe it was a trick he was playing on Momma, too. You couldn't trust him. Mary Lynda stood there on the steps so long, not able to move, not able to breathe, at last Momma came to see where she was.

Soft as a whisper coming up behind Mary Lynda.

"Honey? Is something wrong?"

7.

The Eagle House Tavern, Yewville, NY.
October 16, 1960.

He told her to come to the Eagle House at noon, he wanted to see her. He'd leave the rear door unlocked. He was pissed as hell at her not answering the phone, almost he'd come over there and broken down the door and the hell with her little girl or any other witness. So she came by. She saw she had no choice. She parked the Chevy on Front Street, by the Lafayette Hotel. A dead-end street. She wasn't seen walking to the Eagle House through the alley. She wore a raincoat and a scarf tied tight around her head and she walked swiftly, in a way unusual for Elsie Kenelly. She entered by the rear door. At this time of day no one was around. There was a raw, egg-white look to the day. High clouds were spitting rain cold enough to be ice. The clouds would be blown away, and the sky would open into patches of bright blue, by the time she left. The Eagle House wasn't open for lunch; it opened, most days, around four P.M. and it closed at two A.M. Beechum was waiting for her just inside. "About time, Elsie." He was angry, but relieved. She'd come as he had commanded: The woman had done his bidding. He grabbed at her. She pushed him off, laughing nervously. She'd washed her hair and put on crimson lipstick. Perfume that made her nostrils pinch. She'd brought a steak knife, one of that set her mother-in-law Maudie Donaldson had given them, in her handbag but she knew she wasn't brave enough to use a knife. She was terrified of blood, and of the possibility of Bud Beechum wrenching the knife out of her fingers. He was strong, and for a man of his size he was quick. She knew he was quick. And he was shrewd. She would have to say the right things to him, to placate him. Because he was pissed from last night, she knew that. She told him that Mary Lynda had been sick, an ear infection. She told him she was sorry. He squeezed her breasts, always there was something mean in this man's touch. And when he kissed her, there was meanness in his kiss. His beery breath, his ridiculous thrusting tongue like an eel. His teeth that needed brushing. The wire-whiskers she'd come to hate though at one time (had she been crazy?) she'd thought they were sexy, and Bud Beechum was "sexy—sort of." She'd always been curious about this guy married to her cousin Joanie, even back in high school it was said all the Beechum men were built like horses which was fine if you liked horses. Drunk, she'd thought just maybe she might. But only part-drunk, and stone-cold sober, she'd had other thoughts.

Mary Lynda was at school. She'd be at school until three-fifteen.

"Look. I got kids, too. You think I don't have my own kids?"

Now he was blaming her for—what? Mary Lynda? The bastard.

There was the doorway to the cellar. Like a dream doorway. *Pass through to an adventure! But you must be brave.* She laughed, and wrenched her mouth free of his. She was breathing quickly as if she'd been running. She lifted her heavy dark-blond hair in both her hands and let it sift through her fingers as it fell, in that way he liked. She could see in his eyes, dilated with desire, he liked. He led her urgently toward the cellar steps, where a bare light bulb was screwed into a ceiling fixture filmy with cobweb. It was both too bright here and smudged-seeming. It smelled of

36

piss from the men's room in the back hall, and of damp
dark earth. All the cellars in these old "historic" buildings
were earthen. Things died in these cellars and rotted away.
Beechum was talking excitedly, laughing, that warning edge
to his voice. He was sexually charged up like a battery. But
he didn't like tricky women, he wanted her to know that.
He'd hinted at things about her old man she wouldn't want
generally known in Yewville. She'd got that, right? He was
leading her down the steps, ahead of her, to this place
they'd gone before, this was the third time in fact. She was
disgusted and ashamed and she pushed him, suddenly
pushed him hard, and he lost his balance and fell forward.
Elsie's fingers with the painted nails, which were strong fingers, you'd better believe they were strong, at the small of
the man's fattish back, and he fell.

He fell hard. He fell onto the wooden steps limp and
lumpy as a sack of potatoes, sliding down. Horrible to
watch, and fascinating, the big man's body helpless, thump-
ing against the steps that swayed dangerously with his
weight. Beechum was six feet three, weighed two hundred
twenty pounds at least. Yet now, falling, he was helpless as
a giant baby. He lay on the earthen floor, stunned. A groan
of utter astonishment escaped his throat. If Beechum wasn't
seriously hurt, if he got hold of Elsie now, he'd kill her.
He'd beat her to death with his fists. She'd seen a pipe amid
a pile of debris. Beechum was writhing, groaning, possibly
the bastard had injured his back in the fall, maybe his spine
or his neck was broken, maybe the bastard was dying but
Elsie hadn't faith this could be so easy. Almost, she was
willing—she was wanting—to work a little harder. Her father Willie Kenelly had killed men in Okinawa, gunfire and
bayonet, he hadn't boasted of it, he'd said it was Goddamned dirty work, it was hard work, killing was hard work,

nothing to be proud of but not ashamed either. That had been his job, and they'd given him medals for it, but in his own mind he'd just done his job. *Do it right, girl, or not at all. Don't screw up.*

She knew. She'd known, making up her mind to drive over here.

Afterward, she wrapped the pipe in newspaper. It was bloody, and there were hairs on it. But nothing had splattered onto her. She would bathe anyway. For the second time that day. She wiped the dead man's mouth roughly, thoroughly, removing all traces of crimson lipstick. She took his wallet, stuffed with small bills. She unbuckled his belt and removed it. She unlaced his shoes. She was feverish yet calm. Whispering aloud, "Now. I want this. These. One, two. The shoe. Three, four. Shut the door. *Don't screw up.*" In a paper bag she carried Beechum's things to her car parked on Front Street beside the Lafayette Hotel. This had been an ideal place to park: a side street above the river, a dead end used mainly by delivery trucks. No one had seen her, and no one would see her. It wasn't yet one P.M. The sky was clearing rapidly. Each morning, as winter neared, the sky was thick with clouds like broken concrete but the wind from Lake Ontario usually dislodged them by midday, patches of bright blue glared like neon. Elsie drove north along the River Road humming the theme from *Moulin Rouge*. It had snagged in her brain and would recur throughout her life, reminding her of this day, this hour. She surprised herself, so calm. *You're doing good, girl. That's my girl.* Why she would behave so strangely within a few hours, bringing her daughter Mary Lynda to the death scene as if to ascertain yes, yes the man was dead, yes it had really happened, yes she could not possibly be to blame if her own daughter was the one to discover the corpse, she would not know. She would not wish to think. *That's right, girl. Never look back.*

She drove the Chevy bump-bump-bumping along a sandy access road to the river, where fishermen parked, but today there were no fishermen. Scrub willow grew thick on the riverbank here, no one would see her. She was a doctor's wife, not a woman you'd suspect of murder. She threw the bloodied pipe out into the river, about twenty feet from shore. It sank immediately, never would it be recovered. Beechum's fat, frayed pigskin wallet Elsie hadn't glanced into, not wanting the bastard's money, the leather belt he'd been so proud of, like the oversized silver buckle was meant to be his cock, and his shoes, his size-twelve smelly brown fake-leather shoes, these items of Bud Beechum's she left on the riverbank for someone unknown to find.

"Like Hallowe'en," she said. "Trick or treat, in reverse."

8.

Yewville, NY. 1959–1960.

She was just so lonely, couldn't help herself. Missing him.

Crying till she was sick. Lost so much weight her clothes hung loose on her. Even her bras. And her eyes bruised, bloodshot.

At first, her husband was sympathetic. In his arms she lay stiff in the terror of a death she'd never somehow believed could happen. *Can't believe it. I can't believe he's gone. I wake up, and it's like it never happened.*

Couldn't help herself, she began dropping by the Eagle House though he wasn't there. Because, each time she entered, pushing through the rear door which was the door by which he'd entered, she told herself, *It might not have happened yet.* She told herself maybe he was there, at the bar. Waiting.

The other men, his friends, were there. Most were older than Willie Kenelly had been. Yet they were there, they were living, still. Glancing around at her when she entered the barroom, the only woman. And Bud Beechum behind the bar, staring at her. Elsie Kenelly, Willie Kenelly's girl, who'd married the doctor.

God, they'd loved Willie Kenelly: Nobody like him.

Except: He'd left without saying goodbye.

Short of breath, sometimes. The heel of his big calloused hand against his chest. And that faraway look in his eyes. She'd asked her father what was wrong, and he hadn't heard her. She asked again, and he turned his gaze upon her, close up, those faded blue eyes, and laughed at her. *What's wrong with what? The world? Plenty.*

Except he'd given Elsie, one evening at the bar of the Eagle House, those worn ivory dice he liked to play with, he'd brought back from Okinawa. His Good Luck Dice he called them.

"Don't lose 'em, honey."

That had been a clear sign, hadn't it? That he was saying goodbye. But Elsie hadn't caught on.

No one would speak of how Willie Kenelly died. One of the papers, not the Yewville paper, printed he'd "stepped or fallen" off the girder of a bridge being repaired upriver at Tintern Falls; there was water in his lungs, yet he'd died of "cardiac arrest." In any case Willie Kenelly's death was ruled "accidental." But Elsie knew better, her father wasn't a man to do anything by accident.

In the Eagle House that summer, she drank. Few women came alone into Yewville taverns, and never any woman who was a doctor's wife and lived in one of the handsome brick houses on Church Street. Yet Elsie was Willie Kenelly's daughter long before she'd become Dr. Donaldson's wife. She'd gone to Yewville High School, everyone knew her in the neighborhood. Bud Beechum leaned his high, hard belly against the edge of the bar, talking with her. Listening sympathetically. Beechum, greasy thinning dark hair worn like he was still in high school, sideburns like Presley's and something of Presley's sullen expression. And those eyes, deep-socketed, black and moist and intense. Elsie had always thought Bud Beechum was an attractive guy, in his way. By Yewville standards. She remembered him in his dress-up G.I. uniform. He'd been lean then. He'd had good posture then. He'd been fox-faced, sexy. They'd kissed, once. A long time ago in somebody's backyard. A beer party. A picnic. When?

Bud Beechum had liked her father. He'd "really admired" Willie Kenelly, he said. Elsie's father was a guy "totally lacking in bullshit," he said. Elsie's father had been in World War II, as it was called, and Beechum in the Korean War. They had that in common: a hatred of the army, of officers, of anybody telling them what to do. And Willie Kenelly hadn't had a son. When Beechum wiped at his eyes with his fist, Elsie felt her heart pierced.

It was hard for men to speak of loss. Of grief. Of what scared them. Better not to try, it always came out clumsy, crude.

But Elsie could tell Beechum, and her father's friends, that he'd been her best friend, not just her father. He'd loved her without wanting anything from her and without judging her. That had always been his way. Maybe she hadn't deserved it but it was so. She'd seen his body at the funeral director's, and she'd seen his coffin lowered into the ground, and she saw his death reflected in others' eyes as in the draining of color during a solar eclipse, yet still it wasn't real to her. So she found herself drifting to the places he'd gone, especially in the late afternoon as fall and winter came on, as the sun turned the western sky hazy, rust-red, reflected in somber ripples on the Yewville River. Never would Elsie drive to Tintern Falls, never would she cross over that bridge. Never again in her lifetime. And this time, the melancholy time, dusk: Never would she not think of him, waiting at the Eagle House for her. She should have been home with Mary Lynda, her daughter. She should have been preparing supper for her husband. She should have been a wife and a mother, not a daughter any longer.

This was the dangerous time.

Possibly Dr. Donaldson wasn't so sympathetic with his wife's grief as people thought, when they were alone. Between him and the older man there'd been rivalry. Donaldson disapproved of Kenelly's business practices. Kenelly had owned a lumberyard in Yewville, but it hadn't been very prosperous. He gave customers credit and rarely collected. The tarpaper roofs of his sheds leaked, his lumber warped and rotted. When customers came to buy single planks, a handful of spikes, he'd say, airily, "Oh hell, just take 'em." His son-in-law Tim Donaldson was a very different kind of man and after Willie Kenelly's death Elsie began to hate him. Her husband! His teeth-brushing, his bathroom noises, his sighs, his chewing, his frowns, his querying of Mary Lynda: "Did you and Mommy go out in the car today? Did you go shopping? Where?" Tim Donaldson never spoke meanly. Always, Dr. Donaldson spoke pleasantly. As he did at his office with his nurse-assistant, and with his patients, the majority of whom were women. His sand-colored hair was trimmed neatly every two weeks and he was a dignified, intelligent man yet after Willie Kenelly's death his jealousy of the old man quickened. Worse, Kenelly had left several thousand dollars to Elsie and Mary Lynda, without so much as mentioning him in the will. And he'd married Elsie, who hadn't been a virgin! Who'd had a certain reputation in Yewville, as a girl. He'd thought the old man would be grateful to him for that, at least.

One night when he touched Elsie in their bedroom, she shrank from him with a look of undisguised dislike. She began crying, not in grief but in anger. *Leave me alone, you disgust me. I don't love you, I love him.*

Next day, in the dusk of an early autumn, Elsie dropped by the Eagle House for just a single drink. She would stay only a few minutes. But Bud Beechum was alone there, waiting. Seeing her face as she entered the barroom, her eyes snatching at the place where her father should have been. "Elsie! Hey." Beechum spoke almost gently. Elsie saw his eyes on her, she saw how he wanted her.

That first time, she'd been drunk. Beechum shut up the Eagle House early. Running his hands over her, greedy and excited and a little scared. Murmuring, "Oh baby, baby." Like he couldn't believe his good luck. Like he was fearful he'd explode, too soon. He led Elsie down into the cellar. A bare light bulb shone in her eyes, screwed into a ceiling fixture amid cobwebs. There was a smell here of stale beer, a stink of cigarettes. She was sexually aroused as she hadn't been in months. What a strange, dirty thing to do; what a wicked thing to do, instead of preparing supper for a hard-working, hungry husband and a sweet little daughter. Elsie and Bud Beechum laughed like kids, and pulled at each other's clothing. This was high-school be-havior, this was teen rock music, oh God how they'd been missing it, these years of being adults.

Somehow it hadn't taken with either of them, adulthood.

Next afternoon, repentant, disgusted with herself, Elsie returned to the Eagle House determined it would be only for a single beer, only so she'd feel less lonely, and she'd take the opportunity to explain to Bud Beechum why yesterday had been a mistake, a terrible mistake, and she hoped he wouldn't think poorly of her . . . but this time, too, somehow it happened that Bud Beechum led Elsie down the unsteady wooden steps into the cellar, to the filthy sofa she recognized as a castoff from her cousin Joanie's living room. "Bud, no. I can't, Bud. I . . ." Elsie heard her voice, plausible and alarmed, and yet there she was in Beechum's rough embrace, and closing her arms about him another time. *It's just I'm so lonely.*

So it happened that, when Elsie changed her mind about seeing Beechum again, Beechum laughed at her, and said, "Elsie. C'mon. I was there. I remember how it was." He knew and she knew, he'd felt her clutching at him, her helpless thrashing and yearning, he'd seen her tears; and so when she stayed away from the Eagle House naturally he began to telephone her at home, "Hey Elsie, c'mon. Don't play hard to get. This is me, Bud. *I know you.*" When she hung up the receiver he began to drive past the handsome brick house on Church Street. Elsie shouldn't have been surprised, she knew who Beechum was, yet somehow she couldn't believe it: what was happening, spinning out of her control. *I made a mistake, I guess. Oh Daddy.*

When she drove to the grocery store, with Mary Lynda, and she glanced up to see Beechum's car in her rearview mirror, she knew—she'd made a serious mistake.

One evening Elsie stopped her car at the Sunoco station.

And Beechum stopped his. And they talked together at the edge of the pavement, Elsie brushing wind-whipped hair out of her eyes, Beechum hunching close in a zip-up jacket, bareheaded. Elsie was talking quickly now. There was a smile she had, a smile girls cultivated for such circumstances, desperate, not quite begging, and Elsie smiled this smile, and told Beechum she'd changed her mind about "seeing him," the mistake had been hers. "See? I'd been drinking. I was drunk." Beechum stared at Elsie, not hearing. She understood that the man was sexually aroused, even now. Her breathy words meant nothing to him, only his arousal had meaning, concentrated in his groin but suffused through his tense, quivering body. She saw it in his eyes, angry and triumphant. For the first time she realized that Bud Beechum, her cousin Joanie's tavern-owner husband, might be dangerous. Like Willie Kenelly, he'd killed men in combat. He'd had the power to kill in his hands, and that power had been sweet. Hoping to placate him, to soften the expression on his flushed, sullen face, Elsie said, almost shyly, "Bud, I just feel wrong, doing this to Joanie. If—" "Screw 'Joanie,' " Beechum said savagely. "This has got nothing to do with 'Joanie.' " Beechum's lips twisted, pronouncing his wife's name. Elsie was shocked at the hatred in his voice. For Joanie? She tried to move away, but Beechum caught her by the arm. His fingers were powerful as hooks. "Your father told me some things, baby," Beechum said suggestively. His breath was warm and beery. "What things?" Elsie asked uneasily. "Things you wouldn't want known," Beechum said, smirking, as if Elsie and her deceased father were co-conspirators in some shame. Elsie asked, "About—what? What?" Beechum said, "How your old man felt about—things. Like, wanting to step in front of a train, or off a bridge. This time he told me—" Elsie lost control and slapped Beechum. The bastard's smug fat face! She was too upset even to scream and when Beechum tried to grab her she wrenched free of him, and ran back to her car. Driving away she trembled with rage, and panic at what was happening to her. *Maligning the dead! Beechum would pay.*

9.

Yewville, NY. July 12, 1959.

The call came late at night: two-twenty A.M. Naturally you'd think it was one of Dr. Donaldson's patients.

Through a haze of sleep, resentfully Elsie heard her husband's calm condescending voice. He loved such late-night calls, obviously; if he didn't, he could leave the damned phone off the hook. (The Donaldsons were sleeping, at this time, in the same bed, of course. Technically, at that time, in the summer of 1959, they were still man-and-wife, with all that applies of marital intimacy and obligation.) Then Donaldson's voice sharpened in surprise. "When? *How?*" Elsie was fully awake in an instant. This was something personal, urgent. And yet there was a thrill to her husband's voice, a quavering she knew meant triumph of a kind, vindication. And when Donaldson put the palm of his hand over the receiver, and said gently, as if he were speaking not to his wife but to his nine-year-old daughter, "Elsie, I'm afraid there's bad news. Your father—in Tintern Falls—" Already Elsie was out of bed, and backing away from him, clumsy as a frightened cow in her aqua nylon nightgown with the lacy straps and bodice, shaking her head. *I already knew. Nothing could hurt me, after this.*

10.

Yewville, NY. March 29, 1957.

This call, Elsie had been expecting.

"Honey? Your mother has—" (there was a moment's pause, delicate as her father's fingers touching her wrist in that way he had, as if to steady her, or caution her, or simply to alert her that something crucial was being communicated) "—passed away."

Elsie surprised herself, beginning to cry. The tears, the childish sobs, burst from her.

Elsie's father disliked women crying, on principle. But he didn't interrupt Elsie. He let her cry for a while, then told her he was at the hospital if she wanted to come by.

Elsie tasted panic. No, no! She didn't want to see her mother's dead, wasted body, her skin the color of yellowed ivory, any more than she'd wanted to see her mother while the woman was alive, and disapproving of her. "Daddy, I can't. I just can't. I'll come by the house, later."

"Suit yourself, Elsie." Her father laughed, she could imagine him rubbing at his nose, a brisk upward gesture with his right forefinger that signaled the end of a conversation he felt had gone on long enough.

11.

Yewville, NY. 1946–1957.

Elsie and her mother hadn't gotten along. It happened in Yewville sometimes, a girl and her mother, living too close, recoiled from each other, hurt and unforgiving.

Elsie's mother hadn't approved of her. Even her marriage to Dr. Donaldson's son Timothy (as Tim was known at that time in Yewville). Mrs. Kenelly had been furious and disgusted with her youngest daughter since she'd caught Elsie, aged seventeen, with her boyfriend Duane Cadmon, in Elsie's attic bedroom, the two of them squirming partly undressed in each other's arms, French-kissing on Elsie's rumpled bed beneath the eaves. Never would Mrs. Kenelly forgive her for such behavior: being cheap, "easy," soiling her reputation, bringing "disgrace" into the Kenelly household. Elsie, who'd had reason to think her mother would be gone from the house for hours, lay pretzel-sprawled in Duane's grip, in a thrumming erotic haze like drowning, and her eyes sprang open in horror to see, past Duane's flushed face, her pinch-faced mother staring at her with ice-pick eyes. In that instant, Mrs. Kenelly slammed the door, hard enough to make Duane wince. Later, they would have it out. Mrs. Kenelly and Elsie. (Where was Willie Kenelly at such times? Nowhere near. Keeping his distance. He never intervened in such female matters.) Elsie's mother spoke bitterly and sarcastically to her, or refused to speak to her at all, even to look at her, as if the sight of Elsie disgusted her; Elsie slammed around the house, sullen, trembling with rage. "How'd anybody get born, Momma, for Christ's sake," Elsie said, her voice rising dangerously so the neighbors might hear, "you act like people don't do things like Duane and I were doing, well God *damn,* Momma, here's news for you: People *do.*"

You didn't talk to your mother like this in Yewville in those days. If you did, you were trailer trash. But here was Elsie Kenelly screaming at her mother. And Mrs. Kenelly screaming back calling Elsie "tramp," "slut," telling her "no decent boy" would respect her, or marry her.

Elsie brooded for weeks, months. Years.

Even after Elsie was married to Tim Donaldson, who'd gone away to medical school in Albany, and was eight years older than Elsie; even after she'd married, not just some high school boyfriend, or a guy from the neighborhood, but a "family physician" with a good income who brought her to live with him on Church Street, still Mrs. Kenelly withheld her approval, as she withheld her love. For that was a mother's sole power: to withhold love. And Elsie recoiled with yet more resentment.

Goddamn, Momma! I married a man of a higher class than you did so maybe you're jealous. My husband's a doctor not a lumber-yard owner, see?

She didn't love Timothy Donaldson. But she took pride in being Dr. Donaldson's wife.

After Mary Lynda was born, and Elsie's mother had a beautiful baby granddaughter she wished to see, and to hold, and to fuss over, then Elsie realized her power: to exclude her mother from as much of her life as she could. (Of course, Elsie's father was always welcome in the Church Street house. Invited to "drop by" after work. Anytime!) Though in public when it couldn't be avoided, Elsie and her mother hugged stiffly, and managed to kiss each other's cheek. In Mrs. Kenelly's presence Elsie was lightheaded, giddy. She laughed loudly. She drank too much. *Momma I hate you. Momma why don't you die.*

12.

Wolf's Head Lake, NY. Summer 1946.

Those evenings at the lake. Where Yewville families went for picnics in the summer. Some of the men fished but not Willie Kenelly who thought fishing was boring— "Almost as bad as the army. Almost as bad as life." He laughed his deep belly laugh that made anybody who listened laugh with him.

Elsie was proud of her dad who'd returned home from the War with burn scars and medals to show for his bravery though he dismissed it all as bullshit and rarely spoke of it with anyone except other veterans. And at such times the men spoke in a way that excluded others. They were profane, obscene. They shouted with laughter. Summer nights, they liked most just to sit drinking beer and ale on the deck of the Lakeside Tavern. Often they played cards (poker, euchre) or craps. These could get to be rowdy, raucous times. The sun set late in summer and so, toward dusk, when the sky was bleeding out into night, red-streaked, bruised-looking clouds, serrated and rough-seeming as a cat's tongue, and the surface of the lake had grown calm except for erratic, nervelike shivers and an occasional leap of a fish, the men would have been drinking for hours, ignoring their wives' pleas to come eat supper. "Daddy, can I?" There was Elsie Kenelly on the deck at her father's elbow teasing him for sips of ale from his glass, or a puff of his cigarette, or asking could she play his hand at cards, just once. Could she take his turn at craps, just once. Elsie in her new white two-piece swimsuit with the halter top, ponytailed dark-blond hair and long tanned legs, nails painted frost-pink to match her lipstick: Elsie was sixteen that summer, and very pretty lounging boldly on the deck against the railing by the men's table, liking the attention her dad gave her, and the other men, which meant more to her than the attention she got from boys her own age. Elsie regarded her good-looking father with pride: how muscled his bare shoulders and his bare, heavy torso, covered in a pelt of hairs, mysteriously tattooed and scarred. She was his girl for life. She blushed and squealed with laughter if he teased her. She bit her lip and came close to crying if he spoke harshly to her. Always it was a risk, hanging by her father, you couldn't predict when Willie Kenelly might speak sarcastically, or suddenly lose patience. He'd come back from the War with an air of speechless rage like a permanent twitch or tic somewhere in his body you couldn't detect, though you knew it was there. You felt it, if you touched him. Yet you had to touch him.

"Sure, honey: Toss 'em."

Willie Kenelly spoke negligently, handing his daughter the ivory dice, as if fate were nothing more than the crudest, meanest chance requiring no human skill. Always she would remember those ivory dice! As the men's eyes move onto her young eager body in the white swimsuit, taking in her snub-nosed profile, the graceful fall of her ponytail partway down her back, Elsie is laughing self-consciously, her heart swelling with happiness, and the excitement of the moment as the dice are released from her hand to tumble, roll, come to rest on the sticky tabletop and there's that anxious moment before you dare look to see what, as your Dad says, the dice have to tell you.

Blood Paths

Clark Howard

When Grant Kenner got out of bed, the first thing he did was look out the window to see what the weather was like. It was beautiful. A splendid spring day. Postcard pretty.

Kenner cursed quietly to himself. Pleasant weather always made it harder. Overcast skies, some fog, even a good steady downpour of rain would have been nice. Might have kept some of the protesters away, at least. And set a better scene for the whole thing.

Then another thought struck him. It wasn't going to be very enjoyable going down to breakfast this morning, either. This was the day his daughter, Susan, was going her own way in life, much to the disapproval of her mother, Kenner's wife, Elaine. There was tension between them.

Difficulties, Kenner decided, always seemed to come in bunches. Anything good came along, it was usually just a dribble.

In the bathroom, as he shaved, Kenner listened to the radio.

". . . in less than twelve hours," a news broadcaster said, "barring a federal court order or a commutation from the governor, husband and wife convicted killers Jack and Ginger Tatum are scheduled to die in the electric chair at Scrubb State Prison." The reporter went on to summarize a story that everyone in the state and probably half the people in the nation had heard at least a dozen times.

More than a decade earlier, Jack and Ginger had been high-school sweethearts, Jack from a poor family, Ginger from affluence. Ginger's parents had, naturally, not approved, and after graduation insisted she enroll in an Ivy League college well removed from Jack's influence. The young lovers rebelled.

For money to run away together, Jack and Ginger tried to rob the safe in her father's study. The father caught them and held Jack at gunpoint while his wife summoned the police. Jack jumped the father, there was a struggle for the gun, and the father was shot.

Jack and Ginger fled in the new car Ginger had received as a graduation present. At a roadblock some hours later, there was a shootout with two sheriff's deputies and one of the officers was killed. The young couple escaped again. While on the run, they kidnapped a justice of the peace and forced him to marry them, then committed a series of convenience-store holdups, one of which resulted in yet another killing, this one a part-time clerk who rashly pulled a gun from under the cash register and was shot point-blank by Jack.

Although Ginger's father had survived his gunshot wound, when the couple was caught in a massive manhunt a week later they were charged with the deaths of the deputy and the store clerk. Tried and convicted in separate trials, they were both sentenced to death. Now, after ten years on their respective Death Rows, Jack and Ginger were facing imminent execution. Odds were, it was going to happen.

After his shave, and a shower, Kenner dressed and went downstairs to face whatever he had to face on the domestic front before going out to face what he had to face on the professional front. In the kitchen, he could tell by the look on his wife's face that the tension had been exacerbated. Elaine, scrambling eggs at the stove, barely glanced at him, her expression cloudy, lips compressed. Toast and coffee were on the table, which was set only for two.

"Susan gone already?" Kenner asked, surprised there was no setting for her.

"No, she's putting a garment bag in her car. She said she wasn't hungry." When the eggs were ready, Elaine dished them up and brought the plates to the table. "I don't think I'll ever forgive you for this, Grant," she said evenly, an emotionless tone that Elaine used only for the most serious denunciations.

"Forgive *me?*" Kenner said. "For what?"

"You know very well for what. For what she's doing, that's for what."

"Elaine, you can't very well blame *me* for what *she* is doing," he said. "Susan is twenty-one years old. She's a grown woman making her own decisions. She knows what she's doing."

"You could stop her if you wanted to, Grant," his wife challenged. "You know it and I know it. She's been her daddy's girl all her life. One word of discouragement from you and she'd forget this ridiculous idea and go back to school. One more year and she'd have her degree—"

"And then what, Elaine?" Kenner asked, as nonconfrontationally as possible. "Teach elementary school for a few years, like you did? Then go back and get a master's degree, like you did? Become a high-school American history teacher and then a vice-principal, like you did?"

"And what, may I ask, is wrong with that?" Elaine continued to challenge. She was an especially attractive woman, with hair not particularly stylish but singularly suited to her, and eyes that were direct and always wide with interest. But in moments of anger, her comeliness was overshadowed by her own malevolence. This was one of those moments.

"There's nothing wrong with it, nothing at all," Kenner answered her protest. "But that's you, Elaine. That's not Susan."

"What's not Susan?" a voice asked from the doorway as their daughter entered the room. She was a younger, not quite as attractive version of her mother, with a firmer line of jaw that had come from her father. "I'm going to have to make you two eat separately if you don't stop arguing at the table," she said lightly, sitting down and taking a bite of her father's toast.

"This is *not* funny, young lady!" Elaine snapped. "You might very well be ruining your life."

"Well, it's mine to ruin, isn't it, Mother?" Susan replied in a much more subdued tone.

Elaine ignored Susan and drilled her husband with an unblinking stare. "Grant, you know how I feel about this. Are you going to support me on it or not?"

Kenner shook his head. "No, Elaine, I'm sorry, I'm not."

"Fine." Elaine tossed her napkin down and left the table. Several minutes later, the front door slammed and her car backed out of the driveway.

"Can't manage to stay out of trouble, can you, Dad?" Susan commented.

"Not with you around, I can't," her father replied.

Susan sighed heavily. "I'm sorry, Daddy. I really am. I just don't know how to act around her anymore."

"Sometimes I don't either," Grant agreed quietly, almost to himself. He thought of their bed upstairs and how infrequently it was used for anything except sleeping.

"I think the only way I could make her happy," Susan said, "is to let her run my life exactly the way she wants it to run."

"Your mother loves you, honey," Kenner rationalized. "And she's convinced that what you're doing is wrong for you. She wouldn't be much of a mother if she didn't try to make you see that."

"Do you think what I'm doing is wrong?"

"I have no idea," Kenner admitted. "We'll all just have to wait and see. But I know this: If *you* think it's right, then you owe it to yourself to try it—no matter what anybody says."

"Thanks, Daddy." Susan rose and kissed him on the cheek. "I think I'll leave now. I want to be early. First day and all."

"Good idea."

Susan left the kitchen, and presently her car, too, backed out of the drive.

Kenner sat in silence for a few minutes, finishing his coffee, wondering how she would do, trying to remember how it felt to be young and unsure, taking the first step on a new path.

But she would be all right, he told himself. He was sure she would.

He cleared the table, put the dishes in the dishwasher, and went out to his own car.

At Scrubb State Prison, Jack Tatum paced up and down

in the execution holding cell.

"Hey, man," he said to a muscular young death-watch officer sitting outside the bars, "what time does the DWC get here?" He was asking about the deputy warden of custody, who was in charge of his execution.

"Can't say, Tatum," the officer answered. "He don't work for me."

"Well, when does Ginger get here from the women's prison?"

"Don't know that either," the officer replied.

"Am I going to be able to visit with her when she gets here?"

"Don't know."

"You don't know much of anything, do you?" Tatum said scornfully.

"I know one thing," the officer replied evenly. "I'll probably be here tomorrow and you won't."

"I'm going to report that!" Tatum snapped. "You're not supposed to say *nothing* about me dying! No comments at all! That's a *rule!*" He stepped close to the bars and put a Marlboro between his lips. "Get your ass over here and light my cigarette," he ordered.

The officer sauntered over and fired up a Zippo for Tatum. As they stood close together, there was a striking difference in their appearance. The officer, a member of the elite prison death squad, was curly-haired, tanned, buffed. Tatum was balding in front from a nervous habit of pulling at his hair when he worried, his body was flaccid from lack of exercise, and his complexion, from a decade without sunshine, resembled provolone.

Smoking now, the condemned man grew quiet and began to pace again. He wore soft felt slippers, so his movement was soundless. The cell he was in, thirty feet from the execution chamber, had a solid rear wall and was barred floor to ceiling on the other three sides. There was a metal bunk against one set of bars, a new cotton-ticking mattress and pillow on it, and a stainless-steel combination sink and toilet on the solid back wall. A cardboard box on the cement floor contained personal photographs and rubber-banded bundles of letters, all he had been allowed to bring with him from his old cell on Death Row. His legal papers from that cell were in a file box in the DWC's office, waiting to be turned over to the United Civil Liberties lawyer who had been handling Tatum's appeal at the federal level and was now rushing final pleas through the appellate courts as well as pursuing a commutation request with the governor.

As Tatum paced and smoked, his thoughts focused again on Ginger. He had not seen her, except in occasional television news clips, since he testified at her trial more than ten years earlier, testimony that he and Ginger's lawyers had hoped, by him saying that he had forced her to go with him, would result in a sentence less than death. But felony murder was felony murder, and Ginger had been packing the dead convenience-store clerk's pistol when they were finally caught, naked in bed in a Holiday Inn, by a small army of lawmen. By the time Ginger was tried, Jack had already been convicted and given the max, so Ginger's jury saw no reason to let the little rich girl off after sentencing the poor boy to ride the lightning of Old Sparky. Ginger was given a death sentence also, and the poolroom and newsroom odds were that she would be the first woman electrocuted in the state in half a century.

But it was not the memory of her at the trial that surfaced in Jack's mind as he paced in his holding cell this morning, it was the memory of their last night together in that Holiday Inn. They had been intimate in an awkward but improving fashion since they were seventeen, but only in the month following high-school graduation, in a makeshift place fixed up in a shed behind Jack's ramshackle home, did they begin to align themselves in a physical union so exact, so precise, that they were certain it had reached perfection. But they were wrong. Only after they had participated in murder, only after they had been hunted like animals by men with guns, only with the new emotions of panic, fear, and dread being introduced into their mutual desire, did they, that last night, reach a summit of gratification unlike any they could have imagined.

It was that last night, Tatum thought as he paced, that had been worth whatever price he had to pay: the killings, the long years on the Row, the electric chair—*anything*.

That had been his time in heaven. Now if he had to go to hell as payment, so be it.

Grant Kenner could see the milling crowd of people and the state-police cars from a full mile away as the highway dipped down into the barren valley where Scrubb State Prison was situated. As he got closer to the perimeter-fence gate, he was able to read some of the signs the people carried: SAVE JACK & GINGER! and ABOLISH THE CHAIR! and CAPITAL PUNISHMENT IS MURDER! and numerous others. In a smaller group, kept separate by a loose cordon of state troopers, were those with signs that read HAVE A SEAT, JACK! and EYE FOR AN EYE! and BURN, GINGER, BURN! At the moment, everyone appeared to be reasonably peaceful. But Kenner knew that in a few hours there would be twice as many people, maybe more, and their collective dispositions would become unruly. Especially after the media got there. Everyone would have a point—and everyone would want to make it, loud and clear, for the whole world.

As Kenner pulled up to the gate, the perimeter officer gave him a casual salute and said, "Morning, sir."

"Morning," said Kenner. "Any problems?"

"Not as long as these boys are here," the officer replied, bobbing his chin at the troopers.

"I'll have an extra half-dozen men down here beginning at noon anyway," Kenner told him, "just in case." As he was speaking, a state-police lieutenant walked over from a radio cruiser parked nearby.

"Morning, sir," he said, saluting the same way the gate officer had.

"Morning, Lieutenant. Crowd under control?"

"Peaceful and quiet," the lieutenant said, "just like good citizens ought to be. But we have standby officers ready to report if we need them."

"Sounds good. I'll have some of my officers down here around noon to help close to the gate. Make sure your men know they're welcome to come up to our officers' dining room for coffee and sandwiches whenever they have a break."

"Thank you, sir. Appreciate that."

He saluted again, and Kenner drove on through the gate. He passed through a second, interior, perimeter fence, this one electrified and topped with four feet of razor wire. Then, a hundred yards farther along, he came to the walled prison itself, fronted by a large parking lot, one side for visitors, one side for personnel. The first three spaces in the latter section were marked WARDEN, DEPUTY WARDEN—CUSTODY, and DEPUTY WARDEN—ADMINISTRATION. Kenner parked in the middle space.

Scrubb State Prison's administrative offices were literally

built into the wall of the prison, half of them outside, half inside, the two areas separated by a deadlock corridor that could be opened only one end at a time, by separate officers. Kenner's office was inside the wall. As he passed through it this morning, he suddenly realized that he had been walking that passageway for half his life—twenty-four years: first as a trainee corrections officer, then as a gate officer, tower officer, yard officer, tier officer, block officer, sergeant, lieutenant, captain, and finally deputy warden. He knew he would never be appointed warden; that always went to the administrative deputy, the one who knew about things like budgets, purchase orders, monthly reports, annual projections. Kenner knew about discipline, rules, punishment. And executions. As far as the warden's job was concerned, he didn't want it anyway. In another seven years, when he was fifty-five, he'd take his retirement, pick up a couple of soft consultant jobs with private security firms, buy himself a new cabin cruiser, and try to set a record for consecutive days of catching albacore.

Passing out of the deadlock corridor, Kenner entered the anteroom of his office, where Mildred Daley, his secretary, was at her desk.

"Morning, Millie," he said. "Everything on schedule?"

"Like clockwork," Mildred said. Already past her own retirement age, she had been a fixture at Scrubb for many years. Her husband and two sons, all corrections officers, had been taken hostage and killed in the bloody four-day riot that had occurred there during Kenner's fourth year on the job. No one had thought Millie would want to come to work at the prison after that, but she had. She told Kenner once it was the only place she could really stay close to her lost loved ones.

"What's the word from the holding cell?" Kenner asked.

"Last report was that Jack wanted to know if he was going to get to play kissy-face with Ginger when she gets here. Warden says it's your call."

Kenner shook his head. "Against policy. They'll each have separate areas to visit with their respective families. Blood relatives are allowed to visit briefly if they're both condemned, but not husbands and wives. Anyway, there's still a difference of opinion as to whether these two are even legally married. The justice of the peace *did* have a gun to his head."

"Is that our official position?"

"It is. What's the status on Ginger?"

"Lieutenant Geary and four death-watch officers went over to Waverly to get her. They have a state-police escort coming back." Waverly was the women's prison twenty miles away.

"Okay," Kenner said. "Get my execution staff in here for a run-through."

Kenner's execution staff, four officers of varying age and experience, sat in a tight semicircle around the front of his desk, each holding a clipboard which held a copy of the official execution schedule of Jack and Ginger Tatum.

"Okay," Kenner said to open the meeting, "barring any unexpected court order or possible commutation from the governor, Jack will go at six o'clock this evening and Ginger at seven. When Ginger arrives from Waverly, she will be kept, under Lieutenant Geary's control, in an isolation wing of the hospital that has been cleared out for her. After Jack's execution, she will be brought at once to the death-watch holding cell. Up until that time, everything on their schedule will be staggered timewise by an hour, except for the final family visits. Those will be from two to four for both of them.

"As usual, I will be in operational charge of the execution process, and Bob," he nodded at his assistant deputy warden of custody, Robert Simms, "will be in logistical command. Bob, let's go over the visits first."

"Right," said Simms. "Jack's will be in the Death Row visiting area, which is closed for the day to other visitors. Ginger's will be in the hospital dining room, which will be secured immediately after the noon meal. Both areas will be configured in standard final-visit layout: a long table down the middle of the room, a single chair on one side for the condemned person, four chairs on the opposite side to accommodate the maximum number of visitors allowed at one time. A death-watch officer will be stationed in a standing position at each end of the table throughout the visits. A third officer will be at the door on the visitors' side and will supervise the entry and exit of each visitor. One embrace and one kiss will be allowed at the beginning of the visit, one of each at the end. Hands must be kept on top of the table at all times, but may not touch. All visitors will be strip-searched prior to entering. No food or drink will be allowed during the visits. No smoking is allowed. As stated, the visits will begin at two o'clock this afternoon and terminate promptly at four o'clock with the condemned persons being taken back to their respective holding areas. Lieutenant Briar will be in charge of the entire procedure."

Kenner looked at Lieutenant Edward Briar. "Ed, everything clear? Any questions?"

"I'm all set," said Briar. "I'll meet with my people at one o'clock to go over our checklist, and we'll begin strip-searching visitors at one-thirty. Three female officers will search women visitors in a separate area."

"Okay," said Kenner. "Bob, last meals?"

"Taken care of," said Simms. "Jack's will be served at four-thirty in his death-watch cell. He's ordered cheeseburgers, French fries, onion rings, a couple of chocolate shakes, and cherry pie *à la mode*. Ginger gets her meal at five-thirty in the hospital isolation wing. Her order was telephoned over from Waverly yesterday: New York cut steak cooked medium well, creamed asparagus, baked potato with sour cream and chives, dinner rolls, butter, and iced mint tea. Lieutenant Kramer is in charge of this detail."

Kenner turned to Lieutenant K. C. Kramer. "Casey, all set?"

"Yes, sir. Running smoothly. We sent an officer into town last night for the mint tea."

"Okay," Kenner nodded. "Showers and shaves?"

"Jack showers at five-fifteen, puts on a new set of clothes in the shower room, and is returned to his holding cell to be shaved," said Simms. "Prior to that, the barber will have shaved his right calf and his head. Jack's picked a lot of his hair out in front, but still has fairly thick hair in back. He's asked if we can just shave a spot large enough for the electrode."

"Negative," said Kenner. "Shave his whole head. They tried spot-shaving down in Florida a while back and the guy's hair caught on fire. Even the witnesses could smell it. The result was a lot of bad press."

Simms made a note on his clipboard. "What about Ginger?" he asked. "She showers at five forty-five under the watch of four female officers, then dresses in a new set of clothes sent over from Waverly. She hasn't arrived yet, but I understand from a telephone conversation with the warden over there that she's got a jungle of thick red hair."

"Shave her head," Kenner ordered. A couple of his staff looked down self-consciously. Kenner drummed his fingers, not entirely comfortable with the order.

"Ginger also requested through the warden at Waverly that she be allowed to wear some, uh, personal underwear that she's bringing with her today."

Kenner pursed his lips slightly and continued to drum his fingers silently. A thought of his daughter Susan flared in his mind. She and Ginger were in the same generation.

"Okay," he said. "But let's do it discreetly. Don't mention it to the public-relations officer. I don't want the press getting this." Kenner turned to Lieutenant Beau Spangler. "You running this detail, Bo? Make sure the female officers handling Ginger do this underwear thing quietly. I'll pass the word to Lieutenant Geary myself."

"Yessir."

Kenner sat back in his big chair. "What else?"

"Clergymen," said Simms. "Ed will take charge of that. Each condemned person will have one clergyman in attendance from the end of the family visits all the way to the door of the death chamber."

"Okay. Witnesses?"

"That'll be Casey's job after the final meals. He and his crew will check credentials and ID, and escort everyone to assigned seating in the viewing room. Families of the condemned will sit on the left, families of the victims on the right, official witnesses, law enforcement representatives, and selected media will be in the middle."

Mildred stuck her head in the door. "Ginger Tatum just got here. Lieutenant Geary wants to know if you'd like to have coffee in the dining room before you see her?"

"Sure," said Kenner. "About ten minutes." His eyes swept the faces of his staff. "Anything else we need to deal with right now?" There was nothing. "Okay," said Kenner, "let's run this show nice and smoothly. Everybody check in with me either in person or by phone at three and five o'clock. Unless the warden decides differently, Bob and I will handle the last walks at six and seven."

He stood up, a signal that the staff meeting was over.

In the officers' dining room, Kenner drew a mug of coffee from a large self-serve urn and took it over to a table where Lieutenant Geary was sitting.

"Morning, Rachel," he said.

"Good morning, Grant." She looked up, smiling, a broad-shouldered woman with sensible short hair, only a trace of makeup, and steady russet eyes. The grey-and-green combination of her uniform was in her color season and gave her complexion a nice balance that some other female officers did not enjoy.

"Ginger settled in?" Kenner asked.

"Yes."

"How did the transfer from Waverly go?"

"Nice and easy. The state police kept the media vultures at bay, and Ginger put a sweater over her head to prevent pictures at the gate."

"What's she like?"

Rachel shrugged. "Pretty. Personable. But still a lot like any other female con. She's been inside long enough to have a convict mentality working. I get the impression she never really expected today to come."

"Do any of them?" Kenner asked rhetorically. He drummed his fingers again. "Listen, I've given tentative permission for her to, uh, wear some kind of, uh, personal stuff—"

"The underwear she brought," Rachel said knowingly. "You're getting easy, Grant," she chided good-naturedly.

"Maybe I am," he admitted. "Her hair is bothering me,

too. I don't particularly want to have her head shaved, but I don't want a burning incident either. Do you think we can get away with a patch shave?"

"I don't know," Rachel replied doubtfully. "She's got a real mop. If we could pull it back tightly, maybe braid it—I don't know."

"Work on it, will you?" Kenner asked. "Technically, Bo Spangler is heading up the detail for this, but for the most part he'll probably leave Ginger to the women officers."

"I'll see what I can do," Rachel said. "You going over to see her before or after her family visits?"

"Before, I think."

Now it was Rachel who drummed her fingers briefly. "How'd it go with Elaine today?" she asked.

"Not well," Kenner admitted. "She's determined not to accept Susan's decision on her future, and she's holding me responsible for it."

"You never encouraged Susan, did you?"

"No, but apparently I was expected to *dis*courage her." Kenner looked searchingly at Rachel Geary. "What would you have done?" he asked, almost an appeal.

"You're asking the wrong person," Rachel quickly demurred. "I've been through two unsuccessful marriages and have a teenage daughter from each of them that thinks I'm unreasonable and overprotective. On top of that, I just ended a longtime relationship with a man they both liked very much, so now they also think I'm mentally unstable and need therapy of some kind. I am the *last* person you need to ask for advice about domestic relations."

"You broke up with—what's his name, Don? The insurance man?" Kenner was staring incredulously at her.

"Yes, I did," she replied, a hint defensively.

"I thought you two were on the verge of getting married," Kenner said, perplexed.

"We were. Then the subject of my job came up. Don has been promoted to regional vice president. He didn't feel that a 'prison guard,' as he calls it, was the proper job for a regional vice president's wife to have. So," she shrugged her broad shoulders, "we called it off."

"You wouldn't give up your job for him?"

"No, why should I?" Almost miffed now. "My job is as important to me as his is to him. I put in a lot of hard work to get these lieutenant's bars. More hard work than the men have to put in—you know that as well as I do, Grant."

"I do know that," he agreed.

"No," she reiterated, "I won't give up my job for anyone." She stared off into space for a moment. "He had no right to ask me to do that."

Kenner reached over and briefly squeezed one of her hands. "Well, I'm sorry," he said earnestly. "Sorry it didn't work out for you."

Rachel fixed him in a curious stare. "Are you?" she asked quietly. "Are you really sorry?"

Kenner, surprised by her candor, parted his lips to speak, but found no appropriate words. Before he could conjure up any, his assistant deputy, Bob Simms, hurried up to him.

"Warden wants to see you, Grant. The size of the crowd at the front gate and along the outer fence is increasing very fast. We may not have access to enough state troopers to control it. And the men on the Row are starting to get a little unruly."

"Unruly how?"

"Just noise so far."

"All right." Kenner rose and drank the last of his coffee. "Send six officers out to the gate right away, Bob. I'll go see the warden. Then I'll run over to the Row."

"I'll take care of that other matter for you," Rachel Geary said, finishing her own coffee.

Leaving the dining room, the three parted.

Kenner's counterpart, Martin Raddis, the deputy warden of administration, was already in the warden's second-floor office when Kenner arrived.

"Everything on schedule?" the warden asked the moment Kenner entered.

"So far," Kenner replied. "What's up with the crowd?"

"Martin just drove in from his budget meeting with the auditors. You tell him, Martin."

"The trooper in charge at the outer-perimeter fence almost wasn't able to clear a path to the gate for me," Raddis said. "He told me the crowd's doubled in just the last hour. They've got all their standby officers on duty, but it doesn't look like that'll be enough. They're worried about how the final visitors and the witnesses will get in."

Kenner went to a wide picture window behind the warden's desk and raised a pair of high-powered binoculars that were always there. Through them, he could see across the main prison yard, on beyond the high wall, across the no-man's-land between the two razor-wire fences, to the perimeter gatehouse, which now presented a milling mob scene of people who not only were spreading out in both directions along the perimeter fence itself, but overflowing onto the two-lane highway, backing up traffic in both directions.

"What do you think, Grant?" the warden asked.

"I hate to say it," said Kenner, "but we're probably going to need the National Guard. I don't see any way around it." He looked at Raddis. "What do you think, Martin?"

"I agree. In addition to final visitors and witnesses, you've got a shift change in a few hours. The day shift has to be able to get out, and the night shift has to be able to get in. It'll put a dent in this month's budget if the shifts overlap." Raddis reduced every problem to dollars.

"What if I keep the day shift on duty until after the executions?" Kenner asked. "Can we afford an extra four hours' pay for everyone on days?"

Raddis shrugged. "If absolutely necessary," he said reluctantly.

"Take the money out of the public-relations budget," the warden groused. "That doesn't seem to be working anyway." He looked at Kenner. "Shall I ask the governor to call out the National Guard?"

"I think we have to." Kenner put down the binoculars and moved away from the window. "I'm going over to the Row. Simms says they're getting noisy."

The warden, shaking his head, picked up the phone. "Let's at least try to keep things under control inside," he said, "even if we can't outside."

"Yes, sir," Kenner and Raddis said in unison, and left.

In the hall, Raddis asked, "You seen Ginger yet?"

"No," said Kenner. "I'm going over there in a little while."

"You have all the fun," said Raddis, who was a bachelor and aware that Ginger Tatum had been sought as the first Death Row centerfold by several magazines.

"Yeah, right," said Kenner.

The two men parted and Kenner went back through the deadlock corridor, which he had come through to get to the warden's office, and left the inner-wall building to walk across a beautifully groomed inner yard intersected by two sidewalks which formed four squares of manicured lawn bordered by a myriad of seasonal flowers. Half a dozen convicts were at work clipping, trimming, and edging. In charge of them was a lean, gray-haired wife killer whose death sentence had been commuted the year Kenner became a corrections officer. He stood up from his gardening when Kenner approached.

"Morning, Mr. Kenner," he said.

"Morning, Franklin. How are you?"

"Arthritis is acting up again," the old convict said, rubbing his upper arm. "I'm going to need an easier job one of these days."

"Anytime you want it, Franklin," Kenner said. "You've earned it."

"I know. But I can't stand the thought of being away from my flowers." Franklin glanced over his shoulder. "Heading for the Row?"

"Yes. Rumors of unrest."

"It's going to be a little more than that," Franklin said very quietly, barely moving his lips now in practiced convict fashion. Kenner said nothing. He could not ask Franklin for information; Franklin had to volunteer it. Any other way would have compromised Kenner's position of authority and involuntarily indebted him to Franklin. On the other hand, if Franklin *offered* information without being asked, Kenner would still be indebted to him, but it would be an obligation he voluntarily accepted rather than solicited. A fine line, but a line nevertheless. And in a maximum-security prison, such lines were vital.

So Kenner waited. And Franklin volunteered.

"Word I have is that a major disturbance will break out at four-thirty, when Jack gets his last meal. They're going to wreck the Row. It's a protest that's really for Ginger, but the thinking is that if the commotion causes the governor to

72

commute Ginger, he'll automatically have to commute Jack."

"Interesting theory," Kenner allowed. "Not a chance of working, but still interesting." He nodded his thanks. "You let me know when you want that new job, and what it is."

"I'll want to sell this one," Franklin said. Good jobs in prison were customarily sold from convict to convict.

"No problem," Kenner told him. "Just make sure you get me someone who'll keep the place looking as good as you do."

"Check," said the old convict, and resumed his work.

When Kenner got to the wing that housed Death Row, he went through a mini-deadlock similar to the main corridor through the wall, where only one steel door at a time opened, and each was controlled by a separate officer. Some disorganized shouting could be heard by Kenner as soon as he passed the inner door. Lieutenant Bart Munro, the day-watch Row commander, came out of his office to meet Kenner.

"I hope you're not here to tell me that Tatum's been commuted," Munro said by way of greeting. "He's one of the biggest pains in the ass I've ever had in here and I definitely do not want him back."

"No commute so far," Kenner said, leading Munro back into the office. "But you may have a riot today at four-thirty."

"How good's the tip?" Munro asked, frowning.

"Get your fire hoses unrolled," Kenner instructed. "That's how good."

"Shit," said Munro. "I was planning to leave early today. My oldest boy is in a Little League tournament that begins this afternoon."

"We've also got an increasing crowd-control problem at

the main gate," Kenner said, "so keep your day-shift crew on board until we see if any night-shift arrivals are delayed. We may keep both shifts here until after the executions anyway."

"Okay," Munro said, disgruntled.

"Your boy pitching?" Kenner asked.

"Yeah."

"Well, listen, try to reach Chris if you want to. See if he can come in early." He was talking about Chris Jacoby, the night-watch Death Row lieutenant. "If he can get here to relieve you, go ahead and take off. We don't need two lieutenants here. But make sure you tell him about the possibility of trouble this afternoon, understand?"

"Yeah, sure. Thanks, Grant." As Kenner started to leave, Munro asked, "You seen Ginger yet?"

"No."

"She sure looked good in those TV clips last night. What a great rack. You going to let Tatum see her?"

"No."

"Good. Bastard doesn't deserve to."

"I'll check back with you about four," Kenner said, and left.

Rachel Geary was working with Ginger Tatum's lush red hair when Kenner got to the hospital isolation wing to see her. Not yet thirty, she had a drop-dead figure and was buffed but not muscular from years of in-cell aerobics. Wearing a tank top, she clearly had, as Bart Munro said, a great rack. Two other women officers stood nearby. All four of them were chit-chatting about hair problems, but the conversation ceased when Kenner appeared.

"Ginger, this is Deputy Warden Kenner," Rachel introduced them.

"Hi there, Mr. Kenner," said Ginger. Not a trace of nervousness. On the surface anyway.

"Hello, Ginger," Kenner said. "I'm here to see you more or less officially as head of custody for the prison, but also to find out if everything's going all right for you here and if there's anything I can do for you."

"Everything's okay," the condemned woman said. "I'm fine. Miss Geary and the other ladies are treating me real nice."

"How's the hair problem working out, Lieutenant?" Kenner asked Rachel.

"Not well, so far." Rachel brushed Ginger's mane back. "She's got enough hair to upholster a couch."

"Well, keep trying," Kenner said. "There must be something we can do to avoid—uh, you know."

Ginger put a hand on Kenner's arm, and all three officers tensed because it was a glaring violation of prison rules. But it was such a natural gesture that everyone, including Kenner, let it pass as Ginger began saying, "Listen, don't worry about it, Mr. Kenner. If I have to lose it, I have to lose it. Long as it's after my family visit is all I care about."

"It will be," Kenner assured her.

"Will you be going with me, you know, tonight?" Ginger asked.

"Yes, that's part of my duties," Kenner said. "I'll be there to take care of any last messages you have, any notes or letters, that kind of thing. And if there's anything at all you need during the day—visitors added to your list, something else on your last meal, things like that—have Lieutenant Geary get in touch with me."

"Am I going to be able to say goodbye to Jack?" she asked.

Kenner shook his head. "I'm afraid not, Ginger. That's a

regulation we just can't get around. If we made an exception in your case, convict litigation over it in the future would be endless."

"I understand," she said, removing her hand at last. Her bare arms, like the deep cleavage disappearing into her tank top, were lightly freckled. When she smiled, she had a dimple in each cheek. "Just tell him I said 'So long' then, I guess."

"I'll do that."

As he was leaving, Kenner took the other two women officers aside and asked quietly, "Has that, uh, matter of the, uh, underwear been taken care of?"

"Yes, sir. She'll go in lime-green panties and bra from Victoria's Secret. Under a prison-issue blouse and skirt, of course."

"Of course." Kenner cleared his throat. "All right. Carry on."

As he left, he thought: *Carry on?* What in hell made him say that? He sounded like some strait-laced British army colonel. Damn!

Between two and four in the afternoon, each of the condemned prisoners had their final family visits.

In the hospital wing's dining room, which was closed off immediately following the eleven-thirty lunch serving, Ginger visited with her father, mother, two older brothers, and one older sister. Kenner had approved an exception to the maximum four visitors to allow all of them to visit at once. The regular dining room furniture had been moved to the side walls, and a long serving table had been set lengthwise in the middle of the room, several clean white tablecloths spread to cover its full length, and folding chairs lined up on one side for the visitors. Ginger, wearing prison-issue skirt and blouse from Waverly, sat on a folding chair on the opposite side. She had been moved from the hospital isolation ward in shackles, handcuffs, and a waist chain, but they had been removed just outside the door before she was taken into where her visitors waited. One woman from among her escort officers stood at each end of the visiting table, two others were posted at the door, one inside, one outside. Ginger had made a request, through Rachel Geary, that her visitors be allowed at least soft drinks and, "You know, peanuts or pretzels or something," to break up the starkness of the bare white table. Kenner had granted the request and instructed the inmate kitchen help to prepare an urn of Kool-Aid and half a dozen bowls of popcorn, along with paper cups and napkins.

In the Death Row wing, the visiting room was already configured for maximum-security screened visits, with a long counter running wall to wall, its undersection cemented to the floor, and a tightly interlaced metal grille extending from its countertop to the ceiling. A large room, which could accommodate a dozen condemned men having visits at one time, it was always reserved exclusively for the use of one person on the day of his execution, and a section of the grille was removed for final visits to allow the permitted kiss and embrace at the beginning and end of the two-hour period. There were vending machines for soft drinks and snacks on the visitor side, and on normal visiting days condemned men were allowed to bring something from the commissary supply in their cells if they chose to. But under the rules of no food or drink for final visits, as had been discussed at Kenner's staff meeting, the vending machines were usually disabled by closing and locking a security face on each of them, and the man awaiting execution could bring nothing into the room with him because he had nothing in the holding cell to bring. As Kenner had done with Ginger, however, and as was his policy with final visits, he usually relaxed the rule long enough for Death Row officers to supervise the purchase of snacks and drinks and to allow a reasonable amount to be passed to the prisoner. This was done for Jack Tatum, even though, as Lieutenant Bart Munro had said, Tatum had been an ongoing behavior problem for them during most of his decade on the Row, and Munro would have kept strictly to the book in his case. But it was Kenner's decision, and Kenner decided to allow it, particularly since Jack's visit was being kept simple anyway: just his widowed father and an older sister and her husband.

During the period when the visits were occurring, two emergency companies of National Guardsmen arrived and restored some semblance of order at and around the main prison gate. Kenner drove out to the gate and conferred with a colonel in charge of the troops, and was given assurance that crowd order would be maintained. Guardsmen were already separating the protesters from the supporters and moving them onto two different areas of the barren open plain across from the prison, while establishing a fifty-foot neutral zone between them.

On the way back to the walls, Kenner reported by radio to the warden that all was secure at the gate, then contacted Lieutenant Ed Briar, who was overseeing the final visits, and learned that both of them, now concluded, had transpired without incident except at the very end when Ginger's father had hyperventilated and had to be removed to a nearby vacant hospital room to be stabilized. On Jack's side, the condemned man had become somewhat defiant in heatedly demanding to be allowed to personally say goodbye to Ginger, and had to be forced back into his holding cell. He was now calm, however, his attorney and the prison chaplain were with him, and his last meal was on its way from the main kitchen on a steam cart.

When Kenner got back inside the walls and parked, before leaving the car, he radioed in to the Death Row lieutenant's desk. Chris Jacoby, the Death Row night lieutenant, answered.

"I guess you and Bart made a deal," Kenner said when he heard Jacoby's voice.

"Yeah, my little girl's got a dance recital in a couple weeks," said Jacoby. "Bart's going to pay me back the time then."

"He fill you in on the possible problem this afternoon?"

"Yes, sir."

"Okay. What's the situation up there at the moment?"

"Warming up. Listen—" Jacoby held the receiver toward the open door of his office. Through it, Kenner could hear a cacophony of cadence-like chants interspersed with sounds of aluminum cups being tapped in loud staccato against steel bars. The singsong incantation was a mixed verse of "NO MORE ELECTRIC CHAIR!" and "KILL ONE OF OURS, WE'LL KILL ONE OF YOURS!"

"Hear it?" Jacoby asked.

"I heard," said Kenner. "Got your hoses out?"

"Connected and ready."

"Okay. Let them make all the racket they want, but the first sign of anything burning—magazines, pillow cases, mattress ticking, anything—I want the cell it comes out of hosed down—totally. Not just a warning spray; I want the cell drenched. See if we can neutralize the protest before it builds up momentum. I'd like to keep it from reaching the general population if we can."

"Got you, Chief," said Jacoby. "Bart said you wanted the day shift to stay on. That still go?"

"Until further notice. I'll be in my office if you need me."

Kenner's assistant deputy, Bob Simms, was waiting when he got inside. "Media's just been let in," he told Kenner. "Warden's going to give his canned statement in conference room two, then turn it over to Laney for the rest of the day." Laney was Darlene Laney, the official prison spokesperson and public-relations supervisor, through whom all information about the execution schedule and events would, with the media as a conduit, begin to flow.

"Lawyers and ministers been advised where the media will be?"

"Yeah, I just called the death watch and had them pass the word."

"Make sure we have enough escort officers posted between the holding cell and the conference room, and the hospital wing and the conference room. I don't want any lawyers or preachers wandering around unescorted. Ginger's lawyer here?"

"Not yet." Simms shook his head. "He telephoned a couple times. Apparently he's at the state house making a final personal plea to the governor."

Kenner nodded. "Conference room one all set up for the witnesses to wait in?"

"Yes. Some of them are here already."

"What's the final count on victim witnesses?"

"Thirteen. Widow, two grown children, two brothers of the deputy sheriff. Widow, three grown children, husbands of two of them, two grandchildren of the clerk."

"Grandchildren? How old?"

"Girl nineteen, boy twenty."

Jacoby, "after you hose down their cells, get on the loud-speaker and announce that further incidents of burning will result in *all* cells being hosed. Maybe we can get Lindholm and Canteno and some of the other heavyweights to put a stop to it."

"Good idea," said Jacoby. "Might work." Lindholm was a big-time holdup man who had to kill a bank guard who got heroic on him, and Canteno was a mob hit man who whacked a guy in a restaurant where a former high-school teacher of his happened to be dining and subsequently identified him. Along with half a dozen other professional criminals, they were the heavyweights of Death Row, as opposed to the child murderers, spouse killers, junkies, psychopathic home invaders, and convenience store–service station stickup freaks who made up most of the rest of the condemned population. Rarely did someone in the lowlife ranks get in the face of a heavyweight. A person like the hit man Canteno would kill another inmate without blinking, and everyone knew it.

"Keep me posted," Kenner advised. "I'll come up there personally if you want me to, but I'd rather not make it look that important."

"I'll handle it, Chief," Jacoby assured him.

Another call came in, from Lieutenant Briar, who was now in the holding cell area. "Jack's just finished his last meal. The lawyer and minister who were with him have gone up to the conference room to do their dog-and-pony show for the media. Bo Spangler and his boys are standing by to give Jack his shave, take him down to the shower, and dress him out. The chamber crew just came through to get Old Sparky ready."

"Make sure Bo gets a diaper on Jack; I want the chair clean for Ginger. Call the supply room and have them send over some spray deodorant, too."

"Will do."

Kenner then called Rachel Geary in the hospital isolation wing. "How's it going?"

"No problems," Rachel said. "Her meal was just delivered and she's eating it. A Catholic priest from her family's parish is sitting with her. They're talking about movies."

"Were you able to fix her hair?"

"I'm afraid not." Ginger's voice lowered. "We'll have to do a full shave. But one of the other ladies has a baseball cap in her locker. Do you suppose Ginger could wear that? At least until she's being strapped in?"

"Sure," Kenner consented at once. "Tell her I'm sorry about her hair. No, wait, don't tell her that. It's not in my job description to be sorry."

"Tough guy. Listen, there's one other thing, Grant. She's asked if I can walk with her. I know I'm not part of the chamber detail, and I know everything's very precise and regimented down there, but—"

"You can go with her all the way up to the door, Rachel. And it's very good of you to do it."

"Well, my daughters think I need therapy anyway, remember?"

"Yes, you told me that. Do you?"

"Do I what?"

"Need therapy."

"All I need is a good man, Grant. That's all I've *ever* needed." She sighed quietly. "Listen, this personal talk is getting kind of heavy. I'll see you over there, okay?"

"Okay."

Kenner hung up, feeling an odd wave of sadness.

Both men looked up at the clock on the office wall. It

was five-twenty. The phone rang again. It was Lieutenant Jacoby.

"The loudspeaker announcement worked," he reported. "Canteno and a couple of the other heavyweights issued a general threat that if anyone caused *their* cells to be hosed, the person wouldn't have to worry about waiting for Old Sparky. So everything's quiet now. Even the noise has stopped."

"Okay, Chris, thanks. Good work."

When Kenner relayed the information to Simms, the assistant deputy warden grunted quietly. "Death Row sure isn't what it used to be. Twenty years ago, when the death penalty was first reinstated, we would have had a full-scale disruption, everything that would burn would've been set on fire, toilets and sinks would've been smashed and the porcelain pieces thrown at officers, there would've been complete turmoil. Killers don't seem to have any loyalty to each other anymore. I think television in the cells changed everything."

"Whatever it was, I'm glad it happened," said Kenner. He looked at the clock again and stood up. "Come on, let's get it done."

Jack Tatum, fed, shaved, dressed in new prison issue, right trouser leg slit up the seam to the knee, paced up and down, speaking in clipped tones to his attorney and the chaplain, who had returned from the media room and stood outside the holding cell. He looked over as Kenner and Simms entered the area.

"How's Ginger doing?" he wanted to know at once.

"She's doing fine," Kenner said. He turned to the lawyer. "You'll have to say goodbye now, Counselor." Then to the death-watch officer, "Have the doctor and the rest of the chamber team come in."

"There's still some hope," the lawyer said to Tatum, as encouragingly as he could. "Your appeal for a stay of execution is with a federal judge, and your petition for a commutation is on the governor's desk right now." He and the condemned man shook hands through the bars. As the lawyer walked away, Tatum turned to Kenner.

"Ginger write me a letter, a note, anything like that?"

"No," Kenner said. He looked around as his six-man chamber team entered, preceded by the prison doctor, who carried a small black bag. "He's all yours, Doc," Kenner told him, then nodded to the death-watch officer. "Open the holding cell." And to the senior officer of the chamber team, "Open the entryway and the chamber door."

Simms, with the hand radio to his ear, said, "Witnesses are going in."

Kenner nodded. He watched closely as the doctor entered the holding cell with two officers, unbuttoned Tatum's light blue cotton shirt, and removed a two-piece stethoscope from the black bag. With adhesive tape, he attached one section—the sound-detector head and an eighteen-inch length of tubing—to Tatum's chest, rebuttoning the shirt with the tubing hanging out. Then the doctor departed the cell and walked toward the death-chamber entryway door, which had now been opened.

Tatum started to put a final cigarette between his lips, changed his mind, and tossed it onto the bunk. "Didn't Ginger give you no kind of message at all for me?" he asked Kenner imploringly.

Kenner repeated what Ginger had told him. "She just said to tell you 'So long,' that was all."

Tatum looked dumbstruck. "*So long?* That's it? Just 'So long'?"

"That's it," replied Kenner. To an officer, he said, "Remove the box of personal belongings and turn them over to the chaplain." Tatum's photographs and bundled letters were given to the chaplain, a Presbyterian minister, who placed them on a table across the room from the holding cell.

Tatum was shaking his head in astonishment. "So long," he repeated. "After all this."

Kenner, Simms, the chaplain, and all six members of the chamber team looked at the condemned man in silence. He continued shaking his head, helpless, bewildered, a pale, lost being at the edge of eternity. Finally Kenner looked at a wall clock above the death-watch officer's desk. It was five-fifty.

"Time to go, Jack," he said quietly.

Two of the chamber team stepped into the holding cell and gently guided Tatum out of it. The team formed a cordon around him, two behind, one on each side, two in front. The chaplain stepped into the queue, Kenner went to the front of it. On a nod from Kenner, they all began to move, Simms bringing up the rear with the hand radio to his ear.

They proceeded through the entryway door into the room which housed the execution chamber. It stood like some ugly, monolithic mistake, its hatchway door opened all the way back, revealing the squat, solid-oak electric chair it held, a three-sided viewing window behind it covered by closed venetian blinds. A long length of rubber tubing, for the stethoscope, lay across one arm of the chair and extended through a port to the outside of the chamber.

"Plug in the phone," Kenner ordered. An officer opened the door of a floor cabinet and removed a telephone which he set on top of the cabinet and plugged into a jack just above it. Kenner picked up the receiver and pressed the operator button. The prison switchboard responded on one ring.

"This is Deputy Warden Kenner in the execution chamber anteroom. Please verify that this line is in service to the governor's mansion and the clerk's office of the federal appeals court." All was silent while he waited for confirmation. "Thank you," he said after a moment, and hung up. As he stepped away, the officer who had plugged the phone in moved next to it and placed a hand on the receiver for immediate answering. "All right," said Kenner.

Three officers entered the chamber; each of them raised a blind on one side of the viewing window. Beyond the window, a sea of eyes widened as the witnesses looked into the chamber for the first time. The two officers outside the door of the chamber guided Tatum inside, turned him, and sat him in the chair. One of them attached the stethoscope tubing hanging from his shirt to the long length running through the chamber wall. Then they both stepped back out as the other three began strapping Tatum's arms, chest, and legs in place. Kenner entered the chamber and watched closely as an ankle electrode at the end of a thick black electrical cord was strapped in place on Tatum's right leg. Made of soft leather, with a natural sea-sponge lining that had been spread liberally with saline salve, this electrode was the return path of the current after it passed through the condemned person's body. When it was in place, Kenner knelt to inspect the fit. As he did so, the telephone rang in the antechamber.

Kenner rose quickly and squeezed past two officers to get out of the chamber. Behind him, he heard Jack Tatum say gleefully, "I knew it! I knew I'd get commuted! I knew I wouldn't go! Unstrap me!"

Kenner got to the telephone, which had already been answered by the officer next to it. Quickly taking the receiver, he said, "Deputy Warden Grant Kenner speaking." A pause as he listened intently. Then: "Yes, sir." Another pause, and: "Yes, sir. I understand, sir." A final pause, then: "Yes, sir. It's clear, sir. Yes, sir."

Kenner hung up. All eyes were on him as he moved over to the open door and back into the chamber. Jack Tatum was grinning at him like a madman. "Get me out of this goddamned chair, Kenner!" he demanded.

"Attach the head electrode," Kenner ordered the officer directly behind the chair.

"What?" Tatum shouted.

The officer quickly fitted to Tatum's shaved head a skullcap made of firmer leather than the ankle electrode, with a similar lining of natural sea sponge spread with saline salve, this one held in place by a mesh screening of copper wire for maximum conduction of the electricity.

"What the hell are you doing?" Tatum asked frantically, struggling against his restraints as the officer fastened a strap under his chin to hold the cap in place.

"Your execution will proceed as scheduled," Kenner said. "Attach the feeder," he told the officer.

A bolt was loosened in a spike on top of the skullcap, a bare six-ampere contact inserted, and the bolt retightened to hold it in place.

"But what about that call?" Tatum pleaded. The officers in the chamber filed out now and Kenner stepped behind the chair to inspect the head electrode. "Wasn't that call from the governor's office?" Tatum asked, nearing hysteria.

"Yes, it was." Kenner bent down to speak quietly in his ear. "But it wasn't about you, Jack. It was about Ginger. The governor has commuted her sentence to life in prison."

"What! But that can't be!"

Kenner stepped around the chair and snapped a soft leather mask in place over Tatum's face.

"How could he do that! It was all her idea! Everything we did!"

"Goodbye, Jack," said Kenner. He stepped to the door and out of the chamber.

"Wait a minute! She's even the one who killed the deputy! I was driving the car!"

An officer swung the big steel door—

"Wait a minute! Please wait a—!"

—closed, silencing the rest of Tatum's words.

Kenner moved to three officers who stood at an electrical panel with three switches on it. At his nod, each of them threw a switch. Only one switch was connected to the electric-chair generator, so the assigned officers never knew which of them activated the current.

In the chamber, twenty-four hundred volts of electricity, at five amps, surged into Jack Tatum's body, through his skull, for a full minute, and exited at his right ankle. He was unconscious in four milliseconds, which was twenty-four times faster than his central nervous system could record pain. Tatum's body pushed forward against the restraints that held him. After a full minute, the current stopped automatically, and the three switches on the control panel snapped back to their previous position.

With his stethoscope attached to the tubing running into the chamber, the doctor listened intently for sounds within Tatum's chest. "The heart is in spasm," he said after fifteen seconds. "The current didn't fully seize it."

Kenner nodded to the three officers at the panel and they each threw a switch again. The electrocution process was repeated. Another twenty-four hundred volts. Another full minute. The body lurching, then stopping limply. The doctor listening. Then: "He's dead."

"Record the time," Kenner instructed.

"Six-eleven," the doctor said.

As officers entered the chamber to close the blinds, Kenner walked back into the area of the holding cell, Bob Simms keeping pace briskly just behind him.

"Where's Ginger?" asked Kenner.

"On her way over."

"Have her taken back. She's been commuted. I'll be in the warden's office."

He walked away quickly as Simms began speaking urgently into his radio.

Three hours later, Kenner ran into Rachel Geary as they were both leaving to go home. They fell in step together walking toward the parking lot.

"Get Ginger back over to Waverly all right?" he asked.

"Yes, we did. Had her back in her old cell by seven-thirty. Still wearing her lime-green undies—but *without* all that beautiful hair. How'd Jack go?"

"Complaining about injustice," Kenner replied drily.

"I'll bet." Rachel laughed softly. "You should have seen the people at the gate when we left. With the day turning out to be a draw for them, the protesters became part supporters, and the supporters became part protesters. They didn't know quite how to act. Finally they just left."

"I can imagine what the media is already doing with the story," Kenner said. "Poor boy goes to the chair, rich girl gets commuted. Our esteemed governor really threw a hand grenade into the public's feelings today; something for everybody, but nobody got everything. Now everybody can wonder which mistake he made: killing Jack or letting Ginger live."

"I had a grandmother who was half Sioux Indian," Rachel said. "She believed that the mistakes made in life were just so people could enjoy getting over them. Without mistakes, she said, no one could ever be happy. And she didn't believe that mistakes had anything to do with how people end up in life. She said everybody followed a blood path handed down by all the ancestors that came before them; that those blood paths would lead people to the same place no matter what they did. Her grandfather told her that when she was a little girl, and she believed it until she died."

"Blood paths," Kenner said thoughtfully. "Interesting philosophy. I didn't know you were part Indian, Rachel."

"Lots of things about me you don't know, Grant."

They reached the parking lot and at once came to Kenner's car. Rachel paused to say goodnight, but Kenner gently took her arm and continued walking down the lot toward her parking space. The vapor lights over the lot gave a smoky cast to their faces. At Rachel's car, Kenner took the keys from her hand, unlocked the door, and held it open for her. She slid behind the wheel and he handed her the keys.

"You off shift for the weekend?" he asked, leaning down with one arm on the roof of the car.

"Yes, I am. You?"

"Yes."

"Got anything planned?"

"Probably drive over to the coast and take my old boat out, do a little fishing."

"Do you and Elaine enjoy the boat?" Rachel asked.

"Elaine never goes out on the boat," he said as neutrally as possible. "She doesn't like the ocean."

"So you go alone?"

"Yes. I go alone." He paused a beat, then asked, "You

like the water, Rachel? You like boats?"

She shrugged. "I've never tried it."

"Would you like to try it? With me?"

Their eyes met and each saw something in the other that neither had seen before in the ten years they had known each other.

"Yes, I would, Grant," she answered. "I'd like to try it with you."

Both of them tried to suppress self-conscious smiles, but neither of them was successful.

"You, uh, know the Lucky Prices all-night supermarket on the coast highway?" Kenner asked, his tone gaining enthusiasm.

"Sure. I've driven past it."

"Well, there's a little coffee shop inside. We could meet there for breakfast. Then we can pick up food for lunch, leave our cars on the lot, and walk to the mooring dock; it's right across the highway."

"Sounds great."

"The boat's not fancy or anything. I'm going to get a new one in a few years when I retire."

"I'll bet the boat is just fine," Rachel said.

"Is six too early?"

"No, six is okay." Their eyes met again. "I like to do things early in the morning."

"Okay," Kenner said. "See you then."

He closed the car door. She smiled through the car window at him as she started the engine, turned on the headlights, and drove away.

When Kenner got home, his daughter was sitting on the porch glider waiting for him. She was wearing her new correction officer's uniform from her first day on the job at

Waverly Prison for women.

"Hi, Daddy." She stood and posed for him in the porch light. "What do you think?"

"Looks great, honey," he said warmly. "How did the day go?"

"It couldn't have been better, Daddy," she told him, sounding extremely pleased. "Of course, everyone *knows* I'm the only child of the DWC at Scrubb, so they treat me like I'm one of the family already. But, Daddy, it was so *exciting*. It's a whole different world in there."

"Yes, it is. And you like it?"

"I *love* it! I just wish—well, you know—" She nodded toward the second floor, where her mother's lights were already out.

"She'll come around," Kenner assured her. "It's just hard for her to understand, that's all. We're all part of the same system. But she's in the part that tries to make the world better by teaching. You and I are in the part that does it by helping to thin the predators. People like your mother haven't accepted yet that the job we do is as important as the job they do. It may even be *more* important. We could exist without them, but I'm not sure they could exist without us. Highly educated people usually find that theory impossible to admit. But the main thing is that *we* understand it." Kenner embraced his daughter and kissed her on the cheek. "Welcome to the team, *Officer.*"

They sat together on the glider, looking out at the calm spring night.

"Everyone at Waverly was so surprised to get Ginger Tatum back at the last minute this evening," Susan said. "They couldn't believe she had been so close that her head was already shaved. How did her husband's execution go?"

"Overall, very well," Kenner said. "We got it done by

eleven minutes after six."

"How does it feel, Daddy? To be in charge of a person's execution?"

"It feels good, honey," Kenner admitted. "It makes me feel like I imagine it must make your mother feel to produce an honor student. She's part of molding somebody good, I'm part of eliminating somebody bad. It's gratifying."

Susan took her father's hand and laid her head on his shoulder. "I'm glad I'm going to be like you, Daddy. I hope I can be in charge of an execution someday."

"I hope you can too, honey."

Kenner patted Susan's hand, remembering what Rachel had said about blood paths. He was glad his daughter was following the blood path he had followed.

Piranha to Scurfy

Ruth Rendell

It was the first time he had been away on holiday without Mummy. The first time in his life. They had always gone to the Isle of Wight, to Ventnor or Totland Bay, so, going alone, he had chosen Cornwall for the change that people say is as good as a rest. Not that Ribbon's week in Cornwall had been entirely leisure. He had taken four books with him, read them carefully in the B and B's lounge, in his bedroom, on the beach, and sitting on the cliff top, and made meticulous notes in the loose-leaf notebook he had bought in a shop in Newquay. The results had been satisfactory, more than satisfactory. Allowing for the anger and disgust making these discoveries invariably aroused, he felt he could say he had had a relaxing time. To use a horrible phrase much favoured by Eric Owlberg in his literary output, he had recharged his batteries.

Coming home to an empty house would be an ordeal. He had known it would be and it was. Instead of going out into the garden, he gave it careful scrutiny from the dining room window. Everything outside and indoors was as he had left it. The house was as he had left it, all the books in their places. Every room contained books. Ribbon was not one to make jokes, but he considered it witty to remark that while other people's walls were papered, his were booked. No one knew what he meant, for hardly anyone except himself ever entered 21 Grove Green Avenue, Leytonstone, and those to whom he uttered his little joke smiled uneasily. He had put up the shelves himself, buying them from Ikea. As they filled he bought more, adding to those already there until the shelves extended from floor to ceiling. A strange appearance was given to the house by this superfluity of books as the shelves necessarily reduced the size of the rooms, so that the living room, originally fifteen feet by twelve, shrank to thirteen feet by ten. The hall and landing were "booked" as densely as the rooms. The place looked like a library, but one mysteriously divided into small sections. His windows appeared as alcoves set deep in the walls, affording a view at the front of the house of a rather gloomy suburban street, thickly treed. The back gave on to the yellow brick rears of other houses and, in the foreground, his garden, which was mostly lawn, dotted about with various drab shrubs. At the far end was a wide flowerbed the sun never reached and in which grew creeping ivies and dark-leaved flowerless plants which like the shade.

He had got over expecting Mummy to come downstairs or walk into a room. She had been gone five months now. He sighed, for he was a long way from recovering from his loss and his regrets. Work was in some ways easier without her and in others immeasurably harder. She had reassured him, sometimes she had made him strong. But he had to press on, there was really no choice. Tomorrow things would be back to normal.

He began by ranging before him on the desk in the

study—though was not the whole house a study?—the book review pages from the newspapers which had arrived while he was away. As he had expected, Owlberg's latest novel, **Paving Hell**, appeared this very day in paperback, one year after hardcover publication. It was priced at £6.99 and by now would be in all the shops. Ribbon made a memo about it on one of the plain cards he kept for this purpose. But before continuing he let his eyes rest on the portrait of Mummy in the plain silver frame that stood on the table where used, read, and dissected books had their temporary home. It was Mummy who had first drawn his attention to Owlberg. She had borrowed one of his books from the public library and pointed out to Ribbon with indignation the mass of errors, solecisms, and abuse of the English language to be found in its pages. How he missed her! Wasn't it principally to her that he owed his choice of career as well as the acumen and confidence to pursue it?

He sighed anew. Then he returned to his newspapers and noted down the titles of four more novels currently published in paperback, as well as the new Kingston Marle, **Demogorgon**, due to appear this coming Thursday in hardcover with the maximum hype and fanfares of metaphorical trumpets, but almost certainly already in the shops. A sign of the degeneracy of the times, Mummy had said, that a book whose publication was scheduled for May appeared on sale at the end of April. No one could wait these days, everyone was in a hurry. It certainly made his work harder. It increased the chances of his missing a vitally important novel which might have sold out before he knew it was in print.

Ribbon switched on his computer and checked that the printer was linked to it. It was only nine in the morning. He had at least an hour before he need make his trip to the bookshop. Where should it be today? Perhaps the City or the West End of London. It would be unwise to go back to his local shop so soon and attract too much attention to himself. Hatchard's, perhaps then, or Books Etc. or Dillon's, or even all three. He opened the notebook he had bought in Cornwall, reread what he had written, and with the paperback open on the desk reached for the **Shorter Oxford Dictionary**, **Brewer's Dictionary of Phrase and Fable**, and **Whittaker's Almanack**. Referring to the first two and noting down his finds, he began his letter.

21 Grove Green Avenue,
London E11 4ZH
Dear Joy Anne Fortune,

I have read your new novel **Dreadful Night** with very little pleasure and great disappointment. Your previous work has seemed to me, while being without any literary merit whatsoever, at least to be fresh, occasionally original, and largely free from those errors of fact and slips in grammar which, I may say, characterise **Dreadful Night**.

Look first at page 24. Do you really believe "desiccated" has two s's and one c? And if you do, have your publishers no copy editor whose job it is to recognise and correct these errors? On page 82 you refer to the republic of Guinea as being in *East* Africa and as a former British possession, instead of being in West Africa and formerly French, and on page 103 to the late General Sikorski as a one-time prime minister of Czechoslovakia rather than of Poland. You describe, on page 139, "hadith" as being the Jewish prayers for the dead instead of what it correctly means, the body of tradition and legend surrounding the Prophet Mohammed and his followers, and on the following page "tabernacle" as an entrance to a temple. Its true meaning is a portable sanctuary in which the Ark of the Covenant was carried.

Need I go on? I am weary of underlining the multifarious mistakes in your book. Needless to say, I shall buy no more of your work, and shall advise my highly literate and discerning friends to boycott it.

Yours sincerely,
Ambrose Ribbon

The threat in the last paragraph was an empty one. Ribbon had no friends and could hardly say he missed having any. He was on excellent, at least speaking, terms with his neighbours and various managers of bookshops. There was a cousin in Gloucestershire he saw occasionally. Mummy had been his friend. There was no one he had ever met who could approach replacing her. He wished, as he did every day, she was back there beside him and able to read and appreciate his letter.

He addressed an envelope to Joy Anne Fortune care of her publishers—she was not one of "his" authors unwise enough to reply to him on headed writing paper—put the letter inside it, and sealed it up. Two more must be written before he left the house, one to Graham Prink pointing out mistakes in **Dancing Partners**, "lay" for "lie" in two instances and "may" for "might" in three, and the other to Jeanne Pettle to tell her that the plot and much of the dialogue in **Southern Discomfort** had been blatantly lifted from **Gone With the Wind**. He considered it the most flagrant plagiarism he had seen for a long while. In both letters he indicated how distasteful he found the authors' frequent use of obscenities, notably those words beginning with an *f* and a *c,* and the taking of the Deity's name in vain.

At five to ten Ribbon took his letters, switched off the computer, and closed the door behind him. Before going downstairs, he paid his second visit of the day to Mummy's room. He had been there for the first time since his return from Cornwall at seven the previous evening, again before he went to bed, and once more at seven this morning. While he was away his second greatest worry had been that something would be disturbed in there, an object removed or its position changed, for though he did his own housework, Glenys Next-door had a key, and often in his absence, in her own words, "popped in to see that everything was okay."

But nothing was changed. Mummy's dressing table was exactly as she had left it, the two cut-glass scent bottles with silver stoppers set one on each side of the lace-edged mat, the silver-backed hairbrush on its glass tray alongside the hair-tidy and the pink pincushion. The wardrobe door he always left ajar so that her clothes could be seen inside, those dear garments, the afternoon dresses, the coats and skirts—Mummy had never possessed a pair of trousers—the warm winter coat, the neatly placed pairs of court shoes. Over the door, because he had seen this in an interiors magazine, he had hung, folded in two, the beautiful white and cream tapestry bedspread he had once given her but which she said was too good for daily use. On the bed lay the dear old one her own mother had worked, and on its spotless if worn bands of lace, her pink silk nightdress. He lingered, looking at it.

After a moment or two, he opened the window two inches at the top. It was a good idea to allow a little fresh air to circulate. He closed Mummy's door behind him and, carrying his letters, went downstairs. A busy day lay ahead.

His tie straightened, one button only out of the three on his linen jacket done up, he set the burglar alarm. Eighteen fifty-two was the code, one-eight, five-two, the date of the first edition of **Roget's Thesaurus**, a compendium Ribbon had found useful in his work. He opened the front door and closed it just as the alarm started braying. While he was waiting on the doorstep, his ear to the keyhole, for the alarm to cease until or unless an intruder set it off again, Glenys Next-door called out a cheery, "Hiya!"

Ribbon hated this mode of address, but there was nothing he could do to stop it, any more than he could stop her calling him Amby. He smiled austerely and said good morning. Glenys Next-door—this was her own description of herself, first used when she moved into 23 Grove Green Avenue fifteen years before, "Hiya, I'm Glenys Next-door"—said it was the window cleaner's day and should she let him in.

"Why does he have to come in?" Ribbon said rather testily.

"It's his fortnight for doing the back, Amby. You know how he does the front on a Monday and the back on the Monday fortnight and inside and out on the last Monday in the month."

Like any professional with much on his mind, Ribbon found these domestic details almost unbearably irritating. Nor did he like the idea of a strange man left free to wander about his back garden. "Well, yes, I suppose so." He had never called Glenys Next-door by her given name and did not intend to begin. "You know the code, Mrs. Judd." It was appalling that she had to know the code, but since Mummy passed on and no one was in the house it was inevitable. "You do know the code, don't you?"

"Eight one five two."

"No, no, no." He must not lose his temper. Glancing up and down the street to make sure there was no one within earshot, he whispered, "One eight five two. You can remember that, can't you? I really don't want to write it down. You never know what happens to something once it has been put in writing."

Glenys Next-door had started to laugh. "You're a funny old fusspot, you are, Amby. D'you know what I saw in your garden last night? A fox. How about that? In *Leytonstone*."

"Really?" Foxes dig, he thought.

"They're taking refuge, you see. Escaping the hunters. Cruel, isn't it? Are you off to work?"

"Yes, and I'm late," Ribbon said, hurrying off. "Old fusspot" indeed. He was a good ten years younger than she.

Glenys Next-door had no idea what he did for a living and he intended to keep her in ignorance. "Something in the media, is it?" she had once said to Mummy. Of course "for a living" was not strictly true, implying as it did that he was paid for his work. That he was not was hardly for want of trying. He had written to twenty major publishing houses, pointing out to them that by what he did, uncovering errors in their authors' works and showing them to be unworthy of publication, he was potentially saving the publishers hundreds of thousands of pounds a year. The least they could do was offer him some emolument. He wrote to four national newspapers as well, asking for his work to receive publicity in their pages, and to the Department of Culture, Media, and Sport, in the hope of recognition of the service he performed. A change in the law was what he wanted, providing something for him in the nature of the Public Lending Right (he was vague about this) or the Value Added Tax. None of them replied, with the exception of the Department, who sent a card saying that his communication had been noted, not signed by the Secretary of State, though, but by some underling with an indecipherable signature.

It was the principle of the thing, not that he was in need of money. Thanks to Daddy, who, dying young, had left all the income from his royalties to Mummy, and thus, of course, to him. No great sum, but enough to live on if one was frugal and managing as he was. Daddy had written three textbooks before death came for him at the heartbreaking age of forty-one, and all were still in demand for use in business schools. Ribbon, because he could not help himself, in great secrecy and far from Mummy's sight, had gone through those books after his usual fashion, looking for errors. The compulsion to do this was irresistible, though he had tried to resist it, fighting against the need, conscious of the disloyalty, but finally succumbing, as another man might ultimately yield to some ludicrous autoeroticism. Alone, in the night, his bedroom door locked, he had perused Daddy's books and found—nothing.

The search was the most shameful thing he had ever done. And this not only on account of the distrust in Daddy's expertise and acumen that it implied, but also because he had to confess to himself that he did not understand what he read and would not have known a mistake if he had seen one. He put Daddy's books away in a cupboard after that and, strangely enough, Mummy had never commented on their absence. Perhaps, her eyesight failing, she hadn't noticed.

Ribbon walked to Leytonstone tube station and sat on the seat to wait for a train. He had decided to change at Holborn and take the Piccadilly Line to Piccadilly Circus. From there it was only a short walk to Dillon's and a further few steps to Hatchard's. He acknowledged that Hatchard's was the better shop, but Dillon's guaranteed a greater anonymity to its patrons. Its assistants seemed indifferent to the activities of customers, ignoring their presence most of the time and not apparently noticing whether they stayed five minutes or half an hour. Ribbon liked that. He liked to describe himself as reserved, a private man, one who minded his own business and lived quietly. Others, in his view, would do well to be the same. As far as he was concerned, a shop assistant was there to take your money, give you your change, and say thank you. The displacement of the high street or corner shop by vast impersonal supermarkets was one of few modern innovations he could heartily approve.

The train came. It was three-quarters empty, as was usually so at this hour. He had read in the paper that London Transport was thinking of introducing Ladies Only carriages in the tube. Why not Men Only carriages as well? Preferably, when you considered what some young men were like, Middle-aged Scholarly Gentlemen Only carriages. The train stopped for a long time in the tunnel between Mile End and Bethnal Green. Naturally, passengers were offered no explanation for the delay. He waited a long time for the Piccadilly Line train, due apparently to some signalling failure outside Cockfosters, but eventually arrived at his destination just before eleven-thirty.

The sun had come out and it was very hot. The air smelt of diesel and cooking and beer, very different from Leytonstone on the verges of Epping Forest. Ribbon went into Dillon's, where no one showed the slightest interest in his arrival, and the first thing to assault his senses was an enormous pyramidal display of Kingston Marle's **Demogorgon**. Each copy was as big as the average-sized dictionary and encased in a jacket printed in silver and two shades of red. A hole in the shape of a pentagram in the front cover revealed beneath it the bandaged face of some mummified corpse. The novel had already been reviewed and the poster on the wall above the display quoted the *Sunday Express*'s encomium in exaggeratedly large type: *"Readers will have fainted with fear before page 10."*

The price, at £18.99, was a disgrace, but there was no help for it. A legitimate outlay, if ever there was one. Ribbon took a copy and, from what a shop assistant had once told him were called "dump bins," helped himself to two paperbacks of books he had already examined and commented on in hardcover. There was no sign in the whole shop of Eric Owlberg's **Paving Hell**. Ribbon's dilemma was to ask or not to ask. The young woman behind the counter put his purchases in a bag and he handed her Mummy's Direct Debit Visa card. Lightly, as if it were an afterthought, the most casual thing in the world, he asked about the new Owlberg.

"Already sold out, has it?" he said with a little laugh.

Her face was impassive. "We're expecting them in tomorrow."

He signed the receipt B. J. Ribbon and passed it to the girl without a smile. She need not think he was going to make this trip all over again tomorrow. He made his way to Hatchard's, on the way depositing the Dillon's bag in a litter bin and transferring the books into the plain plastic hold-all he carried rolled up in his pocket. If the staff at Hatchard's had seen Dillon's name on the bag he would have felt rather awkward. Now they would think he was carrying his purchases from a chemist or a photographic store.

One of them came up to him the minute he entered Hatchard's. He recognised her as the marketing manager, a small, good-looking blond woman with an accent. The very faintest of accents but still enough for Ribbon to be put off her from the start. She recognised him, too, and to his astonishment and displeasure addressed him by his name.

"Good morning, Mr. Ribbon."

Inwardly he groaned, for he remembered having had forebodings about this at the time. On one occasion he had ordered a book, he was desperate to see an early copy, and had been obliged to say who he was and give them his phone number. He said good morning in a frosty sort of voice.

"How nice to see you," she said. "I rather think you may be in search of the new Kingston Marle, am I right? **Demogorgon**? Copies came in today."

Ribbon felt terrible. The plastic of his carrier was translucent rather than transparent, but he was sure she must be able to see the silver and the two shades of red glowing through the cloudy film that covered it. He held it behind his back in a manner he hoped looked natural.

"It was **Paving Hell** I actually wanted," he muttered, wondering what rule of life or social usage made it necessary for him to explain his wishes to marketing managers.

"We have it, of course," she said with a radiant smile, and picked the paperback off a shelf. He was sure she was going to point out to him in schoolmistressy fashion that he had already bought it in hardcover, she quite distinctly remembered, and why on earth did he want another copy. Instead she said, "Mr. Owlberg is here at this moment, signing stock for us. It's not a public signing but I'm sure he'd love to meet such a constant reader as yourself. And be happy to sign a copy of his book for you."

Ribbon hoped his shudder hadn't been visible. No, no, he was in a hurry, he had a pressing engagement at twelve-thirty on the other side of town, he couldn't wait, he'd pay for his book. . . . Thoughts raced through his mind of the things he had written to Owlberg about his work, all of it perfectly justified, of course, but galling to the author. His name would have lodged in Owlberg's mind as firmly as Owlberg's had in his. Imagining the reaction of **Paving Hell**'s author when he looked up from his signing, saw the face and heard the name of his stern judge, made him shudder again. He almost ran out of the shop. How fraught with dangers visits to the West End of London were! Next time he came up he'd stick to the City or Bloomsbury. There was a very good Waterstones in the Grays Inn Road. Deciding to walk up to Oxford Circus tube station and thus obviate a train change, he stopped on the way to draw money out from a cash dispenser. He punched in Mummy's PIN number, her birth date, 1-5-27, and drew from the slot one hundred pounds in crisp new notes.

Most authors to whom Ribbon wrote his letters of complaint either did not reply at all or wrote back in a conciliatory way to admit their mistakes and promise these would be rectified for the paperback edition. Only one, out of all the hundreds, if not thousands, who had had a letter from him, reacted violently and with threats. This was a woman called Selma Gunn. He had written to her, care of her publishers, criticising, but quite mildly, her novel **A Dish of Snakes**, remarking how irritating it was to read so many verbless sentences and pointing out the absurdity of her premise that Shakespeare, far from being a sixteenth-century English poet and dramatist, was in fact an Italian astrologer born in Verona and a close friend of Leonardo da Vinci. Her reply came within four days, a vituperative response in which she several times used the f-word, called him an ignorant swollen-headed nonentity, and threatened

107

legal action. Sure enough, on the following day a letter arrived from Ms. Gunn's solicitors, suggesting that many of his remarks were actionable, all were indefensible, and they awaited his reply with interest.

Ribbon had been terrified. He was unable to work, incapable of thinking of anything but Ms. Gunn's letter and the one from Evans Richler Sabatini. At first he said nothing to Mummy, though she, of course, with her customary sensitive acuity, could tell something was wrong. Two days later he received another letter from Selma Gunn. This time she drew his attention to certain astrological predictions in her book, told him that he was one of those Nostradamus had predicted would be destroyed when the world came to an end next year and that she herself had occult powers. She ended by demanding an apology.

Ribbon did not, of course, believe in the supernatural, but, like most of us, was made to feel deeply uneasy when cursed or menaced by something in the nature of necromancy. He sat down at his computer and composed an abject apology. He was sorry, he wrote, he had intended no harm, Ms. Gunn was entitled to express her beliefs; her theory as to Shakespeare's origins was just as valid as identifying him with Bacon or Ben Jonson. It took it out of him, writing that letter, and when Mummy, observing his pallor and trembling hands, finally asked him what was wrong, he told her everything. He showed her the letter of apology. Masterful as ever, she took it from him and tore it up.

"Absolute nonsense," she said. He could tell she was furious. "On what grounds can the stupid woman bring an action, I should like to know? Take no notice. Ignore it. It will soon stop, you mark my words."

"But what harm can it do, Mummy?"

"You coward," Mummy said witheringly. "Are you a man or a mouse?"

Ribbon asked her, politely but as manfully as he could, not to talk to him like that. It was almost their first quarrel—but not their last.

He had bowed to her edict and stuck it out in accordance with her instructions, as he did in most cases. And she had been right, for he heard not another word from Selma Gunn or from Evans Richler Sabatini. The whole awful business was over and Ribbon felt he had learnt something from it—to be brave, to be resolute, to soldier on. But this did not include confronting Owlberg in the flesh, even though the author of **Paving Hell** had promised him in a letter responding to Ribbon's criticism of the hardcover edition of his book that the errors of fact he had pointed out would all be rectified in the paperback. His publishers, he wrote, had also received Ribbon's letter of complaint and were as pleased as he to have had such informed critical comment. Pleased, my foot! What piffle! Ribbon had snorted over this letter, which was a lie from start to finish. The man wasn't pleased, he was aghast and humiliated, as he should be.

Ribbon sat down in his living room to check in the paperback edition for the corrections so glibly promised. He read down here and wrote upstairs. The room was almost as Mummy had left it. The changes were only in that more books and bookshelves had been added and in the photographs in the silver frames. He had taken out the picture of himself as a baby and himself as a schoolboy and replaced them with one of his parents' wedding, Daddy in Air Force uniform, Mummy in cream costume and small cream hat, and one of Daddy in his academic gown and mortarboard. There had never been one of Ribbon himself in similar garments. Mummy, for his own good, had decided he would be better off at home with her, leading a quiet, sheltered life, than at a university. Had he regrets? A degree would have been useless to a man with a private income, as Mummy had pointed out, a man who had all the resources of an excellent public library system to educate him.

He opened **Paving Hell**. He had a foreboding before he had even turned to the middle of chapter one, where the first mistake occurred, that nothing would have been put right. All the errors would be still there, for Owlberg's promises meant nothing, he had probably never passed Ribbon's comments on to the publishers; and they, if they had received the letter he wrote them, had never answered it. For all that, he was still enraged when he found he was right. Didn't the man care? Was money and a kind of low notoriety, for you couldn't call it fame, all he was interested in? None of the errors had been corrected. No, that wasn't quite true; one had. On page ninety-nine, Owlberg's ridiculous statement that the One World Trade Center tower in New York was the world's tallest building had been altered. Ribbon noted down the remaining mistakes, ready to write to Owlberg next day. A vituperative letter it would be, spitting venom, catechising illiteracy, carelessness, and a general disregard (contempt?) for the sensibilities of readers. And Owlberg would reply to it in his previous pusillanimous way, making empty promises, for he was no Selma Gunn.

Ribbon fetched himself a small whisky and water. It was six o'clock. A cushion behind his head, his feet up on the footstool Mummy had embroidered, but covered now with a plastic sheet, he opened **Demogorgon**. This was the first book by Kingston Marle he had ever read, but he had some idea of what Marle wrote about. Murder, violence, crime, but instead of a detective detecting and reaching a solution, supernatural interventions, demonic possession, ghosts, as well as a great deal of unnatural or perverted sex, cannibalism, and torture. Occult manifestations occurred side by side with rational, if unedifying, events. Innocent people were caught up in the magical dabblings, frequently going wrong, of so-called adepts. Ribbon had learnt this from the reviews he had read of Marle's books, most of which, surprisingly to him, received good notices in periodicals of repute. That is, the serious and reputable critics engaged by literary editors to comment on his work, praised the quality of the prose as vastly superior to the general run of thriller writing. His characters, they said, convinced, and he induced in the reader a very real sense of terror, while a deep vein of moral theology underlay his plot. They also said that his serious approach to mumbo jumbo and such nonsense as evil spirits and necromancy was ridiculous, but they said it *en passant* and without much enthusiasm. Ribbon read the blurb inside the front cover and turned to chapter one.

Almost the first thing he spotted was an error on page two. He made a note of it. Another occurred on page seven. Whether Marle's prose was beautiful or not he scarcely noticed, he was too incensed by errors of fact, spelling mistakes, and grammatical howlers. For a while, that is. The first part of the novel concerned a man living alone in London, a man in his own situation whose mother had died not long before. There was another parallel: The man's name was Charles Ambrose. Well, it was common enough as surname, much less so as baptismal name, and only a paranoid person would think any connection was intended.

Charles Ambrose was rich and powerful, with a house in London, a mansion in the country, and a flat in Paris. All these places seemed to be haunted in various ways by something or other but the odd thing was that Ribbon could see what that reviewer meant by readers fainting with terror before page ten. He wasn't going to faint, but he could feel himself growing increasingly alarmed. "Frightened" would be too strong a word. Every few minutes he found himself glancing up towards the closed door or looking into the dim and shadowy corners of the room. He was such a reader, so exceptionally well-read, that he had thought himself proof against this sort of thing. Why, he had read hundreds of ghost stories in his time. As a boy he had inured himself by reading first Dennis Wheatley, then Stephen King, not to mention M. R. James. And this **Demogorgon** was so absurd, the supernatural activity the reader was supposed to accept so pathetic, that he wouldn't have gone on with it but for the mistakes he kept finding on almost every page.

After a while he got up, opened the door, and put the hall light on. He had never been even mildly alarmed by Selma Gunn's **A Dish of Snakes**, nor touched with disquiet by any effusions of Joy Anne Fortune's. What was the matter with him? He came back into the living room, put on the central light and an extra table lamp, the one with the shade Mummy had decorated with pressed flowers. That was better. Anyone passing could see in now, something he usually disliked, but for some reason he didn't feel like drawing the curtains. Before sitting down again he fetched himself some more whisky.

This passage about the mummy Charles Ambrose brought back with him after the excavations he had carried out in Egypt was very unpleasant. Why had he never noticed before that the diminutive by which he had always addressed his mother was the same word as that applied to embalmed bodies? Especially nasty was the paragraph where Ambrose's girlfriend Kaysa reaches in semidarkness for a garment in her wardrobe and her wrist is grasped by a scaly paw. This was so upsetting that Ribbon almost missed noticing that Marle spelt the adjective "scaley." He had a sense of the room being less light than a few moments before, as if the bulbs in the lamps were weakening before entirely failing. One of them did indeed fail while his eyes were on it—flickered, buzzed, and went out. Of course, Ribbon knew perfectly well this was not a supernatural phenomenon but simply the result of the bulb coming to the end of its life after a thousand hours or whatever it was. He switched off the lamp, extracted the bulb when it was cool, shook it to hear the rattle that told him its usefulness was over, and took it outside to the wastebin. The kitchen was in darkness. He put on the light and the outside light which illuminated part of the garden. That was better. A siren wailing on a police car going down Grove Green Road made him jump. He helped himself to more whisky, a rare indulgence for him. He was no drinker.

Supper now. It was almost eight. Ribbon always set the table for himself, either here or in the dining room, put out a linen table napkin in its silver ring, a jug of water and a glass, and the silver pepper pot and salt cellar. This was Mummy's standard and if he had deviated from it he would have felt he was letting her down. But this evening, as he made toast and scrambled two large free-range eggs in a buttered pan, filled a small bowl with mandarin oranges from a can, and poured evaporated milk over them, he found himself most unwilling to venture into the dining room. It was, at the best of times, a gloomy chamber, its rather small window set deep in bookshelves, its furnishing largely a reptilian shade of brownish-green Mummy always called Crocodile. Poor Mummy only kept the room like that because the crocodile green had been Daddy's choice when they were first married. There was only a central light, a bulb in a parchment shade, suspended above the middle of the mahogany table. Books covered, as yet, only two sides of the room, but new shelves had been bought and were only waiting for him to put them up. One of the pictures on the wall facing the window had been most distasteful to Ribbon when he was a small boy, a lithograph of some Old Testament scene and entitled *Saul Encounters the Witch of Endor*. Mummy, saying he should not fear painted devils, refused to take it down. He was in no mood tonight to have that lowering over him while he ate his scrambled eggs.

Nor did he much fancy the kitchen. Once or twice, while he was sitting there, Glenys Next-door's cat had looked through the window at him. It was a black cat, totally black all over, its eyes large and of a very pale crystalline yellow. Of course, he knew what it was and had never in the past been alarmed by it, but somehow he sensed it would be different tonight. If Tinks Next-door pushed its black face and yellow eyes against the glass it might give him a serious shock. He put the plates on a tray and carried it back into the living room with the replenished whisky glass.

It was both his job and his duty to continue reading **Demogorgon**, but there was more to it than that, Ribbon admitted to himself in a rare burst of honesty. He *wanted* to go on, he wanted to know what happened to Charles Ambrose and Kaysa de Floris; whose the embalmed corpse was and how it had been liberated from its arcane and archaic (writers always muddled up those adjectives) sarcophagus, and whether the mysterious and saintly rescuer was in fact the reincarnated Joseph of Arimathea and the vessel he carried the Holy Grail. By the time Mummy's grandmother clock in the hall struck eleven, half an hour past his bedtime, he had read half the book and would no longer have described himself as merely alarmed. He was frightened. So frightened that he had to stop reading.

Twice during the course of the past hour he had refilled his whisky glass, half in the hope that strong drink would induce sleep when, finally, at a quarter past eleven, he went to bed. He passed a miserable night, worse even than those he experienced in the weeks after Mummy's death. It was, for instance, a mistake to take **Demogorgon** upstairs with him. He hardly knew why he had done so, for he certainly had no intention of reading any more of it that night, if ever. The final chapter he had read—well, he could scarcely say what had upset him most, the orgy in the middle of the Arabian desert in which Charles and Kaysa had both enthusiastically taken part, wallowing in perverted practices, or the intervention, disguised as a Bedouin tribesman, of the demon Kabadeus, later revealing in his nakedness his hermaphrodite body with huge female breasts and trifurcated member.

As always, Ribbon placed his slippers by the bed. He pushed the book a little under the bed but he couldn't forget that it was there. In the darkness he seemed to hear sounds he had never heard, or never noticed, before: a creaking as if a foot trod first on one stair, then the next; a rattling of the window pane, though it was a windless night; a faint rustling on the bedroom door as if a thing in graveclothes had scrabbled with its decaying hand against the panelling. He put on the bedlamp. Its light was faint, showing him deep wells of darkness in the corners of the room. He told himself not to be a fool. Demons, ghosts, evil spirits had no existence. If only he hadn't brought the wretched book up with him! He would be better, he would be able to sleep, he was sure, if the book wasn't there, exerting a malign influence. Then something dreadful occurred to him. He couldn't take the book outside, downstairs, away. He hadn't the nerve. It would not be possible for him to open the door, go down the stairs, carrying that book.

The whisky, asserting itself in the mysterious way it had, began a banging in his head. A flicker of pain ran from his eyebrow down his temple to his ear. He climbed out of bed, crept across the floor, his heart pounding, and put on the central light. That was a little better. He drew back the bedroom curtains and screamed. He actually screamed aloud, frightening himself even more with the noise he made. Tinks Next-door was sitting on the window sill, staring impassively at the curtain linings, now into Ribbon's face. It took no notice of the scream but lifted a paw, licked it, and began washing its face.

Ribbon pulled the curtains back. He sat down on the end of the bed, breathing deeply. It was two in the morning, a pitch-black night, ill-lit by widely spaced yellow chemical lamps. What he would really have liked to do was rush across the passage—do it quickly, don't think about it—into Mummy's room, burrow down into Mummy's bed, and spend the night there. If he could only do that he would be safe, would sleep, be comforted. It would be like creeping back into Mummy's arms. But he couldn't do it, it was impossible. For one thing, it would be a violation of the sacred room, the sacrosanct bed, never to be disturbed since Mummy spent her last night in it. And for another, he dared not venture out onto the landing.

Trying to court sleep by thinking of himself and Mummy in her last years helped a little. The two of them sitting down to an evening meal in the dining room, a white candle alight on the table, its soft light dispelling much of the gloom and ugliness. Mummy had enjoyed television when a really good programme was on, *Brideshead Revisited*, for instance, or something from Jane Austen. She had always liked the curtains drawn, even before it was dark, and it was his job to do it, then fetch each of them a dry sherry. Sometimes they read aloud to each other in the gentle lamplight, Mummy choosing to read her favourite Victorian writers to him, he picking a book from his work, correcting the grammar as he read. Or she would talk about Daddy and her first meeting with him in a library, she searching the shelves for a novel whose author's name she had forgotten, he offering to help her and finding—triumphantly—Mrs. Henry Wood's **East Lynne**.

But all these memories of books and reading pulled Ribbon brutally back to **Demogorgon**. The scaly hand was the worst thing and, second to that, the cloud or ball of visible darkness that arose in the lighted room when Charles Ambrose cast salt and asafoetida into the pentagram. He reached down to find the lead on the bedlamp where the switch was and encountered something cold and leathery. It was only the tops of his slippers, which he always left just beside his bed, but he had once again screamed before he remembered. The lamp on, he lay still, breathing deeply. Only when the first light of morning, a grey trickle of dawn, came creeping under and between the curtains at about six, did he fall into a troubled doze.

Morning makes an enormous difference to fear and to depression. It wasn't long before Ribbon was castigating himself for a fool and blaming the whisky and the scrambled eggs for his disturbed night rather than Kingston Marle. However, he would read no more of **Demogorgon**. No matter how much he might wish to know the fate of Charles and Kaysa or the identity of the bandaged reeking thing, he preferred not to expose himself any longer to this distasteful rubbish or Marle's grammatical lapses.

A hot shower, followed by a cold one, did a lot to restore him. He breakfasted, but in the kitchen. When he had finished he went into the dining room and had a look at *Saul Encounters the Witch of Endor.* It was years since he had even glanced at it, which was no doubt why he had never noticed how much like Mummy the witch looked. Of course, Mummy would never have worn diaphanous gray draperies and she had all her own teeth, but there was something about the nose and mouth, the burning eyes and the pointing finger, this last particularly characteristic of Mummy, that reminded him of her.

He dismissed the disloyal thought but, on an impulse, took the picture down and put it on the floor, its back towards him, to lean against the wall. It left behind it a paler rectangle on the ochre-coloured wallpaper but the new bookshelves would cover that. Ribbon went upstairs to his study and his daily labours. First, the letter to Owlberg.

21 Grove Green Avenue,
London E11 4ZH
Dear Sir,

In spite of your solemn promise to me as to the correction of errors in your new paperback publication, I find you have fulfilled this undertaking only to the extent of making *one single amendment.*

This, of course, in anyone's estimation, is a gross insult to your readers, displaying as it does your contempt for them and for the TRUTH. I am sending a copy of this letter to your publishers and await an explanation both from you and them.

Yours faithfully,
Ambrose Ribbon

Letting off steam always put him in a good mood. He felt a joyful adrenalin rush and was inspired to write a congratulatory letter for a change. This one was addressed to: The Manager, Dillon's Bookshop, Piccadilly, London W1.

21 Grove Green Avenue,
London E11 4ZH
Dear Sir or Madam, (*There were a lot of women taking men's jobs these days, poking their noses in where they weren't needed.*)

I write to congratulate you on your excellent organisation, management, and the, alas, now old-fashioned attitude you have to your book buyers. I refer, of course, to the respectful distance and detachment maintained between you and them. It makes a refreshing change from the over-familiarity displayed by many of your competitors.

Yours faithfully,
Ambrose Ribbon

Before writing to the author of the novel which had been directly responsible for his loss of sleep, Ribbon needed to look something up. A king of Egypt of the seventh century B.C. called Psamtik I he had come across before in someone else's book. Marle referred to him as Psammetichus I and Ribbon was nearly sure this was wrong. He would have to look it up and the obvious place to do this was the **Encyclopaedia Britannica**.

Others might have recourse to the Internet. Because Mummy had despised such electronic devices, Ribbon did so too. He wasn't even on the Net and never would be. The present difficulty was that Psamtik I would be found in volume eight of the **Micropaedia**, the one that covered

subjects from *Piranha* to *Scurfy*. This volume he had had no
occasion to use since Mummy's death, though his eyes
sometimes strayed fearfully in its direction. There it was
placed, in the bookshelves to the left of where he sat facing
the window, bound in its black, blue, and gold, its position
between *Montpel Piranesi* and *Scurlock Tirah*. He was very
reluctant to touch it but he *had to*. Mummy might be dead,
but her injunctions and instructions lived on. Don't be de-
terred, she had often said, don't be deflected by anything
from what you know to be right, not by weariness, nor in-
difference, nor doubt. Press on, tell the truth, shame these
people.

There would not be a mark on *Piranha Scurfy*, he knew
that, nothing but his fingerprints and they, of course, were
invisible. It had been used and put back and was un-
changed. Cautiously he advanced upon the shelf where the
ten volumes of the **Micropaedia** and the nineteen of the
Macropaedia were arranged and put out his hand to
Volume VIII. As he lifted it down he noticed something different about it, different, that is, from the others. Not a
mark, not a stain or scar, but a slight loosening of the thousand and two pages as if at some time it had been mis-
treated, violently shaken or in some similar way abused. It
had. He shivered a little but he opened the book and turned
the pages to the P's. It was somewhat disappointing to find
that Marle had been right. Psamtik was right and so was
the Greek form, Psammetichus I; it was optional. Still,
there were enough errors in the book, a plethora of them,
without that. Ribbon wrote as follows, saying nothing
about his fear, his bad night, or his interest in **Demogorgon**'s characters:

21 Grove Green Avenue,
London E11 4ZH
Sir,

Your new farrago of nonsense (I will not dignify it with the name of "novel" or even "thriller") is a disgrace to you, your publishers, and those reviewers corrupt enough to praise your writing. As to the market you serve, once it has sampled this revolting affront to English literary tradition and our noble language, I can hardly imagine its members will remain your readers for long. The greatest benefit to the fiction scene conceivable would be for you to retire, disappear, and take your appalling effusions with you into outer darkness.

The errors you have made in the text are numerous. On page 30 alone there are three. You cannot say "less people." "Fewer people" is correct. Only the illiterate would write: "He gave it to Charles and I." By "mitigate against" I suppose you mean "militate against." More howlers occur on pages 34, 67, and 103. It is unnecessary to write "meet with." "Meet" alone will do. "A copy" of something is sufficient. "A copying" is a nonsense.

Have you any education at all? Or were you one of those children who somehow missed schooling because their parents were neglectful or itinerant? You barely seem able to understand the correct location of an apostrophe, still less the proper usage of a colon. Your book has wearied me too much to allow me to write more. Indeed, I have not finished it and shall not. I am too fearful of its corrupting my own prose.

He wrote "Sir" without the customary endearment so

that he could justifiably sign himself "yours truly." He re-read his letters and paused awhile over the third one. It was very strong and uncompromising. But there was not a phrase in it he didn't sincerely mean (for all his refusing to end with that word) and he told himself that he who hesitates is lost. Often when he wrote a really vituperative letter he allowed himself to sleep on it, not posting it till the following day and occasionally, though seldom, not sending it at all. But he quickly put all three into envelopes and addressed them, Kingston Marle's care of his publishers. He would take them to the box at once.

While he was upstairs his own post had come. Two envelopes lay on the mat. The direction on one was typed, on the other he recognised the handwriting of his cousin Frank's wife Susan. He opened that one first. Susan wrote to remind him that he was spending the following weekend with herself and her husband at their home in the Cotswolds, as he did at roughly this time every year. Frank or she herself would be at Kingham station to pick him up. She supposed he would be taking the one-fifty train from Paddington to Hereford which reached Kingham at twenty minutes past three. If he had other plans, perhaps he would let her know.

Ribbon snorted quietly. He didn't want to go, he never did, but they so loved having him he could hardly refuse after so many years. This would be his first visit without Mummy, or Auntie Bee as they called her. No doubt they, too, desperately missed her. He opened the other letter and had a pleasant surprise. It was from Joy Anne Fortune and she gave her own address, a street in Bournemouth, not her publishers' or agents'. She must have written by return of post.

Her tone was humble and apologetic. She began by

thanking him for pointing out the errors in her novel **Dreadful Night**. Some of them were due to her own carelessness but others she blamed on the printer. Ribbon had heard that one before and didn't think much of it. Ms. Fortune assured him that all the mistakes would be corrected if the book ever went into paperback, though she thought it unlikely that this would happen. Here Ribbon agreed with her. However, this kind of letter—though rare—was always gratifying. It made all his hard work worthwhile.

He put stamps on the letters to Eric Owlberg, Kingston Marle, and Dillon's and took them to the postbox. Again he experienced a quiver of dread in the pit of his stomach when he looked at the envelope addressed to Marle and recalled the words and terms he had used. But he drew strength from remembering how stalwartly he had withstood Selma Gunn's threats and defied her. There was no point in being in his job if he was unable to face resentful opposition. Mummy was gone, but he must soldier on alone and he repeated to himself Paul's words about fighting the good fight, running a straight race, and keeping the faith. He held the envelope in his hand for a moment or two after the Owlberg and Dillon's letters had fallen down inside the box. How much easier it would be, what a lightening of his spirits would take place, if he simply dropped that envelope into a litter bin rather than this postbox! On the other hand, he hadn't built up his reputation for uncompromising criticism and stern incorruptible judgment by being cowardly. In fact, he hardly knew why he was hesitating now. His usual behaviour was far from this. What was wrong with him? There in the sunny street a sudden awful dread took hold of him, that when he put his hand to that aperture in the postbox and inserted the letter a scaly paw would reach out of it and seize hold of his wrist. How stupid could he be? How irrational? He reminded himself of his final quarrel with Mummy, those awful words she had spoken, and quickly, without more thought, he dropped the letter into the box and walked away.

At least they hadn't to put up with that ghastly old woman, Susan Ribbon remarked to her husband as she prepared to drive to Kingham station. Old Ambrose was a pussycat compared to Auntie Bee.

"You say that," said Frank. "You haven't got to take him down the pub."

"I've got to listen to him moaning about being too hot or too cold, or the bread being wrong or the tea, or the birds singing too early or us going to bed too late."

"It's only two days," said Frank. "I suppose I do it for my uncle Charlie's sake. He was a lovely man."

"Considering you were only four when he died, I don't see how you know."

Susan got to Kingham at twenty-two minutes past three and found Ambrose standing in the station approach, swivelling his head from left to right, up the road and down, a peevish look on his face. "I was beginning to wonder where you were," he said. "Punctuality is the politeness of princes, you know. I expect you heard my mother say that. It was a favourite dictum of hers."

In her opinion, Ambrose appeared far from well. His face, usually rather full and flabby, had a pasty, sunken look. "I haven't been sleeping," he said as they drove through Moreton-in-Marsh. "I've had some rather unpleasant dreams."

"It's all those highbrow books you read. You've been overtaxing your brain." Susan didn't exactly know what it was Ambrose did for a living. Some sort of freelance editing, Frank thought. The kind of thing you could do from home. It wouldn't bring in much, but Ambrose didn't need much, Auntie Bee being in possession of Uncle Charlie's royalties. "And you've suffered a terrible loss. It's only a few months since your mother died. But you'll soon feel better down here. Good fresh country air, peace and quiet, it's a far cry from London."

They would go into Oxford tomorrow, she said, do some shopping, visit Blackwell's, perhaps do a tour of the colleges and then have lunch at the Randolph. She had asked some of her neighbours in for drinks at six, then they would have a quiet supper and watch a video. Ambrose nodded, not showing much interest. Susan told herself to be thankful for small mercies. At least there was no Auntie Bee. On that old witch's last visit with Ambrose, the year before she died, she had told Susan's friend from Stow that her skirt was too short for someone with middle-aged knees, and at ten-thirty informed the people who had come to dinner that it was time they went home.

When he had said hallo to Frank, she showed Ambrose up to his room. It was the one he always had, but he seemed unable to remember the way to it from one year to the next. She had made a few alterations. For one thing, it had been redecorated, and for another, she had changed the books in the shelf by the bed. A great reader herself, she thought it rather dreary always to have the same selection of reading matter in the guest bedroom.

Ambrose came down to tea looking grim. "Are you a fan of Mr. Kingston Marle, Susan?"

"He's my favourite author," she said, surprised.

"I see. Then there's no more to be said, is there?" Ambrose proceeded to say more. "I rather dislike having a whole shelf full of his works by my bed. I've put them out on the landing." As an afterthought, he added, "I hope you don't mind."

After that, Susan decided against telling her husband's cousin the prime purpose of their planned visit to Oxford next day. She poured him a cup of tea and handed him a slice of Madeira cake. Manfully, Frank said he would take Ambrose to see the horses and then they might stroll down to the Cross Keys for a nourishing glass of something.

"Not whisky, I hope," said Ambrose.

"Lemonade, if you like," said Frank in an out-of-character sarcastic voice.

When they had gone, Susan went upstairs and retrieved the seven novels of Kingston Marle which Ambrose had stacked on the floor outside his bedroom door. She was particularly fond of **Evil Incarnate** and noticed that its dust jacket had a tear in the front on the bottom right-hand side. That tear had certainly not been there when she put the books on the shelf two days before. It looked, too, as if the jacket of **Wickedness in High Places** had been removed, screwed up in an angry fist, and later replaced. Why on earth would Ambrose do such a thing?

She returned the books to her own bedroom. Of course, Ambrose was a strange creature. You could expect nothing else with that monstrous old woman for a mother, his sequestered life, and, whatever Frank might say about his being a freelance editor, the probability that he subsisted on a small private income and had never actually worked for his living. He had never married nor even had a girlfriend, as far as Susan could make out. What did he do all day? These weekends, though only occurring annually, were terribly tedious and trying. Last year he had awakened her and Frank by knocking on their bedroom door at three in the morning to complain about a ticking clock in his room.

Then there had been the business of the dry-cleaning spray. A splash of olive oil had left a pinpoint spot on the (already not very clean) jacket of Ambrose's navy blue suit. He had averred that the stain remover Susan had in the cupboard left it untouched, though Susan and Frank could see no mark at all after it had been applied, and insisted on their driving him into Cheltenham for a can of a particular kind of dry-cleaning spray. By then it was after five, and by the time they got there all possible purveyors of the spray were closed till Monday. Ambrose had gone on and on about that stain on his jacket right up to the moment Frank dropped him at Kingham station on Sunday afternoon.

The evening passed uneventfully and without any real problems. It was true that Ambrose remarked on the silk trousers she had changed into, saying on a slightly acrimonious note that reminded Susan of Auntie Bee what a pity it was that skirts would soon go entirely out of fashion. He left most of his pheasant *en casserole,* though without comment. Susan and Frank lay awake a long while, occasionally giggling and expecting a knock at their door. None came. The silence of the night was broken only by the melancholy hooting of owls.

A fine morning, though not hot, and Oxford particularly beautiful in the sunshine. When they had parked the car they strolled up The High and had coffee in a small select cafe outside which tables and chairs stood on the wide pavement. The Ribbons, however, went inside where it was rather gloomy and dim. Ambrose deplored the adoption by English restaurants of Continental habits totally unsuited to what he called "our island climate." He talked about his mother and the gap in the company her absence caused, interrupting his own monologue to ask in a querulous tone why Susan kept looking at her watch.

"We have no particular engagement, do we? We are, as might be said, free as air?"

"Oh, quite," Susan said. "That's exactly right."

But it wasn't *exactly* right. She resisted glancing at her watch again. There was, after all, a clock on the cafe wall. So long as they were out of there by ten to eleven they would be in plenty of time. She didn't want to spend half the morning standing in a queue. Ambrose went on talking about Auntie Bee, how she lived in a slower-paced and more gracious past, how, much as he missed her, he was glad for her sake she hadn't survived to see the dawn of a new, and doubtless worse, millennium.

They left at eight minutes to eleven and walked to Blackwell's. Ambrose was in his element in bookshops, which was partly, though only partly, why they had come. The signing was advertised in the window and inside, though there was no voice on a public address system urging customers to buy and get the author's signature. And there he was, sitting at the end of a table loaded with copies of his new book. A queue there was, but only a short one. Susan calculated that by the time she had selected her copy of **Demogorgon** and paid for it she would be no further back than eighth in line, a matter of waiting ten minutes.

She hadn't counted on Ambrose's extraordinary reaction. Of course, she was well aware—he had seen to that—of his antipathy to the works of Kingston Marle, but not that it should take such a violent form. At first, the author, and perhaps also the author's name, had been hidden from Ambrose's view by her own back and Frank's and the press of people around him. But as that crowd for some reason melted away, Frank turned round to say a word to his cousin, and she went to collect the book she had reserved, Kingston Marle lifted his head and seemed to look straight at Frank and Ambrose.

He was a curious-looking man, tall and with a lantern-shaped but not unattractive face, his chin deep and his forehead high. A mass of long dark womanish hair sprang from the top of that arched brow, flowed straight back, and descended to his collar in full, rather untidy curves. His mouth was wide and with the sensitive look lips shaped like this usually give to a face. Dark eyes skimmed over Frank, then Ambrose, and came to rest on her. He smiled. Whether it was this smile or the expression in Marle's eyes that had the effect on Ambrose it apparently did, Susan never knew. Ambrose let out a little sound, not quite a cry, more a grunt of protest. She heard him say to Frank, "Excuse me—must go—stuffy in here—can't breathe—just pop out for some fresh air," and he was gone, running faster than she would have believed him capable of.

When she was younger, she would have thought it right to go after him, ask what was wrong, could she help, and so on. She would have left her book, given up the chance of getting it signed, and given all her attention to Ambrose. But she was older now and no longer believed it was necessary inevitably to put others first. As it was, Ambrose's hasty departure had lost her a place in the queue and she found herself at number ten. Frank joined her.

"What was all that about?"

"Some nonsense about not being able to breathe. The old boy gets funny ideas in his head, just like his old mum. You don't think she's been reincarnated in him, do you?"

Susan laughed. "He'd have to be a baby for that to have happened, wouldn't he?"

She asked Kingston Marle to inscribe the book on the

title page "For Susan Ribbon." While he was doing so and adding, "with best wishes from the author, Kingston Marle," he told her hers was a very unusual name. Had she ever met anyone else called Ribbon?

"No, I haven't. I believe we're the only ones in this country."

"And there aren't many of us," said Frank. "Our son is the last of the Ribbons but he's only sixteen."

"Interesting," said Marle politely.

Susan wondered if she dared. She took a deep breath. "I admire your work very much. If I sent you some of my books—I mean, your books—and if I put in the postage, would you—would you sign those for me, too?"

"Of course. It would be a pleasure."

Marle gave her a radiant smile. He rather wished he could have asked her to have lunch with him at the Lemon Tree instead of having to go to the Randolph with this earnest bookseller. Susan, of course, had no inkling of this and, clutching her signed book in its Blackwell's bag, she went in search of Ambrose. He was standing outside on the pavement, staring at the roadway, his hands clasped behind his back. She touched his arm and he flinched.

"Are you all right?"

He spun round, nearly cannoning into her. "Of course I'm all right. It was very hot and stuffy in there, that's all. What have you got in there? Not his latest?"

Susan was getting cross. She asked herself why she was obliged to put up with this year after year, perhaps until they all died. In silence, she took **Demogorgon** out of the bag and handed it to him. Ambrose took it in his fingers as someone might pick up a package of decaying refuse prior to dropping it in an incinerator, his nostrils wrinkling and his eyebrows raised. He opened it. As he looked at the title page, his expression and his whole demeanour underwent a violent change. His face had gone a deep mottled red and a muscle under one eye began to twitch. Susan thought he was going to hurl the book in among the passing traffic. Instead he thrust it back at her and said in a very curt, abrupt voice, "I'd like to go home now. I'm not well."

Frank said, "Why don't we all go into the Randolph— we're lunching there anyway—have a quiet drink and a rest and I'm sure you'll soon feel better, Ambrose. It *is* a warm day and there was quite a crowd in there. I don't care for crowds myself, I know how you feel."

"You don't know how I feel at all. You've just made that very plain. I don't want to go to the Randolph, I want to go home."

There was little they could do about it. Susan, who seldom lunched out and sometimes grew very tired of cooking, was disappointed. But you can't force an obstinate man to go into an hotel and drink sherry if he is unwilling to do this. They went back to the car park and Frank drove home. When she and Frank had a single guest, it was usually Susan's courteous habit to sit in the back of the car and offer the visitor the passenger seat. She had done this on the way to Oxford, but this time she sat next to Frank and left the back to Ambrose. He sat in the middle of the seat, obstructing Frank's view in the rear mirror. Once, when Frank stopped at a red light, she thought she felt Ambrose trembling, but it might only have been the engine, which was inclined to judder.

On their return he went straight up to his room without explanation and remained there, drink-less, lunch-less, and later on, tea-less. Susan read her new book and was soon totally absorbed in it. She could well understand what the reviewer had meant when he wrote about readers fainting with fear, though in fact she herself had not fainted but only felt pleasurably terrified. Just the same, she was glad Frank was there, a large comforting presence, intermittently reading *The Times* and watching the golf on television. Susan wondered why archaeologists went on excavating tombs in Egypt when they knew the risk of being laid under a curse or bringing home a demon. Much wiser to dig up a bit of Oxfordshire as a party of archaeology students were doing down the road. But Charles Ambrose—how funny he should share a name with such a very different man!—was nothing if not brave, and Susan felt total empathy with Kaysa de Floris when she told him one midnight, smoking *kif* on Mount Ararat, *"I could never put my body and soul into the keeping of a coward."*

The bit about the cupboard was almost too much for her. She decided to shine a torch into her wardrobe that night before she hung up her dress. And make sure Frank was in the room. Frank's roaring with laughter at her she wouldn't mind at all. It was terrible, that chapter where Charles first sees the small dark "curled-up" shape in the corner of the room. Susan had no difficulty in imagining her hero's feelings. The trouble (or the wonderful thing) was that Kingston Marle wrote so well. Whatever people might say about only the plot and the action and suspense being of importance in this sort of book, there was no doubt that good literary writing made threats, danger, terror, fear, and a dark nameless dread immeasurably more real. Susan had to lay the book down at six; their friends were coming in for a drink at half-past.

She put on a long skirt and silk sweater, having first made Frank come upstairs with her, open the wardrobe door, and demonstrate, while shaking with mirth, that there was no scaly paw inside. Then she knocked on Ambrose's door. He came at once, his sports jacket changed for a dark grey, almost black suit, which he had perhaps bought new for Auntie Bee's funeral. That was an occasion she and Frank had not been asked to. Probably Ambrose had attended it alone.

"I hadn't forgotten about your party," he said in a mournful tone.

"Are you feeling better?"

"A little." Downstairs, his eye fell at once on **Demogorgon**. "Susan, I wonder if you would oblige me and put that book away. I hope I'm not asking too much. It is simply that I would find it extremely distasteful if there were to be any discussion of that book in my presence among your friends this evening."

Susan took the book upstairs and put it on her bedside cabinet. "We are only expecting four people, Ambrose," she said. "It's hardly a party."

"A gathering," he said. "Seven is a gathering."

For years she had been trying to identify the character in fiction of whom Ambrose Ribbon reminded her. A children's book, she thought it was. *Alice in Wonderland?* *The Wind in the Willows?* Suddenly she knew. It was Eeyore, the lugubrious donkey in *Winnie the Pooh*. He even looked rather like Eeyore, with his melancholy grey face and stooping shoulders. For the first time, perhaps the first time ever, she felt sorry for him. Poor Ambrose, prisoner of a selfish mother. Presumably, when she died, she had left those royalties to him, after all. Susan distinctly remembered one unpleasant occasion when the two of them had been staying and Auntie Bee had suddenly announced her intention of leaving everything she had to the Royal National Lifeboat Institute. She must have changed her mind.

★ ★ ★ ★ ★

Susan voiced these feelings to her husband in bed that night, their pillow talk consisting of a review of the "gathering," the low-key, rather depressing supper they had eaten afterwards, and the video they had watched failing to come up to expectations. Unfortunately, in spite of the novel's absence from the living room, Bill and Irene had begun to talk about **Demogorgon** almost as soon as they arrived. Apparently, this was the first day of its serialisation in a national newspaper. They had read the installment with avidity, as had James and Rosie. Knowing Susan's positive addiction to Kingston Marle, Rosie wondered if she happened to have a copy to lend to them. When Susan had finished reading it, of course.

Susan was afraid to look at Ambrose. Hastily she promised a loan of the novel and changed the subject to the less dangerous one of the archaeologists' excavations in Haybury Meadow and the protests it occasioned from local environmentalists. But the damage was done. Ambrose spoke scarcely a word all evening. It was as if he felt Kingston Marle and his book underlying everything that was said and threatening always to break through the surface of the conversation, as in a later chapter in **Demogorgon** the monstrous Dragosoma, with the head and breasts of a woman and the body of a manatee, rises slowly out of the Sea of Azov. At one point, a silvery sheen of sweat covered the pallid skin of Ambrose's face.

"Poor devil," said Frank. "I suppose he was very cut up about his old mum."

"There's no accounting for people, is there?"

They were especially gentle to him next day, without knowing exactly why gentleness was needed. Ambrose refused to go to church, treating them to a lecture on the death of God and atheism as the only course for enlightened mankind. They listened indulgently. Susan cooked a particularly nice lunch, consisting of Ambrose's favourite foods: chicken, sausages, roast potatoes, and peas. It had been practically the only dish on Auntie Bee's culinary repertoire, Ambrose having been brought up on sardines on toast and tinned spaghetti, the chicken being served on Sundays. He drank more wine than was usual with him and had a brandy afterwards.

They put him on an early afternoon train for London. Though she had never done so before, Susan kissed him. His reaction was very marked. Seeing what was about to happen, he turned his head abruptly as her mouth approached and the kiss landed on the bristles above his right ear. They stood on the platform and waved to him.

"That was a disaster," said Frank in the car. "Do we have to do it again?"

Susan surprised herself. "We have to do it again." She sighed. "Now I can go back and have a nice afternoon reading my book."

A letter from Kingston Marle, acknowledging the errors in **Demogorgon** and perhaps offering some explanation of how they came to be there, with a promise of amendment in the paperback edition, would have set everything to rights. The disastrous weekend would fade into oblivion and those stupid guests of Frank's with it. Frank's idiot wife, good-looking, they said, though he had never been able to see it, but a woman of neither education nor discernment, would dwindle away into the mists of the past. Above all, that lantern-shaped face, that monstrous jaw and vaulted forehead, looming so shockingly above its owner's blood-coloured works, would lose its menace and assume a merely arrogant cast. But before he reached home, while he was still in the train, Ambrose, thinking about it—he could think of nothing else—knew with a kind of sorrowful resignation that no such letter would be waiting for him. No such letter would come next day or the next. By his own foolhardy move, his misplaced *courage,* by doing his duty, he had seen to that.

And yet it had scarcely been all his own doing. If that retarded woman, his cousin's doll-faced wife, had only had the sense to ask Marle to inscribe the book "to Susan," rather than "to Susan Ribbon," little harm would have been done. Ribbon could hardly understand why she had done so, unless from malice, for these days it was the custom, and one he constantly deplored, to call everyone from the moment you met them, or even if you only talked to them on the phone, by their first names. Previously, Marle would have known his address but not his appearance, not seen his face, not established him as a real and therefore vulnerable person.

No letter had come. There were no letters at all on the doormat, only a flyer from a pizza takeaway company and two hire-car cards. It was still quite early, only about six. Ribbon made himself a pot of real tea—that woman used *teabags*—and decided to break with tradition and do some work. He never worked on a Sunday evening but he was in need of something positive to distract his mind from Kingston Marle. Taking his tea into the front room, he saw Marle's book lying on the coffee table. It was the first thing his eye lighted on. The Book. The awful book that had been the ruin of his weekend. He must have left **Demogorgon** on the table when he abandoned it in a kind of queasy disgust halfway through. Yet he had no memory of leaving it there. He could have sworn he had put it away, tucked it

136

into a drawer to be out of sight and therefore of mind.

The dreadful face, fish-belly white between the bandages, leered at him out of the star-shaped hole in the red and silver jacket. He opened the drawer in the cabinet where he thought he had put it. There was nothing there but what had been there before, a few sheets of writing paper and an old diary of Mummy's. Of course there was nothing there, he didn't possess two copies of the horrible thing, but it was going in there now. . . .

The phone rang. This frequent event in other people's homes happened seldom in Ribbon's. He ran out into the hall where the phone was and stood looking at it while it rang. Suppose it should be Kingston Marle? Gingerly he lifted the receiver. If it was Marle he would slam it down fast. That woman's voice said, "Ambrose? Are you all right?"

"Of course I'm all right. I've just got home."

"It was just that we've been rather worried about you. Now I know you're safely home, that's fine."

Ribbon remembered his manners and recited Mummy's rubric. "Thank you very much for having me, Susan. I had a lovely time."

He would write to her, of course. That was the proper thing. Upstairs in the office he composed three letters. The first was to Susan.

21 Grove Green Avenue,
London E11 4ZH
Dear Susan,

I very much enjoyed my weekend with you and Frank. It was very enjoyable to take a stroll with Frank and take in "the pub" on the way. The ample food provided was tip-top. Your friends seemed charming people, though I cannot commend their choice of reading matter!

All is well here. It looks as if we may be in for another spell of hot weather.

With kind regards to you both,
Yours affectionately,
Ambrose

Ribbon wasn't altogether pleased with this. He took out "very much" and put in "enormously," and for "very enjoyable" substituted "delightful." That was better. It would have to do. He was rather pleased with that acid comment about those ridiculous people's reading matter and hoped it would get back to them.

During the weekend, particularly during those hours in his room on Saturday afternoon, he had gone carefully through the two paperbacks he had bought at Dillon's. Lucy Grieves, author of **Cottoning On**, had meticulously passed on to her publishers all the errors he had pointed out to her when the novel appeared in hardcover, down to "on to" instead of "onto." Ribbon felt satisfied. He was pleased with Lucy Grieves, though not to the extent of writing to congratulate her. The second letter he wrote was to Channon Scott Smith, the paperback version of whose novel **Carol Conway** contained precisely the same mistakes and literary howlers as it had in hardcover. That completed, a scathing paean of contempt if ever there was one, Ribbon sat back in his chair and thought long and hard.

Was there some way he could write to Kingston Marle and *make things all right* without grovelling, without apologising? God forbid that he should apologise for boldly telling truths that needed to be told. But could he compose something, without saying he was sorry, that would mollify

Marle, better still that would make him understand? He had a notion that he would feel easier in his mind if he wrote to Marle, would sleep better at night. The two nights he had passed at Frank's had been very wretched, the second one almost sleepless.

What was he afraid of? Afraid of writing and afraid of not writing? Just afraid? Marle couldn't do anything to him. Ribbon acknowledged to himself that he had no absurd fears of Marle's setting some hit man on to him or stalking him or even attempting to sue him for libel. It wasn't that. What was it then? The cliché came into his head unbidden, the definition of what he felt: a nameless dread. If only Mummy were here to advise him! Suddenly he longed for her and tears pricked the backs of his eyes. Yet he knew what she would have said. She would have said what she had that last time.

That *Encyclopaedia Britannica* Volume VIII had been lying on the table. He had just shown Mummy the letter he had written to Desmond Erb, apologising for correcting him when he wrote about "the quinone structure." Of course he should have looked the word up but he hadn't. He had been so sure it should have been "quinine." Erb had been justifiably indignant, as writers tended to be, when he corrected an error in their work that was in fact not an error at all. He would never forget Mummy's anger, nor anything of that quarrel, come to that; how, almost of their own volition, his hands had crept across the desk towards the black, blue, and gold volume . . .

She was not here now to stop him and after a while he wrote this:

Dear Mr. Marle,
    With reference to my letter of June 4th, in which I

pointed out certain errors of fact and of grammar and spelling in your recent novel, I fear I may inadvertently have caused you pain. This was far from my intention. If I have hurt your feelings I must tell you that I very much regret this. I hope you will overlook it and forgive me.

Yours sincerely,

Reading this over, Ribbon found he very much disliked the bit about overlooking and forgiving. "Regret" wasn't right either. Also, he hadn't actually named the book. He ought to have put in its title but, strangely, he found himself reluctant to type the word **Demogorgon**. It was as if, by putting it into cold print, he would set something in train, spark off some reaction. Of course, this was mad. He must be getting tired. Nevertheless, he composed a second letter.

Dear Mr. Marle,

With reference to my letter to yourself of June 4th, in which I pointed out certain errors in your recent and highly-acclaimed novel, I fear I may inadvertently have hurt your feelings. It was not my intention to cause you pain. I am well aware—who is not? of the high position you enjoy in the ranks of literature. The amendments I suggested you make to the novel when it appears in paperback—in many hundreds of thousand copies, no doubt—were meant in a spirit of assistance, not criticism, simply so that a good book might be made better.

Yours sincerely,

Sycophantic. But what could be more mollifying than flattery? Ribbon endured half an hour's agony and self-doubt, self-recrimination and self-justification, too, before writing a third and final letter.

Dear Mr. Marle,

With reference to my letter to your good self, dated June 4th, in which I presumed to criticise your recent novel, I fear I may inadvertently have been wanting in respect. I hope you will believe me when I say it was not my intention to offend you. You enjoy a high and well-deserved position in the ranks of literature. It was gauche and clumsy of me to write to you as I did.

> With best wishes,
> Yours sincerely,

To grovel in this way made Ribbon feel actually sick. And it was all lies, too. Of course it had been his intention to offend the man, to cause him pain and to make him angry. He would have given a great deal to recall that earlier letter but this—he quoted silently to himself those hackneyed but apt words about the moving finger that writes and having writ moves on—neither he nor anyone else could do. What did it matter if he suffered half an hour's humiliation when by sending this apology he would end his sufferings? Thank heaven only that Mummy wasn't here to see it.

Those letters had taken him hours and it had grown quite dark. Unexpectedly dark, he thought, for nine in the evening in the middle of June with the longest day not much more than a week away. But still he sat there, in the dusk, looking at the backs of houses, yellow brick punctured by the bright rectangles of windows, at the big shaggy trees, his own garden, the square of grass dotted with dark shrubs, big and small. He had never previously noticed how unpleasant ordinary privets and cypresses can look in deep twilight when they are not clustered together in a shrubbery or copse; when they stand individually on an otherwise open space, strange shapes, tall and slender or round and squat, or with a branch here and there protruding like a limb, and casting elongated shadows.

He got up abruptly and put the light on. The garden and its gathering of bushes disappeared. The window became dark, shiny, opaque. He switched off the light almost immediately and went downstairs. Seeing **Demogorgon** on the coffee table made him jump. What was it doing there? How did it get there? He had put it in the drawer. And there was the drawer standing open to prove it.

It couldn't have got out of the drawer and returned to the table on its own. Could it? *Of course not.* Ribbon put on every light in the room. He left the curtains open so that he could see the streetlights as well. He must have left the book on the table himself. He must have intended to put it into the drawer and for some reason had not done so. Possibly he had been interrupted. But nothing ever interrupted what he was doing, did it? He couldn't remember. A cold teapot and a cup of cold tea stood on the tray on the coffee table beside the book. He couldn't remember making tea.

After he had taken the tray and the cold teapot away and poured the cold tea down the sink, he sat down in an armchair with **Chambers Dictionary**. He realised that he had never found out what the word "Demogorgon" meant. Here was the definition: *a mysterious infernal deity first mentioned about AD 450. [Appar Gr daimon deity, and gorgo Gorgon, from gorgos terrible].* He shuddered, closed the dictionary, and opened the second Channon Scott Smith paperback he had bought. This novel had been published four

years before, but Ribbon had never read it, nor indeed any
of the works of Mr. Scott Smith before the recently published one, but he thought this fat volume might yield a rich
harvest if **Carol Conway** were anything to go by. But instead of opening **Destiny's Suzerain**, he found that the
book in his hands was **Demogorgon**, open one page past
where he had stopped a few days before.

In a kind of horrified wonder, he began to read. It was
curious how he was compelled to go on reading, considering how every line was like a faint pinprick in his equilibrium, a tiny physical tremor through his body, reminding
him of those things he had written to Kingston Marle and
the look Marle had given him in Oxford on Saturday. Later
he was to ask himself why he had read any more of it at all,
why he hadn't just stopped, why indeed he hadn't put the
book in the rubbish for the refuse collectors to take away in
the morning.

The dark shape in the corner of Charles Ambrose's tent
was appearing for the first time: in his tent, then his hotel
bedroom, his mansion in Shropshire, his flat in Mayfair. A
small curled-up shape like a tiny huddled person or small
monkey. It sat or simply *was*, amorphous but for faintly visible hands or paws and uniformly dark but for pinpoint malevolent eyes that stared and glinted. Ribbon looked up
from the page for a moment. The lights were very bright.
Out in the street a couple went by, hand-in-hand, talking
and laughing. Usually, the noise they made would have an-
gered him but tonight he felt curiously comforted. They
made him feel he wasn't alone. They drew him, briefly, into
reality. He would post the letter in the morning and once it
had gone all would be well.

He read two more pages. The unravelling of the mystery
began on page 423. The Demogorgon was Charles Am-

brose's own mother who had been murdered and whom he had buried in the grounds of his Shropshire house. Finally, she came back to tell him the truth, came in the guise of a cypress tree which walked out of the pinetum. Ribbon gasped out loud. It was his own story. How had Marle known? What was Marle—some kind of god or magus that he knew such things? The dreadful notion came to him that **Demogorgon** had not always been like this, that the ending had originally been different, but that Marle, seeing him in Oxford and immediately identifying him with the writer of that defamatory letter, *had by some remote control or sorcery altered the end of the copy that was in his, Ribbon's, possession.*

He went upstairs and rewrote his letter, adding to the existing text, "Please forgive me. I meant you no harm. Don't torment me like this. I can't stand any more." It was a long time before he went to bed. Why go to bed when you know you won't sleep? With the light on—and all the lights in the house were on now—he couldn't see the garden, the shrubs on the lawn, the flowerbed, but he drew the curtains just the same. At last he fell uneasily asleep in his chair, waking four or five hours later to the horrid thought that his original letter to Marle was the first really vituperative criticism he had sent to anyone since Mummy's death. Was there some significance in this? Did it mean he couldn't get along without Mummy? Or, worse, that he had killed all the power and confidence in himself he had once felt?

He got up, had a rejuvenating shower, but was unable to face breakfast. The three letters he had written the night before were in the postbox by nine and Ribbon on the way to the tube station. Waterstones in Leadenhall Market was his destination. He bought Clara Jenkins's **Tales My Lover Told Me** in hardcover as well as Raymond Kobbo's **The**

Nomad's Smile and Natalya Dreadnought's *Tick* in paperback. Copies of **Demogorgon** were everywhere, stacked in piles or displayed in fanciful arrangements. Ribbon forced himself to touch one of them, to pick it up. He looked over his shoulder to see if any of the assistants were watching him, and having established that they were not, opened it at page 423. It was as he had thought, as he had hardly dared put into words. Charles Ambrose's mother made no appearance, there was nothing about a burial in the grounds of Montpellier Hall or a cypress tree walking. The end was quite different. Charles Ambrose, married to Kaysa in a ceremony conducted in a balloon above the Himalayas, awakens on his wedding night and sees in the corner of the honeymoon bedroom the demon curled up, hunched and small, staring at him with gloating eyes. It had followed him from Egypt to Shropshire, from London to Russia, from Russia to New Orleans, and from New Orleans to Nepal. It would never leave him, it was his for life and perhaps beyond.

Ribbon replaced the book, took up another copy. The same thing, no murder, no burial, no tree walking, only the horror of the demon in the bedroom. So he had been right. Marle had infused this alternative ending into *his* copy alone. It was part of the torment, part of the revenge for the insults Ribbon had heaped on him. On the way back to Liverpool Street Station a shout and a thump made him look over his shoulder—a taxi had clipped the rear wheel of a motorbike—and he saw, a long way behind, Kingston Marle following him.

Ribbon thought he would faint. A great flood of heat washed over him, to be succeeded by shivering. Panic held him still for a moment. Then he dived into a shop, a sweetshop it was, and it was like entering a giant chocolate box.

The scent of chocolate swamped him. Trembling, he stared at the street through a window draped with pink frills. Ages passed before Kingston Marle went by. He paused, turned his head to look at the chocolates, and Ribbon, again almost fainting, saw an unknown man, lantern-jawed but not monstrously so, long-haired but the hair sparse and brown, the blue eyes mild and wistful. Ribbon's heartbeat slowed, the blood withdrew from the surface of his skin. He muttered, "No, no thank you," to the woman behind the counter and went back into the street. What a wretched state his nerves were in! He'd be encountering a scaly paw in the wardrobe next. Clasping his bag of books, he got thoughtfully into the train.

What he really should have done was add a P.S. to the effect that he would appreciate a prompt acknowledgement of his letter. Just a line saying something like *Please be kind enough to acknowledge receipt.* However, it was too late now. Kingston Marle's publishers would get his letter tomorrow and send it straight on. Ribbon knew publishers did not always do this, but surely in the case of so eminent an author and one of the most profitable on their list . . .

Sending the letter should have allayed his fears, but they seemed to crowd in upon him more urgently, jostling each other for preeminence in his mind. The man who had followed him along Bishopsgate, for instance. Of course he knew it had not been Kingston Marle, yet the similarity of build, of feature, of height, between the two men was too great for coincidence. The most likely explanation was that his stalker was Marle's younger brother, and now, as he reached this reasonable conclusion, Ribbon no longer saw the man's eyes as mild but sly and crafty. When his letter came, Marle would call his brother off but, in the nature of things, the letter could not arrive at Marle's home before Wednesday at the earliest. Then there was the matter of The Book itself. The drawer in which it lay failed to hide it adequately. It was part of a mahogany cabinet (one of Mummy's wedding presents, Ribbon believed), well-polished but of course opaque. Yet sometimes the wood seemed to become transparent and the harsh reds and glaring silver of **Demogorgon** to shine through it as he understood a block of radium would appear as a glowing cuboid behind a wall of solid matter. Approaching closely, creeping up on it, he would see the bright colours fade and the woodwork reappear, smooth, shiny, and *ordinary* once more.

In the study upstairs on Monday evening he tried to do some work, but his eye was constantly drawn to the window and what lay beyond. He became convinced that the bushes on the lawn had moved. That small thin one had surely stood next to the pair of tall fat ones, not several yards away. Since the night before it had shifted its position, taking a step nearer to the house. Drawing the curtains helped, but after a while he got up and pulled them apart a little to check on the small thin bush, to see if it had taken a step further or had returned to its previous position. It was where it had been ten minutes before. All should have been well but it was not. The room itself had become uncomfortable and he resolved not to go back there, to move the computer downstairs, until he had heard from Kingston Marle.

The doorbell ringing made him jump so violently he felt pain travel through his body and reverberate. Immediately he thought of Marle's brother. Suppose Marle's brother, a strong young man, was outside the door and when it was opened would force his way in? Or, worse, was merely checking that Ribbon was at home and when footsteps sounded inside, intended to disappear? Ribbon went down. He took a deep breath and threw the door open. His caller was Glenys Next-door.

Marching in without being invited, she said, "Hiya, Amby," and that Tinks Next-door was missing. The cat had not been home since the morning, when he was last seen by Sandra On-the-other-side sitting in Ribbon's front garden eating a bird.

"I'm out of my mind with worry, as you can imagine, Amby."

As a matter of fact, he couldn't. Ribbon cared very little for songbirds, but he cared for feline predators even less. "I'll let you know if I come across him. However—" he laughed lightly "—he knows he's not popular with me so he makes himself scarce."

This was the wrong thing to say. In the works of his less literate authors, Ribbon sometimes came upon the expression "to bridle"—"she bridled" or even "the young woman bridled." At last he understood what it meant. Glenys Next-door tossed her head, raised her eyebrows, and looked down her nose at him.

"I'm sorry for you, Amby, I really am. You must find that attitude problem of yours a real hang-up. I mean socially. I've tried to ignore it all these years but there comes a time when one has to speak one's mind. No, don't bother, please, I can see myself out."

This was not going to be a good night. He knew that before he switched the bedside light off. For one thing, he always read in bed before going to sleep. Always had and always would. But for some reason he had forgotten to take **Destiny's Suzerain** upstairs with him and though his bedroom was full of reading matter, shelves and shelves of it, he had read all the books before. Of course he could have gone downstairs and fetched himself a book, or even just gone into the study, which was lined with books. Booked, not papered, indeed. He *could* have done so, in theory he could have, but on coming into his bedroom he had locked the door. Why? He was unable to answer that question, though he put it to himself several times. It was a small house, potentially brightly lit, in a street of a hundred and fifty such houses, all populated. A dreadful feeling descended upon him as he lay in bed that if he unlocked that door, if he turned the key and opened it, something would come in. Was it the small thin bush that would come in? These thoughts, ridiculous, unworthy of him, puerile, frightened him so much that he put the bedside lamp on and left it on till morning.

Tuesday's post brought two letters. Eric Owlberg called Ribbon "a little harsh" and informed him that printers do not always do as they are told. Jeanne Pettle's letter was from a secretary who wrote that Ms. Pettle was away on an extended publicity tour but would certainly attend to his "interesting communication" when she returned. There was nothing from Dillon's. It was a bright sunny day. Ribbon went into the study and contemplated the garden. The shrubs were, of course, where they had always been. Or where they had been before the small thin bush stepped back into its original position?

"Pull yourself together," Ribbon said aloud.

Housework day. He started, as he always did, in Mummy's room, dusting the picture rail and the central lamp with a bunch of pink and blue feathers attached to a rod, and the ornaments with a clean fluffy yellow duster. The numerous books he took out and dusted on alternate weeks but this was not one of those. He vacuumed the carpet, opened the window wide, and replaced the pink silk nightdress with a pale blue one. He always washed Mummy's nightdresses by hand once a fortnight. Next his own room and the study, then downstairs to the dining and front rooms. Marle's publishers would have received his letter by the first post this morning, and the department which looked after this kind of thing would, even at this moment, probably, be readdressing the envelope and sending it on. Ribbon had no idea where the man lived. London? Devonshire? Most of those people seemed to live in the Cotswolds, its green hills and lush valleys must be chock-full of them. But perhaps Shropshire was more likely. He had written about Montpellier Hall as if he really knew such a house.

Ribbon dusted the mahogany cabinet and passed on to Mummy's little sewing table, but he couldn't quite leave things there, and he returned to the cabinet—to stand, duster in hand, staring at that drawer. It was not transparent on this sunny morning and nothing could be seen glowing in its depths. He pulled it open suddenly and snatched up The Book. He looked at its double redness and at the pentagram. After his experiences of the past days he wouldn't have been surprised if the bandaged face inside had changed its position, closed its mouth, or moved its eyes. Well, he would have been surprised, he'd have been horrified, aghast. But the demon was the same as ever, The Book was just the same, an ordinary, rather tastelessly jacketed, cheap thriller.

"What on earth is the matter with me?" Ribbon said to The Book.

He went out shopping for food. Sandra On-the-other-side appeared behind him in the queue at the checkout. "You've really upset Glenys," she said. "You know me, I

believe in plain speaking, and in all honesty I think you
ought to apologise."

"When I want your opinion I'll ask for it, Mrs. Wilson,"
said Ribbon.

Marle's brother got on the bus and sat behind him. It
wasn't actually Marle's brother, he only thought it was, just
for a single frightening moment. It was amazing, really,
what a lot of people there were about who looked like
Kingston Marle, men and women, too. He had never noticed it before, had never had an inkling of it until he came
face to face with Marle in that bookshop. If only it were
possible to go back. For the moving finger, having writ, not
to move on but to retreat, retrace its strokes, white them
out with correction fluid, and begin writing again. He
would have guessed why that silly woman, his cousin's wife,
was so anxious to get to Blackwell's; her fondness for
Marle's works—distributed so tastelessly all over his bedroom—would have told him, and he would have cried off
the Oxford trip, first warning her on no account to let
Marle know her surname. Yet—and this was undeniable—
Marle had Ribbon's home address, the address was on the
letter. The moving finger would have to go back a week and
erase *21 Grove Green Avenue, London E11 4ZH* from the top
right-hand corner of his letter. Then, and only then, would
he have been safe. . . .

Sometimes a second post arrived on a weekday but none
came that day. Ribbon took his shopping bags into the
kitchen, unpacked them, went into the front room to open
the window—and saw **Demogorgon** lying on the coffee
table. A violent trembling convulsed him. He sat down,
closed his eyes. He *knew* he hadn't taken it out of the
drawer. Why on earth would he? He hated it. He wouldn't
touch it unless he had to. There was not much doubt now

that it had a life of its own. Some kind of kinetic energy lived inside its covers, the same sort of thing as moved the small thin bush across the lawn at night. Kingston Marle put that energy into objects, he infused them with it, he was a sorcerer whose powers extended far beyond his writings and his fame. Surely that was the only explanation why a writer of such appallingly bad books, misspelt, the grammar nonexistent, facts awry, should enjoy such a phenomenal success, not only with an ignorant illiterate public but among the cognoscenti. He practised sorcery or was himself one of the demons he wrote about, an evil spirit living inside that hideous lantern-jawed exterior.

Ribbon reached out a slow wavering hand for The Book and found that, surely by chance, he had opened it at page 423. Shrinking while he did so, holding The Book almost too far away from his eyes to see the words, he read of Charles Ambrose's wedding night, of his waking in the half-dark with Kaysa sleeping beside him and seeing the curled-up shape of the demon in the corner of the room. . . . So Marle had called off his necromancer's power, had he? He had restored the ending to what it originally was. Nothing about Mummy's death and burial, nothing about the walking tree. Did that mean he had already received Ribbon's apology? It might mean that. His publishers had hardly had time to send the letter on, but suppose Marle, for some reason—and the reason would be his current publicity tour—had been in his publishers' office and the letter had been handed to him. It was the only explanation, it fitted the facts. Marle had read his letter, accepted his apology, and, perhaps with a smile of triumph, whistled back whatever dogs of the occult carried his messages.

Ribbon held The Book in his hands. Everything might be over now, but he still didn't want it in the house. Carefully, he wrapped it up in newspaper, slipped the resulting parcel into a plastic carrier, tied the handles together, and dropped it in the wastebin. "Let it get itself out of that," he said aloud. "Just let it try." Was he imagining that a fetid smell came from it, swathed in plastic though it was? He splashed disinfectant into the wastebin, opened the kitchen window.

He sat down in the front room and opened **Tales My Lover Told Me** but he couldn't concentrate. The afternoon grew dark, there was going to be a storm. For a moment he stood at the window, watching the clouds gather, black and swollen. When he was a little boy Mummy had told him a storm was the clouds fighting. It was years since he had thought of that and now, remembering, for perhaps the first time in his life he questioned Mummy's judgment. Was it quite right so to mislead a child?

The rain came, sheets of it blown by the huge gale which arose. Ribbon wondered if Marle, among his many accomplishments, could raise a wind, strike lightning from some diabolical tinderbox, and, like Jove himself, beat the drum of thunder. Perhaps. He would believe anything of that man now. He went around the house closing all the windows. The one in the study he closed and fastened the catches. From his own bedroom window he looked at the lawn, where the bushes stood as they had always stood, unmoved, immoveable, lashed by rain, whipping and twisting in the wind. Downstairs, in the kitchen, the window was wide open, flapping back and forth, and the wastebin had fallen on its side. The parcel lay beside it, the plastic bag that covered it and the newspaper inside torn as if a scaly paw had ripped it. Other rubbish, food scraps, a sardine can, were scattered across the floor.

Ribbon stood transfixed. He could see the red and silver jacket of The Book gleaming, almost glowing, under its torn wrappings. What had come through the window? Was it possible the demon, unleashed by Marle, was now beyond his control?

He asked the question aloud, he asked Mummy, though she was long gone. The sound of his own voice, shrill and horror-stricken, frightened him. Had whatever it was come in to retrieve the—he could hardly put it even into silent words—*the chronicle of its exploits?* Nonsense, nonsense. It was Mummy speaking, Mummy telling him to be strong, not to be a fool. He shook himself, gritted his teeth. He picked up the parcel, dropped it into a black rubbish bag, and took it into the garden, getting very wet in the process. In the wind the biggest bush of all reached out a needly arm and lashed him across the face.

He left the black bag there. He locked all the doors and even when the storm had subsided and the sky cleared he kept all the windows closed. Late that night, in his bedroom, he stared down at the lawn. The Book in its bag was where he had left it, but the small thin bush had moved, in a different direction this time, stepping to one side so that the two fat bushes, the one that had lashed him and its twin, stood close together and side by side like tall heavily-built men gazing up at his window. Ribbon had saved half a bottle of Mummy's sleeping pills. For an emergency, for a rainy day. All the lights blazing, he went into Mummy's room, found the bottle, and swallowed two pills. They took effect rapidly. Fully-clothed, he fell onto his bed and into something more like a deep trance than sleep. It was the first time in his life he had ever taken a soporific.

In the morning he looked through the yellow pages and found a firm of tree-fellers, operating locally. Would they send someone to cut down all the shrubs in his garden? They would, but not before Monday. On Monday morning they would be with him by nine. In the broad daylight he asked himself again what had come through the kitchen window, come in and taken That Book out of the wastebin, and sane again, wondered if it might have been Glenys Next-door's fox. The sun was shining, the grass gleaming wet after the rain. He fetched a spade from the shed and advanced upon the wide flowerbed. Not the right-hand side, not there, avoid that at all costs. He selected a spot on the extreme left, close by the fence dividing his garden from that of Sandra On-the-other-side. While he dug he wondered if it was commonplace with people, this burying of unwanted or hated or threatening objects in their back gardens. Maybe all the gardens in Leytonstone, in London suburbs, in the United Kingdom, in the world, were full of such concealed things, hidden in the earth, waiting . . .

He laid **Demogorgon** inside. The wet earth went back over the top of it, covering it, and Ribbon stamped the surface down viciously. If whatever it was came back and dug The Book out he thought he would die.

Things were better now **Demogorgon** was gone. He wrote to Clara Jenkins at her home address—for some unaccountable reason she was in **Who's Who**—pointing out that in chapter one of **Tales My Lover Told Me** Humphry Nemo had blue eyes and in chapter twenty-one brown eyes, Thekla Pattison wore a wedding ring on page 20 but denied, on page 201, that she had ever possessed one, and on page 245 Justin Armstrong was taking part in an athletics contest, in spite of having broken his leg on page 223, a mere five days before. But Ribbon wrote with a new gentleness, as if she had caused him pain rather than rage.

Nothing had come from Dillon's. He wondered bitterly why he had troubled to congratulate them on their service if his accolade was to go unappreciated. And more to the point, nothing had come from Kingston Marle by Friday. He had the letter of apology, he must have, otherwise he wouldn't have altered the ending of **Demogorgon** back to the original plot line. But that hardly meant he had recovered from all his anger. He might still have other revenges in store. And, moreover, he might intend never to answer Ribbon at all.

The shrubs seemed to be back in their normal places. It would be a good idea to have a plan of the garden with the bushes all accurately positioned so that he could tell if they moved. He decided to make one. The evening was mild and sunny, though damp, and of course, at not long past midsummer, still broad daylight at eight. A deck chair was called for, a sheet of paper, and, better than a pen, a soft lead pencil. The deck chairs might be up in the loft or down here, he couldn't remember, though he had been in the shed on Wednesday evening to find a spade. He looked through the shed window. In the far corner, curled up, was a small dark shape.

Ribbon was too frightened to cry out. A pain seized him in the chest, ran up his left arm, held him in its grip before it slackened and released him. The black shape opened its eyes and looked at him, just as the demon in The Book looked at Charles Ambrose. Ribbon hunched his back and closed his eyes. When he opened them again and looked again he saw Tinks Next-door get up, stretch, arch its back, and begin to walk in leisurely fashion towards the door. Ribbon flung it open.

"Scat! Get out! Go home!" he screamed.

Tinks fled. Had the wretched thing slunk in there when he opened the door to get the spade? Probably. He took out a deck chair and sat on it, but all heart had gone out of him for drawing a plan of the garden. In more ways than one, he thought, the pain receding and leaving only a dull ache. You could have mild heart attacks from which you recovered and were none the worse. Mummy said she had had several, some of them brought on—he sadly recalled—by his own defections from her standards. It could be hereditary. He must take things easy for the next few days, not *worry*, try to put stress behind him.

Kingston Marle had signed all the books she sent him and returned them with a covering letter. Of course she had sent postage and packing as well and had put in a very polite little note, repeating how much she loved his work and what a great pleasure meeting him in Blackwell's had been. But still she had hardly expected such a lovely long letter from him, nor one of quite that nature. Marle wrote how very different she was from the common run of fans, not only in intellect but in appearance, too. He hoped she wouldn't take it amiss when he told her he had been struck by her beauty and elegance among that dowdy crowd.

It was a long time since any man had paid Susan such a compliment. She read and reread the letter, sighed a little, laughed, and showed it to Frank.

"I don't suppose he writes his own letters," said Frank, put out. "Some secretary will do it for him."

"Well, hardly."

"If you say so. When are you seeing him again?"

"Oh, don't be silly," said Susan.

She covered each individual book Kingston Marle had signed for her with cling film and put them all away in a glass-fronted bookcase from which, to make room, she first removed Frank's **Complete Works of Shakespeare**, Tennyson's **Poems**, **The Poems of Robert Browning**, and

Kobbe's **Complete Opera Book**. Frank appeared not to notice. Admiring through the glass, indeed gloating over, her wonderful collection of Marle's works with the secret inscriptions hidden from all eyes, Susan wondered if she should respond to the author. On the one hand a letter would keep her in the forefront of his mind, but on the other it would be in direct contravention of the playing-hard-to-get principle. Not that Susan had any intention of being "got," of course not, but she was not averse to inspiring thoughts about her in Kingston Marle's mind or even a measure of regret that he was unable to know her better.

Several times in the next few days she surreptitiously took one of the books out and looked at the inscription. Each had something different in it. In **Wickedness in High Places** Marle had written, "To Susan, met on a fine morning in Oxford," and in **The Necromancer's Bride**, "To Susan, with kindest of regards," but on the title page of **Evil Incarnate** appeared the inscription Susan liked best. "She was a lady sweet and kind, ne'er a face so pleased my mind—ever yours, Kingston Marle."

Perhaps he would write again, even if she didn't reply. Perhaps he would be *more likely* to write if she didn't reply.

On Monday morning the post came early, just after eight, delivering just one item. The computer-generated address on the envelope made Ribbon think for one wild moment that it might be from Kingston Marle. But it was from Clara Jenkins, and it was an angry, indignant letter, though containing no threats. Didn't he understand her novel was fiction? You couldn't say things were true or false in fiction, for things were as the author, who was all-powerful, wanted them to be. In a magic-realism novel, such as **Tales My**

Lover Told Me, only an ignorant fool would expect facts (and these included spelling, punctuation, and grammar) to be as they were in the dreary reality he inhabited. Ribbon took it into the kitchen, screwed it up, and dropped it in the wastebin.

He was waiting for the tree-fellers who were due at nine. Half-past nine went by, ten went by. At ten past the front doorbell rang. It was Glenys Next-door.

"Tinks turned up," she said. "I was so pleased to see him I gave him a whole can of red Sockeye salmon." She appeared to have forgiven Ribbon for his "attitude." "Now don't say what a wicked waste, I can see you were going to. I've got to go and see my mother, she's fallen over, broken her arm and bashed her face, so would you be an angel and let the washing-machine man in?"

"I suppose so." The woman had a mother! She must be getting on for seventy herself.

"You're a star. Here's the key and you can leave it on the hall table when he's been. Just tell him it's full of pillow-cases and water and the door won't open."

The tree-fellers came at eleven-thirty. The older one, a joker, said, "I'm a funny feller and he's a nice feller, right?"

"Come this way," Ribbon said frostily.

"What d'you want them lovely Leylandiis down for then? Not to mention that lovely flowering currant?"

"Them currants smell of cat's pee, Damian," said the young one. "Whether there's been cats peeing on them or not."

"Is that right? The things he knows, guv. He's wasted in this job, ought to be fiddling with computers."

Ribbon went indoors. The computer and printer were downstairs now, in the dining room. He wrote first to Natalya Dreadnought, author of **Tick**, pointing out in a mild way that "eponymous" applies to a character or object which gives a work its name, not to the name derived from the character. Therefore it was the large blood-sucking mite of the Acarina order which was eponymous, not her title. The letter he wrote to Raymond Kobbo would correct just two mistakes in **The Nomad's Smile**, but for both Ribbon needed to consult *Piranha* to *Scurfy*. He was pretty sure the Libyan caravan centre should be spelt "Sabha," not "Sebha," and he was even more certain that "qalam," meaning a reed pen used in Arabic calligraphy, should start with a k. He went upstairs and lifted the heavy tome off the shelf. Finding that Kobbo had been right in both instances—"Sabha" and "Sebha" were optional spellings and "qalam" perfectly correct—unsettled him. Mummy would have known, Mummy would have set him right in her positive, no-nonsense way, before he had set foot on the bottom stair. He asked himself if he could live without her and could have sworn he heard her sharp voice say, "You should have thought of that before."

Before what? That day in February when she had come up here to—well, oversee him, supervise him. She frequently did so, and in later years he hadn't been as grateful to her as he should have been. By the desk here she had stood and told him it was time he earned some money by his work, by a man's fifty-second year it was time. She had made up her mind to leave Daddy's royalties to the lifeboat people. But it wasn't this which finished things for him, or triggered things off, however you liked to put it. It was the sneering tone in which she told him, her right index finger pointing at his chest, that he was no good, he had failed. She had kept him in comfort and luxury for decade after decade, she had instructed him, taught him everything he knew, yet in spite of this, his literary criticism had not had the slightest effect on authors' standards or effected the least improvement in English fiction. He had wasted his time and his life through cowardice and pusillanimity, through mousiness instead of manliness.

It was that word "mousiness" which did it. His hands moved across the table to rest on *Piranha* to *Scurfy*, he lifted it in both hands and brought it down as hard as he could on her head. Once, twice, again and again. The first time she screamed but not again after that. She staggered and sank to her knees and he beat her to the ground with Volume VIII of the **Encyclopaedia Britannica**. She was an old woman, she put up no struggle, she died quickly. He very much wanted not to get blood on the book—she had taught him books were sacred—but there was no blood. What was shed was shed inside her.

Regret came immediately. Remorse followed. But she was dead. He buried her in the wide flowerbed at the end of the garden that night, in the dark without a torch. The widows on either side slept soundly, no one saw a thing. The ivies grew back and the flowerless plants that liked shade. All summer he had watched them slowly growing. He told only two people she was dead, Glenys Next-door and his cousin Frank. Neither showed any inclination to come to the "funeral," so when the day he had appointed came he left the house at ten in the morning, wearing the new dark suit he had bought, a black tie that had been Daddy's, and carrying a bunch of spring flowers. Sandra On-the-other-side spotted him from her front-room window, and, approving, nodded sombrely while giving him a sad smile. Ribbon smiled sadly back. He put the flowers on someone else's grave and strolled round the cemetery for half an hour.

From a material point of view, living was easy. He had

more money now than Mummy had ever let him have. Daddy's royalties were paid into her bank account twice a year and would continue to be paid in. Ribbon drew out what he wanted on her direct-debit card, his handwriting being so like hers that no one could tell the difference. She had been collecting her retirement pension for years, and he went on doing so. It occurred to him that the Department of Social Security might expect her to die sometime and the bank might expect it, too, but she had been very young when he was born and might in any case have been expected to outlive him. He could go on doing this until what would have been her hundredth birthday and even beyond. But could he live without her? He had "made it up to her" by keeping her bedroom as a shrine, keeping her clothes as if one day she would come back and wear them again. Still he was a lost soul, only half a man, a prey to doubts and fears and self-questioning and a nervous restlessness.

Looking down at the floor, he half expected to see some mark where her small slight body had lain. There was nothing, any more than there was a mark on Volume VIII of **Britannica**. He went downstairs and stared out into the garden. The cypress he had associated with her, had been near to seeing as containing her spirit, was down, was lying on the grass, its frondy branches already wilting in the heat. One of the two fat shrubs was down, too. Damian and the young one were sitting *on Mummy's grave,* drinking something out of a vacuum flask and smoking cigarettes. Mummy would have had something to say about that, but he lacked the heart. He thought again how strange it was, how horrible and somehow wrong, that the small child's name for its mother was the same as that for an embalmed Egyptian corpse.

In the afternoon, after the washing-machine man had

come and been let into Glenys Next-door's, Ribbon plucked up the courage to phone Kingston Marle's publishers. After various people's voice mail, instructions to press this button and that and requests to leave messages, he was put through to the department which sent on authors' letters. A rather indignant young woman assured him that all mail was sent on within a week of the publishers receiving it. Recovering a little of Mummy's spirit, he said in the strongest tone he could muster that a week was far too long. What about readers who were waiting anxiously for a reply? The young woman told him she had said "within a week" and it might be much sooner. With that he had to be content. It was eleven days now since he had apologised to Kingston Marle, ten since his publishers had received the letter. He asked tentatively if they ever handed a letter to an author in person. For a while she hardly seemed to understand what he was talking about, then she gave him a defiant no, such a thing could never happen.

So Marle had not called off his dogs because he had received the apology. Perhaps it was only that the spell, or whatever it was, lasted no more than, say, twenty-four hours. It seemed, sadly, a more likely explanation. The tree-fellers finished at five, leaving the wilted shrubs stacked on the flowerbed, not on Mummy's grave but on the place where The Book was buried. Ribbon took two of Mummy's sleeping pills and passed a good night. No letter came in the morning, there was no post at all. Without any evidence as to the truth of this, he became suddenly sure that no letter would come from Marle now, it would never come.

He had nothing to do, he had written to everyone who needed reproving, he had supplied himself with no more new books and had no inclination to go out and buy more. Perhaps he would never write to anyone again. He unplugged the link between computer and printer and closed the computer's lid. The new shelving he had bought from Ikea to put up in the dining room would never be used now. In the middle of the morning he went into Mummy's bedroom, tucked the nightdress under the pillow and quilt, removed the bedspread from the wardrobe door, and closed the door. He couldn't have explained why he did these things, it simply seemed time to do them. From the window he saw a taxi draw up and Glenys Next-door get out of it. There was someone else inside the taxi she was helping out but Ribbon didn't stay to see who it was.

He contemplated the back garden from the dining room. Somehow he would have to dispose of all those logs, the remains of the cypresses, the flowering currant, the holly, and the lilac bush. For a ten-pound note the men would doubtless have taken them away, but Ribbon hadn't thought of this at the time. The place looked bleak and characterless now, an empty expanse of grass with a stark ivy-clad flowerbed at the end of it. He noticed for the first time, over the wire dividing fence, the profusion of flowers in Glenys Next-door's, the birdtable, the little fish pond (both hunting grounds for Tinks), the red-leaved Japanese maple. He would burn that wood, he would have a fire.

Of course he wasn't supposed to do this. In a small way it was against the law, for this was a smokeless zone and had been for nearly as long as he could remember. By the time anyone complained—and Glenys Next-door and Sandra On-the-other-side would both complain—the deed would have been done and the logs consumed. But he postponed it for a while and went back into the house. He felt reasonably well, if a little weak and dizzy. Going upstairs made him breathless in a way he never had been before, so he postponed that for a while, too, and had a cup of tea, sitting in the front room with his feet up. What would Marle do next? There was no knowing. Ribbon thought that when he was better he would find out where Marle lived, go to him, and apologise in person. He would ask what he could do to make it up to Marle, and whatever the answer was he would do it. If Marle wanted him to be his servant he would do that, or kneel at his feet and kiss the ground or allow Marle to flog him with a whip. Anything Marle wanted he would do, whatever it was.

Of course, he shouldn't have buried the book. That did no good. It would be ruined now and the best thing, the *cleanest* thing, would be to cremate it. After he was rested he made his way upstairs, crawled really, his hands on the stairs ahead of him, took *Piranha Scurfy* off the shelf, and brought it down. He'd burn that, too. Back in the garden he arranged the logs on a bed of screwed-up newspaper, rested Volume VIII of **Britannica** on top of them, and, fetching the spade, unearthed **Demogorgon**. Its plastic covering had been inadequate to protect it and it was sodden as well as very dirty. Ribbon felt guilty for treating it as he had. The fire would purify it. There was paraffin in a can somewhere, Mummy had used it for the little stove that heated her bedroom. He went back into the house, found the can, and sprinkled paraffin on newspaper, logs, and books, and applied a lighted match.

The flames roared up immediately, slowed once the oil had done its work. He poked at his fire with a long stick. A voice started shouting at him but he took no notice, it was only Glenys Next-door complaining. The smoke from the fire thickened, grew dense and grey. Its flames had reached The Book's wet pages, the great thick wad of 427 of them, and as the smoke billowed in a tall whirling cloud an acrid smell poured from it. Ribbon stared at the smoke for, in it now, or behind it, something was taking shape, a small, thin, and very old woman swathed in a mummy's bandages, her head and arm bound in white bands, the skin between fish-belly white. He gave a small choking cry and fell, clutching the place where his heart was, holding on to the overpowering pain.

"The pathologist seems to think he died of fright," the policeman said to Frank. "A bit fanciful that, if you ask me. Anyone can have a heart attack. You have to ask yourself what he could have been frightened *of*. Nothing, unless it was of catching fire. Of course, strictly speaking, the poor chap had no business to be having a fire. Mrs. Judd and her mother saw it all. It was a bit of a shock for the old lady, she's over ninety and not well herself, she's staying with her daughter while recovering from a bad fall."

Frank was uninterested in Glenys Judd's mother and her problems. He had a severe summer cold, could have done without any of this, and doubted if he would be well enough to attend Ambrose Ribbon's funeral. In the event, Susan went to it alone. Someone had to. It would be too terrible if no one was there.

She expected to find herself the only mourner, and she was very surprised to find she was not alone. On the other side of the aisle from her in the crematorium chapel sat Kingston Marle. At first she could hardly believe her eyes, then he turned his head, smiled, and came to sit next to her. Afterwards, as they stood admiring the two wreaths, his, and hers and Frank's, he said that he supposed some sort of explanation would be in order.

"Not really," Susan said. "I just think it's wonderful of you to come."

"I saw the announcement of his death in the paper, with

the date and place of the funeral," Marle said, turning his wonderful deep eyes from the flowers to her. "A rather odd thing had happened. I had a letter from your cousin—well, your husband's cousin. It was a few days after we met in Oxford. His letter was an apology, quite an abject apology, saying he was sorry for having written to me before, asking me to forgive him for criticising me for something or other."

"What sort of something or other?"

"That I don't know. I never received his previous letter. But what he said reminded me that I *had* received a letter intended for Dillon's bookshop in Piccadilly and signed by him. Of course I sent it on to them and thought no more about it. But now I'm wondering if he put the Dillon's letter into the envelope intended for me and mine into the one for Dillon's. It's easily done. That's why I prefer e-mail myself."

Susan laughed. "It can't have had anything to do with his death, anyway."

"No, certainly not. I was going to mention it to him in Blackwell's but—well, I saw you instead and everything else went out of my head. I didn't really come here because of the letter, that's not important, I came because I hoped I might see you again."

"Oh."

"Will you have lunch with me?"

Susan looked around her, as if spies might be about. But they were alone. "I don't see why not," she said.

The Lost Boy

Robert Barnard

The young man in jeans and chunky pullover walked out of the sportswear shop into the broad upper walk of the shopping precinct, his little boy riding high on his shoulders.

"Where to now, Captain?" he asked. "What's the menu: Coke, ice cream, or lemonade?"

The child's eyes sparkled, but he thought long and seriously and when at last he said, "Lemonade, Daddy," the man wondered whether he said it because it was the last option mentioned. Often his apparent pondering was really the sign of his general thoughtfulness.

"Okay, well, we'll go to the ice-cream stall downstairs, shall we? They have drinks as well there, so you can make up your mind finally when you get there."

"Yes!" said the little boy enthusiastically.

They made an attractive sight as they took the escalator down to the lower floor of the shopping precinct, the little boy glorying in his wondrous elevation above really grown-up people, crowing down on them and drawing their attention. The man was about twenty-five, casual altogether, but his jeans were clean and above the neck of the pullover could be seen the bright check of his shirt. The face would not have attracted a second look, but when it did, the passerby would have noted light brown hair cut short around a long, thoughtful face.

"Here we are, Captain," he said as they arrived at the ice-cream stall on the ground level. "Now, take a good look and tell me what it is you'd like."

"What a lovely little boy," said a middle-aged woman, joining the queue behind them.

"Malcolm?" responded the man softly, his hand ruffling the hair of the boy, now on the ground and staring through the side glass of the stall. "He's a cracker. But we don't tell him."

They looked at him. He was oblivious to their conversation, single-mindedly surveying the range of desirables on offer.

"Take your time, Captain," the man said.

"He's got a good father, that's for sure," said the woman, half in love with the man's youth and healthy look. "These days men pretend they're shouldering half the burden, but really they leave most of it to the mother as they always did."

"He's everything to me," said the young man simply. "He's what makes life worth living. We'll be phoning his mother in a while, to tell her we're both all right."

"Oh—don't you come from here?"

"No, we're not from these parts."

"I want the red one," said the little boy, pointing to a bright pink bowl of ice cream.

"The red one, right. I think that's cherry, not strawberry."

"Sherry. I want the sherry one."

So the cherry one it was. The man paid for a double

scoop of ice cream, refused one for himself, and when he'd paid over the money he nodded to the woman and led the boy by the left hand out of the St. James's Mall and into early spring sunlight. The boy walked confidently, his hand in the man's, while the other one held the cornet, which he was licking enthusiastically.

"Don't they make a lovely picture?" said the middle-aged woman wistfully to the girl behind the counter of the stall. The girl looked as if she had seen enough children in her job to last her a lifetime.

"Now then, Captain," said the man, his little boy's hand still warmly in his as they waited on the pavement, then crossed the Headrow and started down towards Boar Lane. "We'll go to the station and phone your mother to tell her we're all right, and then we'll go to the car and find a bed for the night."

Malcolm nodded wisely, and went on licking his ice cream with intense concentration. It lasted him most of the way to Boar Lane, and when it was done he needed his fingers and his chin wiped with a handkerchief.

"Want to ride on my shoulders again?"

"*Yes!*" It was said with the intensity Malcolm reserved for everything he felt most deeply or enthusiastically about. The man took him under the armpits and swung him up. They crossed Boar Lane towards the Yates Wine Bar, then took the side road to the station.

"Now then, Malcolm," the man said, "I think the telephones are through there near the ticket office."

The boy was taking in the large square concourse and the train departure board, his eyes wide. After a second he nodded. They went through to the booking hall, the man bending his knees to get through the door, the child on his shoulders crowing triumphantly. They found a telephone, and the man brought Malcolm down from his point of vantage to sit in the crook of his arm beside the telephone.

"Now, we put some money in . . . That's it. Let's see: 01325. Then 274658 . . . Here we are. It's ringing. Now then, Captain: your call to Mummy."

The phone had been picked up at the other end.

"274658." The voice sounded strained.

"Mummy!"

"Malcolm! Where are you? What—?"

But already the man's strong forefinger had come down on the telephone's cradle.

"There we are, Captain. Mustn't take up too much of Mummy's time."

"I'm getting desperate," said Selena Randall.

Her solicitor, Derek Mitcham, looked at her hands, tugging and tearing at a tiny handkerchief, and could only agree. He had found, though, with desperate clients, that the best thing to do was to keep the tone low and level.

"Everyone's doing everything they can," he said.

The woman's voice rose dangerously.

"Are they? *Are* they? It doesn't look like that to me, I can tell you. The police, for example. What are they doing, actually *doing?* I can't see that they're doing anything."

"You can be quite sure that police forces all over the country have a description of your husband, and of Malcolm. They'll all be on the lookout for them."

In this case the measured tone did not seem to be working.

"But what about publicity? If there was a hue and cry, a proper campaign with publicity in the media, everyone in the country would be looking for them. Carol Parker is everywhere, appealing to people who see her little boy and his father—in all the tabloids, and on daytime television, too."

Mr. Mitcham sighed. He knew Mrs. Randall was not avid for publicity, only anxious to do everything needed to get her son back. But she must give people who knew her less well a very poor impression, and though he had tried to get the message across to her, this still came up at every meeting they had. He tried again.

"Mrs. Parker's husband is German, and he has a history of mental instability. The police are afraid he may take the little boy out of the country, or even harm him wittingly or unwittingly. You must see that your husband is a quite different matter. Children are taken quite frequently by the parent who does not have custody. Usually there is no question of their being in any danger."

He spoke quietly and distinctly, and now it seemed to work. Selena nodded, taking in, at least for the moment, his argument.

"Oh, I know Dick wouldn't harm Malcolm. He loves him to bits. . . . But the fact that he's English doesn't mean he won't take him out of the country."

"You can be sure the police at ports and airports will be especially on the alert."

"These days you can drive through the channel tunnel and no one gives you a second glance."

"That's not true, Mrs. Randall."

She looked down at the ruin of her handkerchief.

"I don't think anybody cares. They just think 'the little boy is bound to be all right,' and don't give it another thought."

"Well, that is something that must be a comfort for you."

"But what about me? I had custody of him, and I haven't

seen him for nearly ten weeks." Her eyes filled with tears and she began dabbing them with the ragged bits of hankie. "Do you know what I fear? I *am* afraid he'll forget me, as a young child like Malcolm is bound to do quite soon. But most of all, I'm afraid I'll forget him. What he sounds like, how he laughs, what it feels like to touch him, have him in my arms." She looked up at Mr. Mitcham, wild-eyed. "I'm afraid if I get him back he'll be a stranger."

"I'm sure you won't forget a thing about him. No mother would."

"Don't be so bloody sentimental! How would you know? . . . sorry." She resumed tugging at the handkerchief. "You said everyone would be on the lookout for Dick and Malcolm, but what is there to be on the lookout *for?* Dick is nice-enough-looking, but there's nothing to distinguish him from thousands of other quite nice-looking young men. Hair colour—that's about the only thing to mark him off: light brown, so that rules out people with black or blond hair. Not much, is it? There's still less with Malcolm."

"They have a photograph."

"I wish it was a better photograph. . . ." She returned obsessively to her theme. "Dick has quite an arrogant look sometimes. Raises his chin and looks out at the world as if he thinks he's a lot better than other people. I don't suppose? . . . No. It's just impression, isn't it, not fact. It's fact you need. Little Anton Parker has a mole on his hip. Malcolm has nothing. She can just pull his pants down and check, whereas I'll have nothing, if I ever see him again. Can you believe it? *Nothing* to distinguish him from thousands and thousands of other boys of his age. . . . Sometimes I think it's hopeless. Sometimes I think I might just as well give up."

"I know you're not serious about that, Mrs. Randall."

"No. . . . It's just a mood. I'll never give up."

"Nor should you."

"I sometimes wonder whether Dick won't come back of his own accord and we can all three be together like we used to be."

"I don't think you should bank on that. But there is going to come a crunch point, and it might come soon. He can't go on running forever. Where did he ring you from?"

"From Leeds. I can't believe Dick would be so cruel. Just one word. . . ."

"The last sighting we had of them that was pretty firm was North Wales. Eventually he's going to run out of money."

There was a pause. Then Mr. Mitcham saw Selena Randall's shoulders stiffen as she made a decision.

"I don't think he will."

"Why not? What do you mean?" He saw the shoulders slacken slightly and he said urgently: "Tell me."

Then it all came out. When she had told her tale, he asked her, already knowing the answer, "Have you told the police this?"

"No. I thought it might get Dick into trouble."

This time Mr. Mitcham's sigh was audible. Sometimes he despaired of fathoming the mysteries of people's hearts.

At the cash desk of The Merry Cook, Dick Randall asked if they had a room vacant. The chain of roadside eateries had at some of their establishments a few overnight rooms—inexpensive, simple, anonymous. It was their anonymity that appealed, because it seemed to spread to the rooms' users. He had a name thought up if he had been asked for one: Tony Wilmslow. He enjoyed thinking up names while he was driving, and sometimes thought he could people a whole novel with the characters he'd invented—though of course it would be an all-male novel, and the idea of that didn't appeal to him. The girl behind the counter nodded, rang up £32.50 on the till, and handed over a key when he paid in cash. Dick's credit card had been unused since he had snatched Malcolm from the front garden of the house he had once shared with his wife.

"Number three," said the girl, then turned her eyes to the next customer in the line, totting up the price of the plates and polystyrene cup on her tray.

I'm not even thought worthy of a second glance, thought Dick wryly, but with an underlying satisfaction. He went out to the car where Malcolm was still strapped in and parked it outside number three.

"Home for the night," he said. "Come along, Captain."

They'd eaten at midday, so they had no use of the cheap and cheerful meals at The Merry Cook. Dick took from the backseat a slice of cold pizza in a plastic bag—something left over from Malcolm's lunch—and a carton of milk. For himself he had bought a sandwich. He never ate much when he had something on, though he was one of those people who burned up calories and never was other than slim. Still, eating made him *feel* bulkier.

They ate companionably on the bed, then played the cat's cradle game Dick had himself always loved when a child, and had taught his son. Malcolm could undress himself for bed, and loved to do it, his face always rapt with concentration. Dick sat him on the lavatory, then chose one of the five or six stories Malcolm always insisted on when he was being read to sleep.

"Remember," Dick said, as he always did, "if you wake in the night and I'm not here, I won't be far away, and I'll soon be back. Just turn over and go to sleep again."

Malcolm nodded, and lay there waiting for **Postman Pat**. Dick wished he could wean him on to a wider choice of stories, but thought that familiarity must be settling to a child's mind at a time when so much of what he was experiencing was unfamiliar. After a page or so, the little head nodded. Dick turned off the light, then lay on the bed beside him, fully clothed.

Dick had marked out the bungalow as they'd driven through the March darkness on the approaches to The Merry Cook. Old, substantial, without alarm, and with token lights obviously switched on by a neighbour. At shortly before midnight, Malcolm sleeping soundly, Dick got carefully off the bed, took the gloves and torch from the little bedside table where he'd left them, collected his old canvas bag from the spindly armchair, and then slipped out of the motel room.

There was no need to take the car. Dick was only interested in portable property. He had a nose for houses inhabited by the sort of people who would have accumulated it. He had a wonderful sense, too, of street geography, acquired during his teenage years: He always knew the best approach to a place, and still better the whole range of possible escape routes. There was no point in subtlety in the approach to number 41 Sheepscar Road, but as he padded along he renewed in the darkness the possible ways of making a quick exit from the area. The lights in the bungalow had been switched off by the obliging neighbour. All the adjacent house lights were off. Once inside the garden he waited in the darkness at the side of the house to make sure he had not been heard or observed. When no lights went on or sounds were heard, he let himself in through the front door with the ease of practice.

Where you could use a credit card to do it, you knew you were dealing with very unworldly owners.

Which everything in the house pointed to. The jewel box was by the dressing-room table in the main bedroom, and yielded modest to good pickings. The inevitable stash of notes under the mattress amounted, his experienced grasp of the bundle told him, to something in the region of two hundred pounds. The sideboard drawer revealed silver cutlery of good quality and an antique candle-snuffer which he suspected was something special. All went into the overnight bag after a torchlight inspection, as did an Art Deco vase in the centre of the dining table. He was out of the house in ten minutes. The rooms he left were to all intents and purposes so similar to their state when he came in that the neighbour would probably not notice that there had been an intruder.

He was back in the little bedroom with Malcolm half an hour after he had left him. As he undressed, the boy stirred in his sleep. Dick got in beside him and cuddled him close. Their future seemed assured for the next week or so.

Inspector Purley looked at Selena Randall with a mixture of sympathy and exasperation. He had always had the feeling that she was holding out on him, either deliberately or unconsciously. In fact, he'd pressed her on this in previous talks they'd had, and she had denied it, but in a way that never quite did away with his suspicion. Now it was going to come out.

"You say there's something about your husband that you've been keeping from us?" he said.

He flustered her further.

"Well, not keeping from you. Just not telling you because I didn't think it was relevant. And I didn't want to hurt Dick, because I always thought—or hoped, anyway—that one day he'd come back and everything would be as it used to be. That's what I really wanted. . . . You see, this could really harm him. . . ."

"Yes. Go on."

"He . . . When I met him, six years ago, he was an accomplished thief. A house burglar."

Inspector Purley bit back any annoyance.

"But he's got no record. We checked."

"No. I said he was very accomplished. He was never caught. . . . You do see why I didn't tell you, don't you? I mean, if he was to be caught with Malcolm, it wouldn't be just the abduction, would it?"

She looked at him, tearfully appealing. Inspector Purley sighed. The story had changed in seconds from not thinking it relevant to not wanting to land her husband with an even longer prison sentence than he'd get anyway.

"Do you know, Mrs. Randall, I think it's time you made up your mind."

"I don't understand you."

"You really have to sort out your priorities. Is your first priority getting your little boy back?"

"*Yes*. Of course it is."

"Then you've got to tell us everything that might be relevant to finding him and your husband. Everything."

"Yes. . . . It's just that I've never felt bitter towards Dick. I loved him when I married him, and I still love him. I can't believe he'd be so cruel as to let me hear Malcolm's voice on the phone and then cut us off after only a single word. It's like he's become another person."

Inspector Purley thought that might be because he was afraid Malcolm would let slip something that could be of use to the police, but he was not in the business of trying to

179

make her think more kindly of her husband. That was the whole problem.

"That's really cruel," he agreed. "Now, about these burglaries: What kind of detail can you give me about them? Your husband isn't on our computer, but the burglaries will be."

She looked at him wide-eyed.

"I don't know any details. I only know he was doing them. That's how he dressed so well, ran a car, did the clubs, and ate at good restaurants. When I found out, of course, I made him stop. That was a condition of our getting engaged. My father got him a job with a business associate. For a time he did very well. He learned quickly, and Dick always had charm. People warmed to him, looked on him as a friend. He was under-manager of the Garrick Hotel in Darlington when the group merged with a larger one, and there were redundancies. . . . That was when things started to go wrong."

"Did he go back to his old ways?"

"No! But he hated being so hard up, and when I got a job he hated being dependent on me."

Inspector Purley considered the matter.

"So how long ago were these burglaries he did?"

"About five years ago—that's when he stopped. But he'd been doing them for years, since he left school."

"And he's how old now?"

"Twenty-six."

"What can you tell us about the burglaries? Surely there must be something about them that sticks in your mind, or one particular job he told you about that stood out?"

"No, there's not. I never knew anything about them. I refused to listen."

She was pulling back, Inspector Purley thought. She

needed to be given a further push to remind her what was at stake.

"He must have been good," he said admiringly, "never to have been caught. Didn't he ever boast? Say what it was that made him so good?"

"Well . . ." She was reluctant, but was being borne along by the tide. "He always said the secret wasn't the technical things, how to break and enter—though he was good at that, too. He said that what mattered was a good eye."

The inspector digested this.

"For what? For stuff that would fetch a tidy sum? Or for an easy target, a likely victim?"

"The last. He always said the best target was a retired couple or a widowed person, someone who had built up a bit of property and was now pottering along." She was putting it more politely than Richard usually had, but suddenly she put aside her protectiveness again. " 'Someone who had done quite nicely for himself and was now coasting towards his dotage'—that's how he described it once. He only said things like that when he was trying to get my goat."

"I see," commented the inspector drily. "He has a nice way with words, your husband. Or a nasty one."

But privately he was pleased to have had contact with the man through his own words. They sounded very adolescent, and he wondered how much of the daredevil boy was in the man still. But most of all he hoped that her willingness to quote her husband's words and show him in an unfavourable light meant that Selena Randall had turned a corner.

"Dick would never hurt Malcolm," said Selena, dashing his hopes. "I've got to believe that. He loves him more than anyone in the world. That's why I don't want to hurt him."

Inspector Purley reserved judgment. He hoped for her sake and the little boy's that what she said about her husband was true.

Dick Randall came out of the little back-street jeweller's with a spring in his step. The man had not hidden his appreciation of the brooch's value, had commented on the workmanship and the quality of the stones, and had offered Dick a very fair price. He was an honest man, and it had been a pleasure to do business with such a person.

Malcolm was still strapped into his seat in the little car park round the corner. It always gave Dick a lift of the heart to see him again. He was solemnly watching a Dalmatian dog in the next car, which was in its turn watching a lazy car-park cat. It struck Dick how lucky he was that Malcolm was the sort of child who could be left on his own for fifteen or twenty minutes, without danger of panic fits or grizzling. He was solemn, watchful, and even, in his childish way, self-confident. Perhaps it was because he had had to be.

"Here I am, Captain," he said, opening his car door and sliding himself into the driver's seat. "A nice little bit of business, very satisfactorily concluded."

He was talking to himself rather than the child, but as usual Malcolm took him up.

"What's bizniz?"

"Business?" he said, starting the car and thinking how he could explain business to a three-year-old. "Well, let's see. Business can be something you've got that someone wants and is willing to pay for. Or it may be some skill or ability that you have that the other man hasn't got, and he'll pay you to use that skill for him. Or it may be a sort of swap: Do this for me, and I'll do that for you."

He'd tried hard to make it simple, but he knew he was

still talking as much to himself as to the child. He often did this, having no one but a child to talk to. *Malcolm is going to grow up too quickly,* he thought, *unless I can settle him down somewhere where he can make friends and lead a normal child's life.*

"So did you have something that the man you went to see wanted?" Malcolm asked after digesting his words.

"That's right, I did. And it means we can eat for a fortnight," said Dick.

"What would we do if we didn't have the money to buy food?"

"Oh, but we always will. That I can promise you, Malcolm. It's what daddies are for—getting money so that you can have food and clothes and a bed for the night."

After a moment Malcolm nodded, seemingly satisfied, and then went off into a light doze. Dick drove on southwards, at a moderate speed.

They stopped for lunch in Grantham. Dick tried to give the little boy a balanced diet, but today, buoyed by the notes bursting the seams of his wallet, he said: "Today you can have just anything you want, Captain."

They found a side-street cafe that looked cosy. Malcolm chose chicken nuggets and chips, and Dick had the day's special: roast beef and Yorkshire pudding. The cafe's owner cooed over Malcolm, but knew better than to ask where his Mummy was: All too often you got a sad tale of marriage breakup. Men alone with children these days usually meant they were using quality time graciously allowed them by the Child Support Agency. Malcolm had a slice of chocolate gâteau for afters, and Dick cleaned him up in the lavatories before going up to the counter, buying some sandwiches and buns for their evening meal, and settling up for everything. When they emerged into the bright afternoon sunlight he felt like a million dollars.

The little jeweller's shop was nearly opposite the cafe.

"Do you know, Malcolm, I feel it's my lucky day," said Dick.

He led the child by the hand the hundred or so yards down the street to where his car was parked. He opened the boot and began to rummage in the canvas bag. Malcolm, standing beside him on the pavement, regarded him wide-eyed: The bag, for him, was beginning to assume the mystic standing of a cornucopia, source of endless goodies.

"Have you got something the man will want?" he asked.

"I think so," said Dick, finally selecting a rather showy diamond ring. "Now, I'll only be five minutes or so, Captain, and then we can be on our way. So you can just sit in your car seat and watch the world go by."

He strapped him in and walked whistling back down the street, the ring wrapped in tissue paper in his trouser pocket. The door of the jeweller's shop opened with an old-fashioned ring.

"Yes, sir. What can I do for you?"

The words were old-fashioned and welcoming, the face less so. There was a suspicion of midnight shadow over the jowls, the eyes were calculating, the mouth mean. Dick nearly turned round there and then, but he had no desire to draw attention to himself needlessly. There seemed to be no alternative but to plunge in.

"I wondered whether you'd be interested in this."

He drew from his pocket the little package and unwrapped it. The central diamond sparkled dangerously, and the rubies of the surround smouldered. The ring was already beginning to seem ill-omened in his eyes. The man behind the counter took it noncommittally.

"Hmm. A rather assertive piece. Not really Grantham.

However, I do have one customer who might . . . and there's a dealer I do business with who sometimes takes this sort of thing. . . ." The tone seemed to Dick professionally disparaging. "I'll just take it into the back, sir, with your permission, and get a better look at the stones."

Dick nodded. The man disappeared through the glass door behind the counter and Dick saw him go behind a little booth in the back room, where he imagined a microscope was set up. He waited, glancing nonchalantly at the rings and pendants on the trays under the counter, and the jewelled clocks and ornaments on the glassed-in shelves behind it.

Suddenly the jeweller's head appeared above the walls of the booth. Dick forced himself to seem to be looking at something else. The man had a telephone at his ear, and he was looking at Dick. When his head disappeared down into the booth again, Dick turned and wrenched open the door.

The shop bell rang.

He began running. In seconds, he was wrenching open the driver's door, had his key in the ignition, and was scorching off down the street. In his mirror he could see the jeweller in the door of his shop. This was probably the most exciting thing to happen in his mean little life for years, Dick thought. *Not too fast. Don't draw attention. Get onto the motorway and then open up.*

"Didn't he want what you had for him?" Malcolm asked.

"Oh, he wanted it," said Dick. "I'm driving fast because I'm excited and pleased."

That night they spent one of their rare nights in the car. Dick had put about a hundred and fifty miles between him and the Grantham police, then had gone off the motorway and cruised around some little Southern English towns and villages. Somehow he felt all shaken up, and he blamed

himself bitterly. He would never indulge in childish super-
stition again. My lucky day, my foot! Like some toothless
old granny reading her horoscope! He hadn't had a worse
one since the day he snatched Malcolm. He just couldn't
face the lies and the performance he always put on at bed-
and-breakfast places, nor going back onto the motorway to
find a Merry Cook with rooms attached. There was also the
matter of organising new number-plates for the car. He
didn't think the man could have seen his—themselves acquired from an abandoned car in Gateshead—but he wasn't
taking any risks.

"Do you mind, Captain?" he asked Malcolm. "I don't
think there's any places round here that take in guests."

"No, I don't mind. I like it," said Malcolm stoutly. "But
I'll need to go to the toilet."

He needed more than that. They found a little coppice
just outside a village called Birley, and Dick drove up the
lane that bisected the trees and found a little open area between it and a field. They ate the sandwiches and the buns
they'd bought at midday, and Malcolm drank a bottle of
pop. That did it. He had to leave the car quickly and be sick
under a tree.

"Not *very* sick," he said, accurately enough.

Then he was ready to sleep.

Dick dozed. He found it difficult to get proper sleep on
the rare occasions that they slept in the car. In the middle of
the night he slipped out and acquired new number-plates in
Birley—he couldn't find an abandoned car, but he took the
plates off the oldest car he could find parked in the road.
When he got back to his own car he spread himself over the
two front seats and tried to sleep again. Sleep was very slow
in coming, but when it did, it brought The Dream again.
The Nightmare.

He dreamt he was driving away from a small town, out onto the wider road, Malcolm beside him, excited and chattering. All was well, wonderfully well, and they were laughing together, making silly jokes, and full of joy in each other's company, as ever.

Then, in his mirror, he saw at a distance a police car. It *couldn't* . . . No, of course it couldn't. Why should he assume they were after him? But he increased his speed a little. Then, with the special tempo of a dream, things began to take on the excitement of a car chase in a film. The police car increased its speed, too—not by very much, but enough to make sure they would catch up with him before long. Dick in his dream was much less cool than the Dick in real life. He could think of nothing else to do but increase his speed again. The police car did the same. "I've got to do something," Dick said to himself. "I've got to do something that shakes them off."

The road stretched straight ahead, but there was an intersection approaching. Dick swerved off onto a winding country road. On the left, though, was a wood, and seeing a lane into it Dick swerved aside again and went into it. Please God the police would go on. The road had been dry and there were no tire marks. But he kept up a good speed. The lane was rutted, the car jolting as it coped with the new conditions. In the seat beside him, Malcolm was crowing with delight and jumping up and down. As the car ploughed ahead down the lane as fast as Dick could push it, Malcolm released his seat belt and strained forward to see.

"Malcolm, belt yourself in again!" he called.

Suddenly, ahead were trees. The end of the lane,

the reassertion of thick woodland. There was space enough between two of the trees, but as he aimed at it the car no longer did what he wanted, diverted by the roughness of the terrain and the thick undergrowth. The left-hand wing bashed with a shattering shock into one of the trees, and the boy in the seat beside him hurtled forward and hit the windscreen with a thud that . . .

Dick woke, sweating and shuddering. He was conscious that his half-waking mind had exerted some kind of control over his sleeping one, and had prevented him from screaming or trying to reach the boy in the backseat. Stiffly he got out of the car. Trees—that was what had set it off, and the little path winding through them. He fumbled in his pocket and lit a rare cigarette. Then soberly he went about his early-morning business, fetching a screwdriver and drill and starting to change the plates. He memorised the numbers as a precaution in case he was stopped. The old plates he buried.

He shivered in the cold of the morning. In the car, Malcolm was stirring. They could be on their way.

"We can treat ourselves tonight," he said to the little boy, who was still rubbing his eyes. "Look at the money we've saved."

"Can we have breakfast soon?" said Malcolm, whose mind focussed on immediate rather than long-term prospects.

When Selena Randall had left the police station, Inspector Purley looked at DC Lackland, who had sat in on the interview.

"What did you think?"

"Still hung up on publicity, using the tabloids, getting on television, that kind of thing."

"Yes. I don't think I got through to her."

"You got through while she was sitting here, but it won't last five minutes once she gets home and is sick with worry. She's bound to clutch at straws."

"I know. But the case of Carol Parker *is* different. While there was a chance her son was in the country, there was a point to the television appeals. Frankly, the appearance Mrs. Randall saw yesterday on daytime television was useless. The woman should be in Germany, not here. That's where the child will be by now."

"And they're not inviting her."

"No. And the police there are doing bugger-all. The boy was born in Germany and as far as they're concerned, he's a German citizen. The father doesn't have him now, but he's a Catholic with family ramifications from one end of the country to another. The boy could be with any of them, and even if they found him, he wouldn't be sent back to his mother. That's German law, and the Common Market hasn't changed that."

"So really, Mrs. Randall is in a more hopeful position?"

"Yes. But try telling that to her. The main thing is, we're pretty sure the child is still in the country. She had one of these tormenting phone calls only three days ago, from Romford. Once we get hold of the child, returning him to her will be a mere formality. If he was abroad, she'd be bogged down in the local judicial system for years."

"On the other hand, we don't seem to be any nearer to discovering where the two of them might be."

"No, and that's because they're *not* anywhere. They're everywhere, zigzagging hither and yon to create confusion. Nevertheless, the indications are that Dick Randall is a good father. I just hope she's not fooling herself about that. If he is, he must be considering the future, facing the fact that the boy needs to be settled, have friends, go to nursery school, live in a house he recognises and relates to. If he finds somewhere and goes on with his burglaries, the local police are going to start seeing a pattern, because he's not going to be able to go very far afield."

DC Lackland screwed up his face sceptically.

"The police up here apparently didn't discover a pattern when he was a teenage Raffles," he said.

"Good point. We need to alert them to the pattern. The other thing is, the balance of sightings and traces seems to be shifting. There's still some zigzagging—Romford was a piece of cheek, to suggest they'd gone to ground in London, but it was a rogue report. The balance is shifting southwards. Nothing in the North for over three weeks. It's been Midlands, South, shifting westwards. I'm going to concentrate on alerting police in Devon, Dorset, Cornwall—that's where he's going to be found."

"The West Country does attract a lot of drifters and oddballs," conceded Lackland.

"Maybe. Though no more than places like Brighton and Tunbridge Wells. The West at this time of year is a good place to be anonymous in."

"So, no television appearances for Selena Randall?"

"No. . . . Even if other things were equal, and even if we could persuade them to slot her in, I'd be doubtful about putting her on the Esther Rantzen programme, or the Richard and Judy show."

"Oh? Why?"

"Mrs. Parker is effective because she's blazingly angry with her ex-husband. She hates him. It comes across white-hot to the listener."

"Whereas Selena Randall is still half in love with hers?"

"Yes. More than half. And not only that: She still thinks

of him as a good man."

"In spite of those phone calls."

"Yes, in spite of them. The message coming from her would be very blurred, or no message at all." He mused, with the wisdom of the police force over the years, unalloyed by feminism, or any other -ism: "Funny things, women."

This was a sentiment DC Lackland could agree with.

The woman who opened the door of Lane's End, in the village of Briscow, was comfortable, attractive, and brightly dressed: a woman in her late forties, neither well-off nor on her uppers, but at ease with life and still full of it.

"Yes?" Good, broad, open smile.

"I wondered if you have a room for the night," said Dick.

She looked at the open face, the lean figure, the little boy on his shoulders. The smile of welcome became still more warming.

"I do that," she said. "Come on in and have a look at it."

She led the way upstairs and pushed open a door. Two single beds pushed together, chintz as a bed covering, chintz at the windows, and the sun streaming through on the gleaming wooden furniture. It looked like heaven.

"This is wonderful," said Dick. "Isn't it, Malcolm?"

"Yes!" said Malcolm, already a connoisseur.

"Are there just the two of you? Is his m—" She stopped on seeing Dick give a tiny shake of the head. "Well, if you take it that will be seventeen pounds fifty a night, and I can do a proper evening meal for six pounds extra—three for the little boy."

They closed the deal at once, there in the sunlight. Already there was a warmth between the three of them which had, in the case of the two adults, a little to do with sex, more to do with aesthetic appreciation, likeness of spirit, a feeling of some kind of reawakening. Dick had consciously begun shaping his story accordingly.

Later in the evening, after a good dinner where his own preferences had been consulted and Malcolm's still more, Dick put the boy to bed, read him to sleep, then by invitation went downstairs to the living room for coffee.

"Will it be coffee, or would you prefer a beer?"

"Coffee, please. I can never get used to beer in cans."

She came forward, her hand held out rather shyly.

"I've been silly, and haven't told you my name. I'm Margaret Cowley—Peggy to my friends."

"And I'm Colin Morton," said Dick, shaking the hand warmly. "I'm sorry I had to stop you, Peggy, when you were going to ask about his mother. It's something I've been trying to stop him thinking about. If he was a little older it would be different."

They were talking in the doorway of the kitchen now, and the percolator was making baritone noises.

"It was silly of me to even think of asking. It's not my business, and these days, with everyone's marriage breaking down, it's much the best plan not to ask."

Dick shook his head. "Oh, it's nothing like that. Malcolm's mother died, in childbirth. We were expecting a little girl, and we knew there were complications, but somehow—"

"Oh, I *am* sorry." She turned to face him. His eyes were full. "So it was a tragedy clean out of the blue?"

"If the doctors suspected anything serious, they kept it from us."

"Poor little boy. And poor you both, of course."

"I'm trying to put it behind us, make a fresh start."

"New place, new life?"

192

"Very much so." He had blinked his eyes free of the tears, and now smiled bravely. "Everything in the old house reminded me . . . and though with a little boy memories fade, still, I do try to keep his mind on other things. *He's* got to look to the future, even if I find it difficult, and keep . . . well, rambling in my mind back to the past. Stop me if I do that."

"Isn't life a bitch?" Peggy Cowley's voice held genuine bitterness. "I lost my husband a couple of years ago. Massive heart attack. He was in his late sixties, but these days that seems no age."

"It doesn't." He thought to himself that she must have married a man fifteen or twenty years older than herself, and his thought showed on his face.

"Yes, he was quite a bit older," Peggy said. "Second marriage for him. But it was a very happy one."

"No children?"

"No. Perhaps that was why it was a happy marriage." They both laughed, but Peggy immediately kicked herself for her tactlessness. "I don't mean it. We'd have loved to have kiddies, but it just didn't happen. I'd have liked to have one to lean on when he died. It would have made all the difference. And even little Malcolm: You'll have found he keeps your mind occupied and stops you grieving too much, I'll be bound."

Dick nodded. He had thought himself into the situation.

"Yes, he does. But sometimes I look at him and . . ." Again there were tears in his eyes and he took out a handkerchief. He shook himself. "That's what I said to stop me doing."

"Not when you're on your own. It will do you good."

"And what about you? Do you have a job? Or can you make ends meet with the bed-and-breakfast trade?"

"Oh, I make ends meet and a bit better than that. I've got the cottage as well."

Peggy's intention had been to drop this information casually into the conversation, but both immediately knew what was at issue.

"You have a cottage?" Dick's voice had an equally bogus neutrality. They didn't look at each other, but they were intensely aware of each other.

"Yes, just a tiny place at the bottom of the garden and across the lane. It doesn't take more than two or three unless they squeeze themselves in. Actually the last of the Easter tenants leave in a couple of days' time. I've got no bookings then until the school holidays start in July."

Dick drained his coffee, and she filled his cup. Then she sat back peaceably and watched him sipping. They needed no words. Dick had half made the decision when he saw her at the door. That was why he had given her the name which was on the false papers he had got from an old contact when he was first contemplating snatching his son. The whole of the last couple of hours had felt like a coming to rest, the thing that all the last few weeks had been leading up to.

"I'd need a job," he said. "That's not easy in the West Country, is it?"

"It's possible, if you'll take the jobs that nobody else wants," said Peggy. Dick was doing sums.

"How much do you charge for the cottage?"

"Oh, we can work something out as far as that goes."

"No, I don't want you to lose out," said Dick emphatically. "There's no earthly reason why you should lose out financially by allowing a stranger to sponge off you."

Though they both knew perfectly well that there was one possible reason. Sex had edged its way more explicitly to the forefront of both their minds.

"I'd give the place at a reasonable rent to anyone who'd take it and look after it in the low season," said Peggy stoutly. "Stands to reason. It's always better to have a place occupied, with a bit coming in for it. Empty, you're just asking for squatters and burglars."

"I suppose that's true," said Dick, who knew better than most. "Where is the nearest job centre?"

"Oh, that's way away, in Truro. You ought to look for something more local first. They're wanting a relief barman at The Cornishman, just down the road."

"Oh? I've never done bar work, but I've worked in hotels, so I know what's involved and I'm pretty sure I could get the hang of it. What's the catch?"

"It's just lunchtime. Eleven to three. That doesn't suit most people. Oh, and there'd be a bit of cellar work in addition."

"I might be able to supplement it with Income Support. Keep on the lookout for other things." Other sources of income flashed through his mind, but he resolved to use those skills only very sparingly, if he used them at all.

"Anyway," said Peggy, getting up to clear away the cups, "I'll just leave the thought with you. We can go and have a look at the cottage tomorrow, if you're interested."

"And maybe go on to The Cornishman for a pub lunch. They do food at lunchtime?"

"Of course. That would be a big part of your work. Could well be a help with feeding the two of you. A lot of food goes to waste in a place like that."

As she washed up the cups and the dinner things in the kitchen Peggy felt a glow of satisfaction. She had gambled, and she felt pretty sure she had won. If she had not told Colin about the cottage, she might have had him and

Malcolm in the house for a few days, maybe for a week. But by mentioning it, she might not have them *with* her, but she would have them *near* her for much longer than that. She'd had no doubt since clapping eyes on the pair of them that that was what she wanted.

That night, as he went up to bed, Dick said, "Better go. Malcolm may be needing me. First night in a strange place."

Unspoken because it did not need to be voiced was the thought that there would be other nights.

Selena Randall pulled a piece of paper towards her. For days she had felt she was going mad, so completely without event had her life become. No news from the police, nothing except attempts at reassurance. No sightings, no media interest, total absence even of those terrible, tantalising phone calls, which did at least tell her where they were at the moment they were made. She had to do something. It had been nagging at her mind for some days that perhaps she should appeal to him though the press, send an open letter to him through the *Daily Mail*, the paper that they had always taken.

"Dear Dick," she began. "I'm writing to tell you how much I miss you both, and how I long to have you back. It's now nearly four months since I saw Malcolm—" Longer than Carol Parker had been without her boy, she thought resentfully, but everyone knows about her loss, and nobody knows about mine. "—and I can't bear the thought that when I see him again he will hardly know me. I will see him again, won't I? Please, Dick, you couldn't be so cruel as to keep him from me forever, could you? I know you love him and will look after him. Please remember that I love him, too. There is not a day goes past, not a minute of the day, when I don't think of him. Remember how happy we were when he was born, you and me and him. I think you loved me then—loved me too much to want me to be so unhappy now. I know I loved you."

She paused. She wanted to add: "I love you still." Was that wise? The policeman would say no. Was it true? She wanted to write nothing but the truth. *Did* she still love him, after what he had done to her? *Could* she?

Seized by a sense of muddle and futility, not in her situation but in herself, her own mind, her own emotions, she laid her head down on the paper and sobbed her heart out.

They went to look at the cottage next morning, after the sort of breakfast dieticians throw up their hands at.

"I never put on weight," said Dick, munching away at his fried bread. "I expect Malcolm will be the same, after he's got over his chubbiness."

They looked at the boy, already tucking in messily to the toast and marmalade.

"Nothing wrong with chubbiness in a child," said Peggy.

When they'd washed up, Peggy only allowing Dick to help under protest, they set off down the back garden, then across the lane and to the tiny cottage. The tenants were just driving off when they got there, and they shouted that they were going to have a last look at Penzance.

"I wondered whether to go on to Penzance," said Dick, "when I was driving around looking for somewhere to stay. Somehow it seemed like the end of the road."

"You've got to give up thoughts like that, Colin," said Peggy urgently. "There's a great wide road ahead of you."

She didn't notice Malcolm looking up at her. He had never heard his father called Colin before.

The cottage was tiny—"bijou," the estate agents would

probably have called it—and there was an ever-present danger of tumbling over the furniture. But it was bright and cheerful, with everything done in the same sort of taste as Peggy's own cottage. Malcolm thought it was wonderful, particularly the strip of lawn at the back, with the apple tree. It was warm enough for him to play in just his shorts, and they watched him as he tried to make friends with a very spry gray squirrel.

"It's ideal," said Dick to Peggy, both of them watching him protectively to see he didn't stray from the garden down towards the riverbank. "Sort of like a refuge."

"Don't think like that," urged Peggy again.

"All right—it's what I've been dreaming about since—you know. Is that positive enough for you? Now, will you let me take us all to the—what was it?—The Cornishman, and we'll have a good pub lunch."

They looked at each other meaningfully.

All the lunchtime regulars in the pub made them welcome for Peggy's sake. She had herself been a regular there when her husband was alive, but had been less frequent since. She was of the generation of women that didn't much like going into a pub on their own. They got themselves a table and settled in. Selecting the food was a big thing, because it was a good menu with plenty to appeal to a child. By the time they had made their decisions they seemed to have spoken to, or had advice from, half the customers in the Saloon Bar. When Jack, the landlord, brought the three piled-high plates to their table, Peggy said: "You still looking for help at lunchtime, Jack?"

"I am. There's folk that are willing, but not folk that are suitable."

Peggy looked in Dick's direction and winked.

"Oh aye?" said the landlord, interested. "Maybe we

could have a chat later, young man, after your meal."

And so it was arranged. The talk was businesslike and decisive: Dick would come down the next couple of nights to learn the business, get into the routine, then he'd start work proper at the weekend. Peggy would look after Malcolm in the middle of the day—"It'll be a pleasure," she said, though she did wonder how she'd cope with the un-accustomed situation. The money was far from wonderful, but it would be welcome. Dick only worried about how much he seemed to be putting on Peggy.

"When we're well settled in, we'll start looking for a play group for Malcolm," he said.

"If it goes well, I might even start one myself," said Peggy.

It certainly went well at The Cornishman. Dick was a good worker and a good listener, and the pub's routines went like clockwork when he was on duty. He never men-tioned his hotel training, but it showed. Jack thought he was manna from heaven and tried to press him into doing longer hours, but Dick was unwilling. The boy came first, he said, and he did. Nobody asked too much about his background. Everyone in the West Country is used to people passing through, casual temporary residents who come from heaven-knows-where and soon pass on. People knew that Dick had lost his wife, because Peggy had revealed that in conversation with a friend and it had got around. Nobody displayed curiosity beyond that.

Dick slept with Peggy the night he got the job. The mu-tual agreement was silent, and Peggy knew she had to go along with any conditions Dick attached to the affair. She knew already that Malcolm would always come first with Dick—and second and third as well. Dick stayed in her room for an hour or so, then went as usual to sleep beside the little boy in the two twin beds put together under the window.

The routine continued when he and Malcolm went to live and fend for themselves in the tiny cottage the other side of the back lane. The boy was used to finding himself alone at nights, and didn't worry about it. He knew it wouldn't be for long. Dick and Peggy developed a code between themselves. When he collected Malcolm, or when he met Peggy casually on his days off, he would say "See you soon" as they parted. That meant that he'd be up that night. Perhaps Peggy should have felt that she was being used, but she didn't. She was happy to have her hours with Malcolm, which were working out better than she could have believed possible with her lack of experience of children. She found him an enchanting child, and she was happy to have the all-too-brief time with Dick at night. She had expected little of her widowhood, and Dick was a wonderful and unexpected bonus.

By the middle of June they were a settled thing, or felt like it. Peggy was refusing all potential summer tenants for the cottage, and had managed to transfer the first bookings she had already accepted to another landlord in the area. Her friends knew what the situation was, and accepted it. Summer would be a lovely time, she knew. It was the time of year she had always enjoyed most, especially as Briscow was that bit off the tourist map. Colin would be working, of course, but he was still resisting the offer of extra hours because he didn't want to leave his son for most of the day. Malcolm was regaining his equilibrium, she felt, though it gave her a start one day when he said: "I haven't spoken to Mummy for *ages*." It wouldn't be long before he forgot her, she thought.

Dick was happy, too. He knew he had landed on his feet.

But always in Eden there lurked the serpent, in wait to spread his poison. Dick knew he was using Peggy—not sexually, because if anything, she was using him that way. But he knew he was getting a free child minder, lots of free meals, and he knew Peggy would be charging a lot more for the cottage if she was letting it on a weekly basis to her usual casual tourist clientele.

It irked him to be dependent—because that was what it was. It had been that that had started the rot between him and Selena. He was old-fashioned, he knew, but that was something he would never apologise for. He'd known when he planned to snatch Malcolm that his feelings for the boy were old-fashioned. And it was the same for his sense that he was becoming too dependent on Peggy.

The truth was, he could do with more money.

"It follows the pattern," said Inspector Purley. "Retired people, away from home, poor security, a nice little haul of jewelry, cash, and small household things—nothing spectacular, but worth having. *And* it's West Country."

"What if the next one's John o' Groats?" asked Lackland. "That's been the pattern so far—zigzagging all over the country."

"Ah, but it won't be from now on, you of little faith."

"Seems to me you're looking at it arse up," countered Lackland. "*You* decided he was headed for the West Country, and now we've got a possible case there, you take it as confirmation, even though we've had other possible cases all over the country. Dick Randall's not the only crook to target respectable retired people."

He did not dent his superior officer's complacent view of things.

"You mark my words," Purley said. "He's come to rest

in the West Country, like all sorts of other people—artists, retired people, ageing hippies, travelling people, and all manner of rag-tag and bobtail. And having come to rest, he can't leave little Malcolm alone for long. The cases we think he was involved in were all over the country because so were they. Now the cases will all be in the West." He walked over and looked at a map on the wall. "This one was in a small village called Monpellon. The area includes Launceston, Bodmin, Padstow—places like that. That's where we'll be looking to, because that's where the two of them will have slung their hook."

"Well, I admire your confidence," said Lackland, who secretly, or not so secretly, did not.

"I'm so certain I'm right that I'll risk ridicule if he does turn up in John o' Groats and I'll alert the local police down there that I think that's where he is. One more strike and he may have given himself away."

Dick was his usual efficient and sympathetic self at lunchtime in The Cornishman, pulling pints now with the sure hand of an expert, bringing three or four laden plates at once from the kitchen into the bar and remembering who had ordered what. But at the back of his mind there was a niggling worry.

Peggy had not been quite her normal self when he had delivered Malcolm that morning, not quite the same in her manner. There hadn't been anything that you could pin down: You couldn't say she'd got the huff, decided she'd gone off him, was feeling she was being exploited. She was minding three or four other toddlers now—children whose mothers had got summer jobs when the holiday season had come upon them. The arrival of one of them at the door had covered over any awkwardness, but also prevented any attempt to sort things out. Dick was sure there was *something*: an alteration in her manner, a slight access of remoteness, even coldness.

"One chicken and chips, one roast pork, one steak-and-kidney pie, and one vegetable bake." He had a cheerful air as he served one of the families who had once been regulars of Peggy's, but had been found an alternative cottage this season. They were a fleshy, forceful family, and they took up their knives and forks with enthusiasm.

"Can hear you're from the North, too," said the wife, smiling at him in a friendly fashion.

"Me father was," said Dick. "Or should I say 'wor'? I can do the accent, and a bit of it has rubbed off onto me. But I come from Cambridge—and all round. I'm a bit of a rolling stone."

"Can't be too much of a rolling stone, now you've got little Malcolm to consider," said the husband. "Champion little lad, that. We saw him when we dropped by to say hello to Peggy."

"Champion's the word for him," said Dick. "I call him 'Captain.' Can't remember how that started, but I certainly have to jump when he gives me orders!"

"Colin—two hamburgers and chips on the bar," called Jack, and Dick resumed his service of the crowded and cheerful bar. He didn't like it when people commented on his very slight Northern accent. He'd told Peggy early on that he came from Cambridge, and that was a lie he was now stuck with.

He got away from The Cornishman shortly after three, and went straight to pick Malcolm up. Peggy had got her manner under control now, and was friendly and pleasant as always. She looked him in the eye, but was—somehow, was he imagining it?—quite keen for an excuse to look away again. *Yes, I am imagining it,* said Dick to himself, settling Malcolm onto his shoulders to ride him piggyback to the cottage.

"See you soon, Peggy," he called. She looked up from the floor where she was playing with one of the other children.

"Oh—yes. Good," she said.

There is something wrong, thought Dick.

"I think this is a call you should take," said DC Lackland, and handed the receiver over to Purley.

"DI Purley speaking."

"Ah, now are you the man who's in charge of the disappearance of that little boy—the one who was snatched by his father in the Darlington area?"

The voice was pure County Durham.

"Yes, I am."

"Well, I'm speaking from Briscow in Cornwall."

"Oh yes?" The heightened interest in his voice was evident.

"That's right, but we're from Stockton, so we read about the case in the local newspapers. There wasn't a great deal in the national papers, was there?"

"No, there wasn't." It seemed as if he was being accused of not pressing for more, so he said: "The North is another country."

"Aye, you're right. Londoners aren't interested in what queer folk like us get up to. They'd rather not know. Any road, we've been coming to Cornwall for four years on the trot up to now, but this year our cottage was taken, let to a young man and a boy."

"Oh yes?" Purley was well trained in police neutrality but he couldn't keep a surge of interest out of his voice.

"Nice-enough-looking fellow, and a lovely little boy. I'm probably way out of order and on the wrong lines altogether, but the little boy is called Malcolm. That was the name of the little boy who was snatched, wasn't it?"

"That's right. The father is Richard Randall."

"This man is calling himself Colin Something-or-other. But the boy is Malcolm. I suppose he thought changing it would cause more problems than it would solve. If it *is* them."

"This man is not a local, I take it."

"No, no, of course not. He's been here since early spring, I believe. And he has a slight Northern accent."

"Really?"

"Yes. Says he got it from his father. But if you were brought up in Cambridge like he says he was, you wouldn't have your father's accent, would you?"

"It sounds unlikely."

"The story is that the little boy's mother died in childbirth. We had that from Peggy, his landlady, the woman who minds the nipper while he works at the pub."

"Right. And Peggy's name and address are?"

"Peggy Cowley, Lane's End Cottage, Deacon Street, Briscow, Cornwall."

"I'm grateful to you, very grateful."

When he had got the man's name and address and his Stockton address, too, Purley banged down the telephone in triumph.

"Got him!"

"You haven't got him at all yet," said Lackland, who enjoyed playing the spoilsport. "And Malcolm's a common enough name."

"I feel a pricking of my thumb," said Purley, refusing to be dampened. "Get me Launceston police."

★ ★ ★ ★ ★

"So how was your day, Captain?" asked Dick, watching Malcolm get his hands very sticky from a jam sandwich. Malcolm, as always, considered at length.

"Jemima was very naughty," he announced.

"Well, I'm sorry to hear that." Jemima was one of the other children Peggy minded, and in Malcolm's opinion she was a Bad Lot.

"She spilt her lemonade and broke the little wooden horse."

"Good Lord, fancy poor old Peggy having to cope with a naughty little girl like that."

"She should have smacked her but she didn't."

After tea, when Malcolm was absorbed in a jigsaw puzzle of Postman Pat with large but bewildering pieces, Dick said: "I'm just popping over to Peggy's, I think we left your pully there."

"My pully's in the—" Malcolm began. But his father was already out of the door.

I want this thing sorted out, thought Dick, as he crossed the lane and ran up the bank and onto Peggy's long back lawn. *It can't wait till tonight. This sort of thing can fester. And if I can't tell her the truth, I'll tell her a lie. It won't be the first time.*

Dick had as great a confidence in his ability to fabricate plausible stories as he had in his eye for a robbable house.

He was about to round the side of Peggy's cottage when he heard voices from outside the front door.

"And when did you say this man and his son took the cottage?"

"Back in March," came Peggy's voice, reassuringly normal. "I'd have the precise dates in my records. They stayed a couple of nights bed-and-breakfast, then took the cottage."

"Are they still there?"

"Yes."

"What name is the man using?"

"The man's name is Colin Morton," came Peggy's voice emphatically.

"And does he say he's divorced?" asked the young sergeant, his hard-looking face intimidating, his eyes like deep, cold lakes.

"Colin is a widower," said Peggy firmly.

"Oh yes? And what does he say his wife died of?"

"His wife died in childbirth. Look, it's not me you should be asking these questions, it's him. He'll have all the papers and things." Thinking she heard movement from the back garden, she went on talking brightly. "But really I *know* that's true. I've seen a picture of the poor girl with little Malcolm. Such a nice face she had, pretty but loving, too. Colin keeps that in his wallet, because he doesn't want the little lad to be reminded of his mother—says that if he'd been a little older when his mother died it would be different, but—"

"And this 'Colin,' he's working locally, is he?" the sergeant interrupted.

"Yes, he's working lunchtimes at The Cornishman. They think the world of—"

"That can't bring in much. He is paying you rent for the cottage, is he?"

The implication was brutally obvious. Peggy chattered on, seeming to take no notice, but really she was speaking from the front of her mind only. The back of her mind was re-membering the night before. The electricity had fused just as she was making her late-night drink. She had no overnighters in the second bedroom, but something—she was reluctant to analyse precisely what—made her want it fixed that night.

Dick had done it before, and made light of it. Surely he wouldn't mind. It would be the first time . . . She rummaged in the dark to find her torch in the kitchen drawer, and then set off across the lawn towards the cottage.

The car was not there. The cottage was in darkness and the little dirt square to the side where Dick kept the car was empty. Malcolm was sleeping in the cottage on his own. The moment she thought this she realized how silly she was being, and what a hypocrite: Malcolm was there on his own asleep all the hours Dick spent in her bed. But that thought raised new fears and doubts. Where was Dick now? In someone's bed? He met all sorts of women while he was serving in the pub. He could have made a date with one of them. The thought that she was nothing more than his piece on the side, and that he'd gone on to more desirable pieces, tormented her. It felt like treachery. It felt like the end of her good life.

She retreated to her garden and stood in the darkness behind a bushy rhododendron. Eventually she heard Dick's car. Well over half an hour had passed since she'd begun waiting. The car came up the lane and was parked in the usual place beside the cottage. She saw Dick's profile before he switched the car lights off, saw him get out of the car. He was wearing a drab jerkin and was carrying that old bag of his. Somehow he didn't look as if he was returning from a sexual assignation.

When he had disappeared into the cottage, she turned and trudged back to her darkened house, somewhat relieved in her mind, but still doubtful. What *did* one look like when one returned from a sexual assignation? she asked herself. And even if he was not, where *had* he been? What *had* he been doing?

"Now, if you'll take us to the cottage—" said the sergeant.

"I can get the key if you like, then you can look over it if they're not in," said Peggy.

She was not betraying them, merely giving Dick time to get them both away. She pottered inside to take as long as possible to find the key. In her heart she knew he was the man they were looking for. In her heart she knew she had lost them both.

"Come on, Captain, we're going for a drive," shouted Dick as he ran through the tiny living room, tripping over a coffee table, then righting himself and dashing up the stairs. When he came down, clutching the bag, heavy from last night, Malcolm was still on the floor with his jigsaw.

"Why are we going for a drive, Daddy? It's nearly my bedtime."

Dick grabbed his jacket, then picked up the little boy and ran out with him.

"It's a lovely evening for a drive," he said, shoving him in the car, but taking care to click the belt in place around him. He ran round to the driver's door, and the key was in the ignition and the car being backed into the lane before Malcolm could make further protest.

He knew he shouldn't drive fast through the village. He tried to moderate his speed, but he was possessed by the urgency of the situation. As he scorched past The Cornishman he saw that one of the local policemen was having an off-duty pint at a little rustic table the landlord had set out for good summer days. In his mirror he saw him getting out his mobile phone.

He knew the roads around Briscow now like a connoisseur. He took a shortcut, then another, then was out not onto the motorway but on the old main road to Bristol. Now he could really open up. If only he had had a new car, or any really powerful one. With a bit of luck the police vehicle wouldn't be much better than his. He put five miles between him and Briscow, then six, seven.

Then he saw the police car in the mirror. Moments later he heard its siren.

The police car wasn't an old banger, or even a sedate family model Ford. It was gaining on him. He pushed the accelerator down to the floor. He was seized momentarily with exhilaration, but at the back of his mind something outside of him seemed to be shouting: The Dream. The Nightmare. And then he began to sweat, and a quieter voice whispered to him: the dead child. He tried to continue, tried to squeeze more speed out of the car, but his heart was not in it. In the mirror he saw the police car gaining on him, its siren gathering in intensity.

He took his foot off the accelerator. The car dropped speed, began coasting. He changed lanes, let the car slow down, then let it chug to the side of the road and stop. As he pulled on the hand brake the police car came to a halt in front of him. Two policemen jumped out and ran over to lean in his window. One had a hard face and piercing cruel eyes. The younger one had unformed features but compassionate eyes.

"Are you Richard Randall, going by the name of Colin Morton?" the sergeant asked, flicking his ID in his face. Dick considered, then nodded.

"You know it all, I expect," he said. "Yes, I am."

"And this is your son Malcolm Randall?"

"Yes, it is."

"Richard Randall, I am arresting you . . ."

The policemen agreed to drop Malcolm off at Peggy's as a temporary measure. Dick knew hard-eyes wouldn't want the embarrassment of a child around him cramping his style. "You must be nice to Mummy when you go home," he said to the boy as Peggy came out to collect him, not looking him in the face. "She must have missed you all this time."

When he was alone with the policemen, driving to the station in Launceston, he suddenly broke down. It was the end of his dream, the very end. Somehow it felt like the end of his life.

He looked up, red-eyed, at the young constable handcuffed to him in the backseat of the car.

"Will you tell his mother I would never have done anything to harm him? That's why I stopped. I love that boy. Tell Selena it's all up to her now. Will you tell her that exactly?"

"Of course I will. What if she asks what you mean?"

He didn't answer directly.

"Tell her I don't want to see her, or the boy. She'll understand. Tell her it's all up to her."

Then they drew into Launceston Police Station and began the long business of interviews and charging.

Having Malcolm back was like a dream for Selena. Inspector Purley had flown down to Bristol the night of Dick's arrest, hired a car, then participated in interviews the next day. He had phoned Selena to say they were sure it was Malcolm and he'd bring him back up North the next day. No point in her coming down.

It was late afternoon when his car had driven up the street and parked outside her Darlington home. She had rushed to the front door just in time to hear the inspector say, "Run to Mummy," and, picking the little bundle up, to hug him, kiss him. Out of the corner of her eye she saw the inspector raise a hand, then get back into his car and drive off.

Malcolm was grown out of all recognition, and was confident beyond belief. He gravely inspected his old toys, told her what he'd most like for tea, and ran around the garden when she told him that Finny the cat was out there. All his talk and memories were of Daddy, and he'd tell her quite disjointedly things they'd done on the road, how Daddy had taken him away, how Jemima at Peggy's was always naughty. When he asked her, "Are you my mummy now?" she had almost choked, and had taken him in her arms and said they'd never be apart again.

Later in the evening she had a phone call from the young constable in Launceston. She was almost incoherent in her joy and thanks, and she was really grateful to get Dick's message to her.

"I suppose they'll be bringing him back up North for trial," she said wistfully. "I could go and see him then."

"He doesn't want that. He doesn't . . . feel he should see you or Malcolm." Being a kind-hearted young man, he added: "Yet. I don't think he feels the time is ripe."

Selena was sad, but she didn't have time to stay sad. Soon it was time for bed, but first she had to wash away the grime and mustiness of travel from the little boy. She ran the bath, just lukewarm as he liked it, and Malcolm insisted on undressing himself, a new departure for Selena, who had always done it in the past. She wondered at his chubbiness—what *had* Dick been feeding him on?—but saw how good and competent he was in all the little things he did for himself.

He climbed into the bath himself, slowly, seriously, but once in, he was more interested in his old rubber duck than in washing himself. Still a child in some things, Selena thought. She worked up a soapy lather on his flannel and began washing him herself. It was pure pleasure, and it felt as if she was washing off all those months when only his father had had him, seen him grow. She leant over the bath to wash the far side of him, and it was then that she saw it.

The birthmark on his hip.

The oval-shaped birthmark, like a rugby ball, on the left hip. Just as she had seen it described in television interviews, in newspaper articles, by Carol Parker. This wasn't Malcolm. This was Anton Parker, born Anton Weissner, when his mother was married to his German father. She let the flannel fall, felt faint, and sank back onto the chair by the wall. Anton played on, oblivious, dipping the duck's head under the water as he had seen ducks do at Briscow.

It was Dick who had snatched Anton. That was six days after he had snatched Malcolm. In that time Malcolm must have died. She felt tears come into her eyes for her lost child, but she suppressed them. She had to think, to be practical. How had he died? Naturally? In a car chase, perhaps? There had been various sightings and police pursuits. Dick had taken this little boy as a substitute, called him Malcolm, taught him to call himself Malcolm. That's why he would not let him say more than a word or two on the phone, in case she recognised or suspected this was not her boy. She thought of Carol Parker, desperate and dispirited, appealing on British television, convinced that her husband had taken their son to Germany, forever.

Then she remembered her husband's words: "It's all up to her now." Suddenly they had quite a new meaning. From the bath came splashings and chuckles of pleasure. She drew her head up straight and opened her eyes.

"Come along, Malcolm—out of the bath now and let Mummy dry you."

Out There in the Darkness

Ed Gorman

1.

The night it all started, the whole strange spiral, we were having our usual midweek poker game—four fortyish men who work in the financial business getting together for beer and bawdy jokes and straight poker. No wild-card games. We hate them.

This was summer, and vacation time, and so it happened that the game was held two weeks in a row at my house. Jan had taken the kids to see her Aunt Wendy and Uncle Verne at their fishing cabin, and so I offered to have the game at my house this week, too. With nobody there to supervise, the beer could be laced with a little bourbon, and the jokes could get even bawdier. With the wife and kids in the house, you're always at least a little bit intimidated.

Mike and Bob arrived together, bearing gifts, which in this case meant the kind of sexy magazines our wives did not want in the house in case the kids might stumble across them. At least that's what they say. I think they sense, and rightly, that the magazines might give their spouses bad ideas about taking the secretary out for a few after-work drinks, or stopping by a singles bar some night.

We got the chips and cards set up at the table, we got the first beers open (Mike chasing a shot of bourbon with his beer), and we started passing the dirty magazines around with tenth-grade glee. The magazines compensated, I suppose, for the balding head, the bloating belly, the stooping shoulders. Deep in the heart of every hundred-year-old man is a horny fourteen-year-old boy.

All this, by the way, took place up in the attic. The four of us got to know each other when we all moved into what city planners called a "transitional neighborhood." There were some grand old houses that could be renovated with enough money and real care. The city designated a ten-square-block area as one it wanted to restore to shiny new luster. Jan and I chose a crumbling Victorian. You wouldn't recognize it today. And that includes the attic, which I've turned into a very nice den.

"Ticks me off," Mike O'Brien said. "He's always late."

And that was true. Neil Solomon *was* always late. Never by that much but always late nonetheless.

"At least tonight he has a good excuse," Bob Genter said.

"He does?" Mike said. "He's probably swimming in his pool." Neil recently got a bonus that made him the first owner of a full-size outdoor pool in our neighborhood.

"No, he's got patrol. But he's stopping at nine. He's got somebody trading with him for next week."

"Oh, hell," Mike said, obviously sorry that he'd complained. "I didn't know that."

Bob's handsome black head nodded solemnly.

Patrol is something we all take very seriously in this newly restored "transitional neighborhood." Eight months ago, the burglaries started, and they've gotten pretty bad. My house has been burglarized once and vandalized once.

Bob and Mike have had curb-sitting cars stolen. Neil's wife Sheila was surprised in her own kitchen by a burglar. And then there was the killing four months ago, man and wife who'd just moved into the neighborhood savagely stabbed to death in their own bed. The police caught the guy a few days later trying to cash some of the traveler's checks he'd stolen after killing his prey. He was typical of the kind of man who infested this neighborhood after sundown: a twentyish junkie stoned to the point of psychosis on various street drugs, and not at all averse to murdering people he envied and despised. He also knew a hell of a lot about fooling burglar alarms.

After the murders there was a neighborhood meeting and that's when we came up with the patrol, something somebody'd read about being popular back East. People think that a nice middle-sized Midwestern city like ours doesn't have major crime problems. I invite them to walk many of these streets after dark. They'll quickly be disabused of that notion. Anyway, the patrol worked this way: Each night, two neighborhood people got in the family van and patrolled the ten-block area that had been restored. If they saw anything suspicious, they used their cellular phones and called police. We jokingly called it the Baby Boomer Brigade. The patrol had one strict rule: You were never to take direct action unless somebody's life was at stake. Always, always use the cellular phone and call the police.

Neil had patrol tonight. He'd be rolling in here in another half-hour. The patrol had two shifts: early, 8–10; late, 10–12.

"Hi, Aaron. Sorry I'm late," Neil Solomon said as he came inside and followed me up to the attic.

"We already drank all the beer," Mike O'Brien said loudly.

Neil smiled. "That gut you're carrying lately, I can believe that *you* drank all the beer."

Neil sat down, I got him a beer from the tiny fridge I keep up here, cards were dealt, seven-card stud was played.

Bob said, "How'd patrol go tonight?"

Neil shrugged. "No problems."

"I still say we should carry guns," Mike said.

"You're not going to believe this, but I agree with you," Neil said.

"Seriously?" Mike said.

"Oh, great," I said to Bob Genter. "Another beer-commercial cowboy."

Bob smiled. "Where I come from we didn't have cowboys, we had 'mothas.' " He laughed. "Mean mothas, let me tell you. And practically *all* of them carried guns."

"That mean you're siding with them?" I said.

Bob looked at his cards again then shrugged. "Haven't decided yet, I guess."

"Play cards," Mike said, "and leave the debate crap till later."

Good idea.

We played cards.

In forty-five minutes, I lost $63.82. Mike and Neil always played as if their lives were at stake. All you had to do was watch their faces. Gunfighters couldn't have looked more serious or determined.

The first pit stop came just after ten o'clock and Neil took it. There was a john on the second floor between the bedrooms, and another john on the first floor.

Neil said, "The good Doctor Gottesfeld had to give me a finger-wave this afternoon, gents, so this may take awhile."

"You should trade that prostate of yours in for a new one," Mike said.

"Believe me, I'd like to."

While Neil was gone, the three of us started talking about the patrol again, and whether we should go armed.

We made the same old arguments. The passion was gone. We were just marking time waiting for Neil and we knew it.

"Guess I'll use the john on the first floor," Bob said, and disappeared downstairs.

The first time I heard it, I thought it was some kind of animal noise from outside, a dog or a cat in some kind of discomfort maybe. Mike, who was dealing himself a hand of solitaire, didn't even look up from his cards. This was about ten minutes after Bob left for downstairs.

But the second time I heard the sound, Mike and I both looked up. And then we heard the exploding sound of breaking glass.

"What the hell is that?" Mike said.

"Let's go find out."

Just about the time we reached the bottom of the attic steps, we saw Neil coming out of the second-floor john. "You hear that?"

"Sure as hell did," I said.

We reached the staircase leading to the first floor. Everything was dark. Mike reached for the light switch but I brushed his hand away.

I put a shushing finger to my lips and then showed him the Louisville Slugger I'd grabbed from Tim's room. He's my nine-year-old and his most devout wish is to be a good baseball player. His mother has convinced him that just because I went to college on a baseball scholarship, I was a good player. I wasn't. I was a lucky player.

I led the way downstairs, keeping the bat ready at all times.

"Damn you!"

The voice belonged to Bob.

More smashing glass.

I listened to the passage of the sound. Kitchen. Had to be the kitchen.

In the shadowy light from the street, I saw their faces, Mike's and Neil's. They looked scared.

I hefted the bat some more and then started moving fast to the kitchen.

Just as we passed through the dining room, I heard something heavy hit the kitchen floor. Something human and heavy.

I got the kitchen light on.

He was at the back door. White. Tall. Blond shoulder-length hair. Filthy tan T-shirt. Greasy jeans. He had grabbed one of Jan's carving knives from the huge iron rack that sits atop the butcher-block island. The one curious thing about him was the eyes: There was a malevolent iridescence to the blue irises, an angry but somehow alien intelligence, a silver glow.

Bob was sprawled facedown on the tile floor. His arms were spread wide on either side of him. He didn't seem to be moving. Chunks and fragments of glass were strewn everywhere across the floor. My uninvited guest had smashed two or three of the colorful pitchers we'd bought the winter before in Mexico.

"Run!" the burglar cried to somebody on the back porch.

He turned, waving the butcher knife back and forth to keep us at bay.

Footsteps out the back door.

The burglar held us off a few more moments, but then I gave him a little bit of tempered Louisville Slugger wood right across the wrist. The knife went clattering.

By this time, Mike and Neil were pretty crazed. They jumped him, hurled him back against the door, and then started putting in punches wherever they'd fit.

"Hey!" I said, and tossed Neil the bat. "Just hold this. If he makes a move, open up his head. Otherwise leave him alone."

They really were crazed, like pit bulls who'd been pulled back just as a fight was starting to get good.

"Mike, call the cops and tell them to send a car."

I got Bob up and walking. I took him into the bathroom and sat him down on the toilet lid. I found a lump the size of an egg on the back of his head. I soaked a clean washcloth with cold water and pressed it against the lump. Bob took it from there.

"You want an ambulance?" I said.

"An ambulance? Are you kidding? You must think I'm a ballet dancer or something."

I shook my head. "No, I know better than that. I've got a male cousin who's a ballet dancer and he's one tough sonofabitch, believe me. You—" I smiled. "You aren't that tough, Bob."

"I don't need an ambulance. I'm fine."

He winced and tamped the rag tighter against his head. "Just a little headache is all." He looked young suddenly, the aftershock of fear in his brown eyes. "Scared the hell out of me. Heard something when I was leaving the john. Went out to the kitchen to check it out. He jumped me."

"What'd he hit you with?"

"No idea."

"I'll go get you some whiskey. Just sit tight."

"I love sitting in bathrooms, man."

I laughed. "I don't blame you."

When I got back to the kitchen, they were gone. All three of them. Then I saw the basement door. It stood open a few inches. I could see dusty light in the space between door and frame. The basement was our wilderness. We hadn't had the time or money to really fix it up yet. We were counting on this year's Christmas bonus from the Windsor Financial Group to help us set it right.

I went down the stairs. The basement is one big, mostly unused room except for the washer and dryer in the corner. All the boxes and odds and ends that should have gone to the attic instead went down here. It smells damp most of the time. The idea is to turn it into a family room for when the boys are older. These days it's mostly inhabited by stray waterbugs.

When I reached the bottom step, I saw them. There are four metal support poles in the basement, near each corner. They had him lashed to a pole in the east quadrant, tied his wrists behind him with rope found in the tool room. They also had him gagged with what looked like a pillowcase. His eyes were big and wide. He looked scared and I didn't blame him. I was scared, too.

"What the hell are you guys doing?"

"Just calm down, Papa Bear," Mike said. That's his name for me whenever he wants to convey to people that I'm kind of this old fuddy-duddy. It so happens that Mike is two years older than I am and it also happens that I'm not a fuddy-duddy. Jan has assured me of that, and she's completely impartial.

"Knock off the Papa Bear crap. Did you call the cops?"

"Not yet," Neil said. "Just calm down a little, all right?"

"You haven't called the cops. You've got some guy tied

up and gagged in my basement. You haven't even asked how Bob is. And you want me to calm down."

Mike came up to me then. He still had that air of pit-bull craziness about him, frantic, uncontrollable, alien.

"We're going to do what the cops *can't* do, man," he said. "We're going to sweat this jerk. We're going to make him tell us who he was with tonight, and then we're going to make him give us every single name of every single bad guy who works this neighborhood. And then we'll turn all the names over to the cops."

"It's just an extension of the patrol," Neil said. "Just keeping our neighborhood safe is all."

"You guys are nuts," I said, and turned back toward the steps. "I'm going up and call the cops."

That's when I realized just how crazed Mike was. "You aren't going anywhere, man. You're going to stay here and help us break this creep down. You're going to do your neighborhood duty."

He'd grabbed my sleeve so hard that he'd torn it at the shoulder. We both discovered this at the same time.

I expected him to look sorry. He didn't. "Don't be such a wimp, Aaron," he said.

I looked over at the prisoner and said, "Let's go upstairs and talk this over."

2.

Once we were back upstairs Mike calmed down a little. He even led the charge at getting the kitchen cleaned up. I think he was feeling guilty about calling me a wimp with such angry exuberance. Now I understood how lynch mobs got formed. One guy like Mike stirring people up by alternately insulting them and urging them on.

After the kitchen was put back in order, and after I'd taken inventory to find that nothing had been stolen, I went to the refrigerator and got beers for everybody. Bob had drifted back to the kitchen, too.

"All right," I said, "now that we've all calmed down, I want to walk over to that yellow kitchen wall phone there and call the police. Any objections?"

"I think blue would look better in here than yellow," Neil said.

"Funny," I said.

They looked themselves now, no feral madness on the faces of Mike or Neil, no winces on Bob's.

I started across the floor to the phone.

Neil grabbed my arm. Not with the same insulting force Mike had used on me. But enough to get the job done.

"I think Mike's right," Neil said. "We should grill him a little."

I shook my head, politely removed his hand from my forearm, and proceeded to the phone.

"This isn't your decision alone," Mike said.

He'd finally had his way. He'd succeeded in making me angry. I turned around and looked at him. "This is my house, Mike. If you don't like my decisions, then I'd suggest you leave."

We both took steps toward each other. Mike would no doubt win any battle we had but I'd at least be able to inflict a little damage, and right now that's all I was thinking about.

Neil got between us.

"Hey," he said. "For God's sake, you two, c'mon. We're friends, remember?"

"This is my house," I said, my words childish in my ears.

"Yeah, but we live in the same neighborhood, Aaron,"

Mike said, "which makes this *our* problem."

"He's right, Aaron," Bob said from the breakfast nook.

"He's not right," I said to Bob. "He's wrong. We're not cops, we're not bounty hunters, we're not trackers. We're a bunch of guys who peddle stocks and bonds. Mike and Neil shouldn't have tied him up downstairs—that happens to be illegal, at least the way they went about it—and now I'm going to call the cops."

"Yes, that poor thing," Mike said, "aren't we just picking on him, though? Tell you what, why don't we make him something to eat?"

"Just make sure we have the right wine to go with it," Neil said. "Properly chilled, of course."

"Maybe we could get him a chick," Bob said.

"With bombers out to here," Mike said, indicating with his hands where "here" was.

I couldn't help it. I smiled. They were all being ridiculous. A kind of fever had caught them. "You really want to go down there and question him?" I said to Neil.

"Yes. We can ask him things the cops can't."

"Scare him a little," Mike said. "So he'll tell us who was with him tonight, and who else works this neighborhood." He came over and put his hand out. "God, man, you're one of my best friends. I don't want you mad at me."

Then he hugged me, which is something I've never been comfortable with men doing, but to the extent I could, I hugged him back.

"Friends?" he said.

"Friends," I said. "But I still want to call the cops."

"And spoil our fun?" Neil said.

"And spoil your fun."

"I say we take it to a vote," Bob said.

"This isn't a democracy," I said. "It's my house and I'm

the king. I don't want to have a vote."

"Can we ask him one question?" Bob said.

I sighed. They weren't going to let go. "One question?"

"The name of the guy he was with tonight."

"And that's it?"

"That's it. That way we get two of them off the street."

"And then I call the cops?"

"Then," Mike said, "you call the cops."

"One question," Neil said.

While we finished our beers, we argued a little more, but they had a lot more spirit left than I did. I was tired now and missing Jan and the kids and feeling lonely. These three guys had become strangers to me tonight. Very old boys eager to play at boy games once again.

"One question," I said. "Then I call the cops."

I led the way down, sneezing as I did so. There's always enough dust floating around in the basement to play hell with my sinuses.

The guy was his same sullen self, glaring at us as we descended the stairs and then walked over to him. He smelled of heat and sweat and city grime. The long bare arms sticking out of his filthy T-shirt told tattoo tales of writhing snakes and leaping panthers. The arms were joined in the back with rope. His jaw still flexed, trying to accommodate the intrusion of the gag.

"Maybe we should castrate him," Mike said, walking up close to the guy. "You like that, scumbag? If we castrated you?"

If the guy felt any fear, it wasn't evident in his eyes. All you could see there was the usual contempt.

"I'll bet this is the jerk who broke into the Donaldson's house a couple weeks ago," Neil said.

Now he walked up to the guy. But he was more ambitious than Mike had been. Neil spat in the guy's face.

"Hey," I said, "cool it."

Neil glared at me. "Yeah, I wouldn't want to hurt his feelings, would I?"

Then he suddenly turned back on the guy, raised his fist, and started to swing. All I could do was shove him. That sent his punch angling off to the right, missing our burglar by half a foot.

"You punk," Neil said, turning back on me now.

But Mike was there, between us.

"You know what we're doing? We're making this jerk happy. He's gonna have some nice stories to tell all his criminal friends."

He was right. The burglar was the one who got to look all cool and composed. We looked like squabbling brats. As if to confirm this, a hint of amusement played in the burglar's blue eyes.

"Oh, hell, Aaron, I'm sorry," Neil said, putting his hand out. This was like a political convention, all the hand-shaking going on.

"So am I, Neil," I said. "That's why I want to call the cops and get this over with."

And that's when he chose to make his move, the burglar. As soon as I mentioned the cops, he probably realized that this was going to be his last opportunity.

He waited until we were just finishing up with the hand-shake, when we were all focused on each other. Then he took off running. We could see that he'd slipped the rope. He went straight for the stairs, angling out around us like a running back seeing daylight. He even stuck his long, tattooed arm out as if he were trying to repel a tackle.

"Hey," Bob shouted. "He's getting away."

He was at the stairs by the time we could gather ourselves enough to go after him. But when we moved, we moved fast, and in virtual unison.

By the time I got my hand on the cuff of his left jean, he was close enough to the basement door to open it.

I yanked hard and ducked out of the way of his kicking foot. By now I was as crazy as Mike and Neil had been earlier. There was adrenaline, and great anger. He wasn't just a burglar, he was all burglars, intent not merely on stealing things from me, but hurting my family, too. He hadn't had time to take the gag from his mouth.

This time, I grabbed booted foot and leg and started hauling him back down the stairs. At first he was able to hold onto the door but when I wrenched his foot rightward, he tried to scream behind the gag. He let go of the door-knob.

The next half-minute is still unclear in my mind. I started running down the stairs, dragging him with me. All I wanted to do was get him on the basement floor again, turn him over to the others to watch, and then go call the cops.

But somewhere in those few seconds when I was hauling him back down the steps, I heard edge of stair meeting back of skull. The others heard it, too, because their shouts and curses died in their throats.

When I turned around, I saw the blood running fast and red from his nose. The blue eyes no longer held contempt. They were starting to roll up white in the back of his head.

"God," I said. "He's hurt."

"I think he's a lot more than hurt," Mike said.

"Help me carry him upstairs."

We got him on the kitchen floor. Mike and Neil rushed around soaking paper towels. We tried to revive him. Bob, who kept wincing from his headache, tried the guy's wrist, ankle, and throat for a pulse. None. His nose and mouth were bloody. Very bloody.

"No way you could *die* from hitting your head like that," Neil said.

"Sure you could," Mike said. "You hit it just the right way."

"He can't be dead," Neil said. "I'm going to try his pulse again."

Bob, who obviously took Neil's second opinion personally, frowned and rolled his eyes. "He's dead, man. He really is."

"No way."

"You a doctor or something?" Bob said.

Neil smiled nervously. "No, but I play one on TV."

So Neil tried the pulse points. His reading was exactly what Bob's reading had been.

"See," Bob said.

I guess none of us was destined to ever quite be an adult.

"Man," Neil said, looking down at the long, cold, unmoving form of the burglar. "He's really dead."

"What the hell're we gonna do?" Mike said.

"We're going to call the police," I said, and started for the phone.

"The hell we are," Mike said. "The hell we are."

3.

Maybe half an hour after we laid him on the kitchen floor, he started to smell. We'd looked for identification, and found none. He was just The Burglar.

We sat at the kitchen table, sharing a fifth of Old Granddad.

We'd taken two votes and they'd come up ties. Two for calling the police, Bob and I; two for not calling the police, Mike and Neil.

"All we have to tell them," I said, "is that we tied him up so he wouldn't get away."

"And then they say," Mike said, "so why didn't you call us before now?"

"We just lie about the time a little," I said. "Tell them we called them within twenty minutes."

"Won't work," Neil said.

"Why not?" Bob said.

"Medical examiner can fix the time of death," Neil said.

"Not that close."

"Close enough so that the cops might question our story," Neil said. "By the time they get here, he'll have been dead at least an hour, hour and a half."

"And then we get our names in the paper for not reporting the burglary or the death right away," Mike said. "Brokerages just love publicity like that."

"I'm calling the cops right now," I said, and got up from the table.

"Think about Tomlinson a minute," Neil said.

Tomlinson was my boss at the brokerage house. "What about him?"

"Remember how he canned Dennis Bryce when Bryce's ex-wife took out a restraining order on him?"

"This is different," I said.

"The hell it is," Mike said. "Neil's right, none of our bosses will like publicity like this. We'll all sound a little— crazy—you know, keeping him locked up in the basement. And then killing him when he tried to get away."

They all looked at me.

"You jerks," I said. "I was the one who wanted to call the police in the first place. And I sure as hell didn't kill him on purpose."

"Looking back on it," Neil said, "I guess you were right, Aaron. We should've called the cops right away."

"Now's a great time to realize that," I said.

"Maybe they've got a point," Bob said softly, glancing at me, then glancing nervously away.

"Oh, great. You, too?" I said.

"They just might kick me out of there if I had any publicity that involved somebody getting killed," Bob said.

"He was a frigging burglar," I said.

"But he's dead," Neil said.

"And we killed him," Mike said.

"I appreciate your saying 'we,' " I said.

"I know a good place," Bob said.

I looked at him carefully, afraid of what he was going to say next.

"Forget it," I said.

"A good place for what?" Neil said.

"Dumping the body," Bob said.

"No way," I said.

This time when I got up, nobody tried to stop me. I walked over to the yellow wall telephone.

I wondered if the cozy kitchen would ever feel the same to me now that a dead body had been laid upon its floor.

I had to step over him to reach the phone. The smell was even more sour now.

"You know how many bodies get dumped in the river that never wash up?" Bob said.

"No," I said, "and you don't either."

"Lots," he said.

"There's a scientific appraisal for you. 'Lots.' "

"Lots and lots, probably," Neil said, taking up Bob's argument.

Mike grinned. "Lots and lots and *lots.*"

"Thank you, professor," I said.

I lifted the receiver and dialed O.

"Operator."

"The police department, please."

"Is this an emergency?" asked the young woman.

"No; no, it isn't."

"I'll connect you," she said.

"You think your kids'll be able to handle it?" Neil said.

"No mind games," I said.

"No mind games at all. I'm asking you a realistic question. The police have some doubts about our story and then the press gets ahold of it and bam. We're the lead story on all three channels."

"Good evening. Police Department."

I started to speak but I couldn't somehow. My voice wouldn't work. That's the only way I can explain it.

"The six o'clock news five nights running," Neil said softly behind me. "And the D.A. can't endorse any kind of vigilante activity so he nails us on involuntary manslaughter."

"Hello? This is the police department," a female voice said.

Neil was there then, reaching me as if by magic.

He took the receiver gently from my hand and hung it back up on the phone again.

"Let's go have another drink and see what Bob's got in mind, all right?"

He led me, as if I were a hospital patient, slowly and carefully back to the table where Bob, over more whiskey, slowly and gently laid out his plan.

★ ★ ★ ★ ★

The next morning, three of us phoned in sick. Bob went to work because he had an important meeting.

Around noon—a sunny day when a softball game and a cold six-pack of beer sounded good—Neil and Mike came over. They looked as bad as I felt, and no doubt looked, myself.

We sat out on the patio eating the Hardee's lunch they'd bought. I'd need to play softball to work off some of the calories.

Birdsong and soft breezes and the smell of fresh-cut grass should have made our patio time enjoyable. But I had to wonder if we'd ever enjoy anything again. I just kept seeing the body momentarily arced over the roaring waters of the dam and dropping into white churning turbulence.

"You think we did the right thing?" Neil said.

"Now's a hell of a time to ask that," I said.

"Of course we did the right thing," Mike said. "What choice did we have? It was either that or get arrested."

"So you don't have any regrets?" Neil said.

Mike sighed. "I didn't say that. I mean, I wish it hadn't happened in the first place."

"Maybe Aaron was right all along," Neil said.

"About what?"

"About going to the cops."

"God damn," Mike said, sitting up from his slouch. We all wore button-down shirts without ties and with the sleeves rolled up. Somehow there was something profane about wearing shorts and T-shirts on a workday. We even wore pretty good slacks. We were those kind of people. "God damn."

"Here he goes," Neil said.

"I can't believe you two," Mike said. "We should be

233

happy that everything went so well last night—and what are we doing? Sitting around here griping and moaning."

"That doesn't mean it's over," I said.

"Why not?" Mike said.

"Because there's still one left."

"One what?"

"One burglar."

"So?"

"So you don't think he's going to get curious about what happened to his partner?"

"What's he gonna do?" Mike said. "Go to the cops?"

"Maybe."

"Maybe? You're crazy. He goes to the cops, he'd be setting himself up for a robbery conviction."

"Not if he tells them we murdered his pal."

Neil said, "Aaron's got a point. What if this guy goes to the cops?"

"He's not going to the cops," Mike said. "No way he's going to the cops at all."

4.

I was dozing on the couch, a Cubs game on the TV set, when the phone rang around nine that evening. I hadn't heard from Jan yet so I expected it would be her. Whenever we're apart, we call each other at least once a day.

The phone machine picks up on the fourth ring so I had to scramble to beat it.

"Hello?"

Nothing. But somebody was on the line. Listening.

"Hello?"

I never play games with silent callers. I just hang up. I did so now.

Two innings later, having talked to Jan, made myself a tuna-fish sandwich on rye, found a package of potato chips I thought we'd finished off at the poker game, and gotten myself a new can of beer, I sat down to watch the last inning. The Cubs had a chance of winning. I said a silent prayer to the god of baseball.

The phone rang.

I mouthed several curses around my mouthful of tuna sandwich and went to the phone.

"Hello?" I said, trying to swallow the last of the bite.

My silent friend again.

I slammed down the phone.

The Cubs got two more singles, I started on the chips, and I had polished off the beer and was thinking of getting another one when the phone rang again.

I had a suspicion of who was calling and then saying nothing—but I didn't really want to think about it.

Then I decided there was an easy way to handle this situation. I'd just let the phone machine take it. If my anonymous friend wanted to talk to a phone machine, good for him.

Four rings. The phone machine took over, Jan's pleasant voice saying that we weren't home but would be happy to call you back if you'd just leave your number.

I waited to hear dead air and then a click.

Instead a familiar female voice said: "Aaron, it's Louise. Bob—" Louise was Bob's wife. She was crying. I ran from the couch to the phone machine in the hall.

"Hello, Louise. It's Aaron."

"Oh, Aaron. It's terrible."

"What happened, Louise?"

"Bob—" More tears. "He electrocuted himself tonight out in the garage." She said that a plug had accidentally

235

fallen into a bowl of water, according to the fire captain on the scene, and Bob hadn't noticed this and put the plug into the outlet and—

Bob had a woodcraft workshop in his garage, a large and sophisticated one. He knew what he was doing.

"He's dead, Aaron. He's dead."

"Oh God, Louise. I'm sorry."

"He was so careful with electricity, too. It's just so hard to believe—"

Yes, I thought. Yes, it was hard to believe. I thought of last night. Of the burglars—one who'd died. One who'd gotten away.

"Why don't I come over?"

"Oh, thank you, Aaron, but I need to be alone with the children. But if you could call Neil and Mike—"

"Of course."

"Thanks for being such good friends, you and Jan."

"Don't be silly, Louise. The pleasure's ours."

"I'll talk to you tomorrow. When I'm—you know."

"Goodnight, Louise."

Mike and Neil were at my place within twenty minutes. We sat in the kitchen again, where we'd been last night.

I said, "Either of you get any weird phone calls tonight?"

"You mean just silence?" Neil said.

"Right."

"I did," Mike said. "Carrie was afraid it was that pervert who called all last winter."

"I did, too," Neil said. "Three of them."

"Then a little while ago, Bob dies out in his garage," I said. "Some coincidence."

"Hey, Aaron," Mike said. "Is that why you got us over here? Because you don't think it was an accident?"

"I'm sure it wasn't an accident," I said. "Bob knew what he was doing with his tools. He didn't notice a plug that had fallen into a bowl of water?"

"He's coming after us," Neil said.

"Oh God," Mike said. "Not you, too."

"He calls us, gets us on edge," I said. "And then he kills Bob. Making it look like an accident."

"These are pretty bright people," Mike said sarcastically.

"You notice the burglar's eyes?" Neil said.

"I did," I said. "He looked very bright."

"And spooky," Neil said. "Never saw eyes like that before."

"I can shoot your theory right in the butt," Mike said.

"How?" I said.

He leaned forward, sipped his beer.

"Here's how. There are two burglars, right? One gets caught, the other runs. And given the nature of burglars, keeps on running. He wouldn't even know who was in the house last night, except for Aaron, and that's only because he's the owner and his name would be in the phone book. But he wouldn't know anything about Bob or Neil or me. No way he'd have been able to track down Bob."

I shook my head. "You're overlooking the obvious."

"Like what?"

"Like he runs off last night, gets his car, and then parks in the alley to see what's going to happen."

"Right," Neil said. "Then he sees us bringing his friend out wrapped in a blanket. He follows us to the dam and watches us throw his friend in."

"And," I said, "everybody had his car here last night. Very easy for him to write down all the license numbers."

"So he kills Bob," Neil said. "And starts making the phone calls to shake us up."

"Does that mean he's coming after us?" Mike said.

"Hell, yes," Neil said. "That's why he's calling us. Shake us up. Sweat us out. Let us know that he's out there somewhere, just waiting. And that we're next."

"I'm going to follow you to work tomorrow, Neil," I said. "And Mike's going to be with me. And then on Saturday you and Neil can follow me. If he's following *us* around, then we'll see it. And then we can start following him. We'll at least find out who he is."

"And then what?" Mike said. "Suppose we do find out where he lives? Then what the hell do we do?"

Neil said, "I guess we worry about that when we get there, don't we?"

In the morning, I picked Mike up early. As agreed, we parked half a block from Neil's house. Also as agreed, Neil emerged exactly at 7:35. Kids were already in the wide streets on skateboards and rollerblades. No other car could be seen, except for a lone silver BMW in a driveway far down the block.

We followed him all the way to work. Nobody followed him. Nobody.

When I dropped Mike off at his office, he said, "You owe me an hour's sleep."

"Two hours," I said.

"Huh?"

"Tomorrow, you and Neil follow me around."

"No way," he said.

There are times when only blunt anger will work with Mike. "It was your idea not to call the police, remember? I'm not up for any of your sulking, Mike. I'm really not."

He sighed: "I guess you're right."

I drove for two and a half hours Saturday morning. I hit a hardware store, a lumberyard, and a K-Mart. At noon, I pulled into a McDonald's. The three of us had some lunch.

"You didn't see anybody even suspicious?"

"Not even suspicious, Aaron," Neil said. "I'm sorry."

"This is all bullshit. He's not going to follow us around."

"I want to give it one more chance," I said.

Mike made a face. "I'm not going to get up early, if that's what you've got in mind."

I got angry again. "Bob's dead, or have you forgotten?"

"Yeah, Aaron," Mike said, "Bob *is* dead. He got electro-cuted. Accidentally."

I said, "You really think it was an accident?"

"Of course I do," Mike said. "When do you want to try it again?"

"Tonight. I'll do a little bowling."

"There's a fight on I want to watch," Mike said.

"Tape it," I said.

" 'Tape it,' " he mocked. "Since when did you start giving us orders?"

"Oh, for God's sake, Mike, grow up," Neil said. "There's no way that Bob's electrocution was an accident or a coincidence. He's probably not going to stop with Bob, either."

The bowling alley was mostly teenagers on Saturday night. There was a time when bowling was mostly a working-class sport. Now it's come to the suburbs and the white-collar people. Now the bowling lane is a good place for teenaged boys to meet girls.

I bowled two games, drank three beers, and walked back outside an hour later.

Summer night. Smell of dying heat, car exhaust, ciga-rette smoke, perfume. Sound of jukebox, distant loud muf-flers, even more distant rushing train, lonely baying dogs.

Mike and Neil were gone.

I went home and opened a beer.

The phone rang. Once again, I was expecting Jan.

"Found the jerk," Neil said. "He followed you from your house to the bowling alley. Then he got tired of waiting and took off again. This time we followed *him*."

"Where?"

He gave me an address. It wasn't a good one.

"We're waiting for you to get here. Then we're going up to pay him a little visit."

"I need twenty minutes."

"Hurry."

Not even the silver touch of moonlight lent these blocks of crumbling stucco apartment houses any majesty or beauty. The rats didn't even bother to hide. They squatted red-eyed on the unmown lawns amidst beer cans and broken bottles and wrappers from Taco John's. And used condoms that looked like deflated mushrooms.

Mike stood behind a tree.

"I followed him around back," he said. "He went up the fire escape on the back. Then he jumped on this veranda. He's in the back apartment on the right side. Neil's in the backyard, watching for him."

Mike looked down at my ball bat. "That's a nice complement," he said. Then he showed me his handgun. "To this."

"Why the hell did you bring that?"

"Are you kidding? You're the one who said he killed Bob."

That, I couldn't argue with.

"All right," I said, "but what happens when we catch him?"

"We tell him to lay off us," Mike said.

"We need to go to the cops."

"Oh, sure. Sure we do." He shook his head. He looked as if he was dealing with a child. A very slow one. "Aaron, going to the cops now won't bring Bob back. And it's only going to get us in trouble."

That's when we heard the shout. Neil; sounded like Neil.

Maybe five feet of rust-colored grass separated us from the alley that ran along the west side of the apartment house.

We ran down the alley, having to hop over an ancient drooping picket fence to reach the backyard where Neil lay sprawled, face down, next to a twenty-year-old Chevrolet that was tireless and up on blocks. Through the windshield, you could see the huge gouges in the seats where the rats had eaten their fill.

The backyard smelled of dog feces and car oil.

Neil was moaning. At least we knew he was alive.

"The punk," he said, when we got him to his feet. "I moved over to the other side, back of the car, so he wouldn't see me if he tried to come down that fire escape. I didn't figure there was another fire escape on the side of the building. He must've come around there and snuck up on me. He tried to kill me but I had this—"

In the moonlight, his wrist and the switchblade knife he held in his fingers were wet and dark with blood. "I got him a couple of times in the arm. Otherwise, I'd be dead."

"We're going up there," Mike said.

"How about checking Neil first?"

"I'm fine," Neil said. "A little headache from where he caught me on the back of the neck." He waved his bloody blade. "Good thing I had this."

The landlord was on the first floor. He wore Bermuda shorts and no shirt. He looked eleven or twelve months pregnant and had enough coarse black hair to knit a sweater with. He had a plastic-tipped cigarillo in the left corner of his mouth.

"Yeah?"

"Two-F," I said.

"What about it?"

"Who lives there?"

"Nobody."

"Nobody?"

"If you were the law, you'd show me a badge."

"I'll show you a badge," Mike said, making a fist.

"Hey," I said, playing good cop to his bad cop. "You just let me speak to this gentleman."

The guy seemed to like my reference to him as a gentleman. It was probably the only name he'd never been called.

"Sir, we saw somebody go up there."

"Oh," he said, "the vampires."

"Vampires?"

He sucked down some cigarillo smoke. "That's what we call 'em, the missus and me. They're street people, winos and homeless and all like that. They know that sometimes some of these apartments ain't rented for a while, so they sneak up there and spend the night."

"You don't stop them?"

"You think I'm gonna get my head split open for something like that?"

"I guess that makes sense." Then: "So nobody's renting it now?"

"Nope, it ain't been rented for three months. This fat broad lived there then. Man, did she smell. You know how fat people can smell sometimes? *She* sure smelled." He wasn't exactly svelte himself.

Back on the front lawn, trying to wend my way between the mounds of dog-doo, I said, " 'Vampires.' Good name for them."

"Yeah, it is," Neil said. "I just keep thinking of the one who died. His weird eyes."

"Here we go again," Mike said. "You two guys love to scare the shit out of each other, don't you? They're a couple of nickel-and-dime crooks, and that's all they are."

"All right if Mike and I stop and get some beer and then swing by your place?"

"Sure," I said. "Just as long as Mike buys Bud and none of that generic crap."

Neil laughed. "Oh, I forgot, he does do that when it's his turn to buy, doesn't he?"

"Yeah," I said, "he certainly does."

I was never sure what time the call came. Darkness. The ringing phone seemed part of a dream from which I couldn't escape. Somehow I managed to lift the receiver before the phone machine kicked in.

Silence. That special kind of silence.

Him. I had no doubt about it. The vampire, as the landlord had called him. The one who'd killed Bob. I didn't say so much as hello. Just listened, angry, afraid, confused.

After a few minutes, he hung up.

Darkness again; deep darkness, the quarter moon in the sky a cold golden scimitar that could cleave a head from a neck.

5.

About noon on Sunday, Jan called to tell me that she was staying a few days extra. The kids had discovered archery and there was a course at the Y they were taking and wouldn't she please please *please* ask good old Dad if they could stay. I said sure.

I called Neil and Mike to remind them that at nine tonight we were going to pay a visit to that crumbling stucco apartment house again.

Around four o'clock *Hombre* was on one of the cable channels so I had a few beers and watched Paul Newman doing the best acting of his career. At least, that was my opinion.

I was just getting ready for the shower when the phone rang.

He didn't say hello. He didn't identify himself. "Tracy call you?"

It was Neil. Tracy was Mike's wife. "Why should she call me?"

"He's dead. Mike."

"What?"

"You remember how he was always bitching about that elevator at work?"

Mike worked in a very old building. He made jokes about the antiquated elevators. But you could always tell the joke simply hid his fears. He'd gotten stuck innumerable times, and it was always stopping several feet short of the upcoming floor.

"He opened the door and the car wasn't there. He fell eight floors."

"Oh God."

"I don't have to tell you who did it, do I?"

"Maybe it's time—"

"I'm way ahead of you, Aaron. I'll pick you up in half an hour. Then we go to the police. You agree?"

"I agree."

Late Sunday afternoon, the second precinct parking lot is pretty empty. We'd missed the shift change. Nobody came or went.

"We ask for a detective," Neil said. He was dark-sportjacket-white-shirt-and-necktie earnest. I'd settled for an expensive blue sport shirt Jan had bought me for my last birthday.

"You know one thing we haven't considered?"

"You're not going to change my mind."

"I'm not *trying* to change your mind, Neil, I'm just saying that there's one thing we haven't considered."

He sat behind his steering wheel, his head resting on the back of his seat.

"A lawyer."

"What for?"

"Because we may go in there and say something that gets us in very deep trouble."

"No lawyers," he said. "We'd just look like we were trying to hide something from the cops."

"You sure about that?"

"I'm sure."

"You ready?" I said.

"Ready."

The interior of the police station was quiet. A muscular bald man in a dark uniform sat behind the information desk.

He said, "Help you?"

"We'd like to see a detective," I said.

"Are you reporting a crime?"

"Uh, yes."

"What sort of crime?"

I started to speak but once again lost my voice. I thought about all the reporters, about how Jan and the kids would be affected by it all. How my job would be affected. Taking a guy down to the basement and tying him up and then accidentally killing him—

Neil said: "Vandalism."

"Vandalism?" the cop said. "You don't need a detective, then. I can just give you a form." Then he gave us a leery look, as if he sensed we'd just changed our minds about something.

"In that case, could I just take it home with me and fill it out there?" Neil said.

"Yeah, I guess." The cop still watched us carefully.

"Great."

"You sure that's what you wanted to report? Vandalism?"

"Yeah; yeah, that's exactly what we wanted to report," Neil said. "Exactly."

"Vandalism?" I said when we were back in the car.

"I don't want to talk right now."

"Well, maybe *I* want to talk."

"I just couldn't do it."

"No kidding."

He looked over at me. "You could've told him the truth. Nobody was stopping you."

I looked out the window. "Yeah, I guess I could've."

"We're going over there tonight. To the vampire's place."

"And do what?"

"Ask him how much he wants."

"How much he wants for what?" I said.

"How much he wants to forget everything. He goes on with his life, we go on with ours."

I had to admit, I'd had a similar thought myself. Neil and I didn't know how to do any of this. But the vampire did. He was good at stalking, good at harassing, good at violence.

"We don't have a lot of money to throw around."

"Maybe he won't *want* a lot of money. I mean, these guys aren't exactly sophisticated."

"They're sophisticated enough to make two murders look like accidents."

"I guess that's a point."

"I'm just not sure we should pay him anything, Neil."

"You got any better ideas?"

I didn't, actually; I didn't have any better ideas at all.

6.

I spent an hour on the phone with Jan that afternoon. The last few days I'd been pretty anxious and she'd sensed it. I had to tell her about their deaths. It was the only way I could explain my tense mood.

"That's awful," she said. "Their poor families."

"They're handling it better than you might think."

"Maybe I should bring the kids home early."

"No reason to, hon. I mean, realistically there isn't anything any of us can do."

"Two accidents in that short a time. It's pretty strange."

"Yeah, I guess it is. But that's how it happens sometimes."

"Are you going to be all right?"

"Just need to adjust is all." I sighed. "I guess we won't be having our poker games anymore."

Then I did something I hadn't intended. I started crying and the tears caught in my throat.

"Oh, honey," Jan said. "I wish I was there so I could give you a big hug."

"I'll be okay."

"Two of your best friends."

"Yeah." The tears were starting to dry up now.

"Maybe you should go do something to take your mind off things. Is there a good movie on?"

"I guess I could check."

"Something light, that's what you need."

"Sounds good," I said. "I'll go get the newspaper and see what's on."

"Love you."

"Love you, too, sweetheart," I said.

I spent the rest of the afternoon going through my various savings accounts and investments, trying to figure out what the creep would want to leave us alone. I settled on five thousand dollars. That was the maximum cash I had to play with. And even then I'd have to borrow a little from one of the mutual funds we had earmarked for the kids and college.

Five thousand dollars. To me, it sounded like an enormous amount of money, probably because I knew how hard I'd had to work to get it.

But would it be enough for our friend the vampire?

Neil was there just at dark. He parked in the drive and came in. Meaning he wanted to talk.

We went in the kitchen. I made us a couple of highballs and we sat there and discussed finances.

"I came up with six thousand," he said.

"I got five."

"That's eleven grand," he said. "It's got to be more cash than this creep has ever seen."

"What if he takes it and comes back for more?"

"We make it absolutely clear," Neil said, "that there is no more. That this is it. Period."

"And if not?"

Neil nodded. "I've thought this through. You know the kind of lowlife we're dealing with? A) He's a burglar, which means, these days, that he's a junkie. B) If he's a junkie, then that means he's very susceptible to AIDS. So between being a burglar and shooting up, this guy is probably going to have a very short lifespan."

"I guess I'd agree."

"Even if he wants to make our life miserable, he probably won't live long enough to do it. So I think we'll be making just the one payment. We'll buy enough time to let nature take its course—his nature."

"What if he wants more than the eleven grand?"

"He won't. His eyes'll pop out when he sees this."

I looked at the kitchen clock. It was going on nine now.

"I guess we could drive over there."

"It may be a long night," Neil said.

"I know."

"But I guess we don't have a hell of a lot of choice, do we?"

As we'd done the last time we'd been here, we split up the duties. I took the backyard, Neil the apartment door. We'd waited until midnight. The rap music had died down by now. Babies cried and mothers screamed; couples fought. TV screens flickered in dark windows.

I went up the fire escape slowly and carefully. We'd talked about bringing guns and then decided against it. We weren't exactly marksmen, and if a cop stopped us for some reason, we could be arrested for carrying unlicensed firearms. All I carried was a flashlight in my back pocket.

As I grabbed the rungs of the ladder, powdery rust dusted my hands. I was chilly with sweat. My bowels felt sick. I was scared. I just wanted it to be over with. I wanted him to say yes, he'd take the money, and then that would be the end of it.

The stucco veranda was filled with discarded toys—a tricycle, innumerable games, a space helmet, a whiffle bat and ball. The floor was crunchy with dried animal feces. At least, I hoped the feces belonged to animals and not human children.

The door between veranda and apartment was open. Fingers of moonlight revealed an overstuffed couch and chair and a floor covered with the debris of fast food: McDonald's sacks, Pizza Hut wrappers and cardboards, Arby's wrappers, and what seemed to be five or six dozen empty beer cans. In the hall that led to the front door I saw four red eyes watching me: a pair of curious rats.

I stood still and listened. Nothing. No sign of life. I went inside. Tiptoeing.

I went to the front door and let Neil in. There in the murky light of the hallway, he made a face. The smell *was* pretty bad.

Over the next ten minutes, we searched the apartment. And found nobody.

"We could wait here for him," I said.

"No way."

"The smell?"

"The smell, the rats; God, don't you just feel unclean?"

"Yeah, guess I do."

"There's an empty garage about halfway down the alley. We'd have a good view of the back of this building."

"Sounds pretty good."

"Sounds better than this place, anyway."

This time, we both went out the front door and down the stairway. Now the smells were getting to me as they'd earlier gotten to Neil. Unclean. He was right.

We got in Neil's Buick, drove down the alley that ran along the west side of the apartment house, backed up to the dark garage, and whipped inside.

"There's a sack in back," Neil said. "It's on your side."

"A sack?"

"Brewskis. Quart for you, quart for me."

"That's how my old man used to drink them," I said. I was the only blue-collar member of the poker-game club. "Get off work at the plant and stop by and pick up two quart bottles of Hamms. Never missed."

I wish I could tell you that I knew what it was right away, the missile that hit the windshield and shattered and starred it, and then kept right on tearing through the car until the back window was also shattered and starred.

But all I knew was that Neil was screaming and I was screaming and my quart bottle of Miller's was spilling all over my crotch as I tried to hunch down behind the dashboard. It was a tight fit because Neil was trying to hunch down behind the steering wheel.

The second time, I knew what was going on: Somebody was shooting at us. Given the trajectory of the bullet, he had to be right in front of us, probably behind the two dumpsters that sat on the other side of the alley.

"Can you keep down and drive this son of a bitch at the same time?"

"I can try," Neil said.

"If we sit here much longer, he's going to figure out we don't have guns. Then he's gonna come for us for sure."

Neil leaned over and turned on the ignition. "I'm going to turn left when we get out of here."

"Fine. Just get moving."

"Hold on."

What he did was kind of slump over the bottom half of
the wheel, just enough so he could sneak a peek at where
the car was headed.

There were no more shots.

All I could hear was the smooth-running Buick motor.

He eased out of the garage, ducking down all the time.

When he got a chance, he bore left.

He kept the lights off.

Through the bullet hole in the windshield I could see an
inch or so of starry sky.

It was a long alley and we must have gone a quarter
block before he said, "I'm going to sit up. I think we lost
him."

"So do I."

"Look at that frigging windshield."

Not only was the windshield a mess, the car reeked of
spilled beer.

"You think I should turn on the headlights?"

"Sure," I said. "We're safe now."

We were still crawling at maybe ten miles per hour when
he pulled the headlights on.

That's when we saw him, silver of eye, dark of hair,
crouching in the middle of the alley waiting for us. He was a
good fifty yards ahead of us but we were still within range.

There was no place we could turn around.

He fired.

This bullet shattered whatever had been left untouched
of the windshield. Neil slammed on the brakes.

Then he fired a second time.

By now, both Neil and I were screaming and cursing
again.

A third bullet.

"Run him over!" I yelled, ducking behind the dashboard.

"What?" Neil yelled back.

"Floor it!"

He floored it. He wasn't even sitting up straight. We might have gone careening into one of the garages or dumpsters. But somehow the Buick stayed in the alley. And very soon it was traveling eighty-five miles per hour. I watched the speedometer peg it.

More shots, a lot of them now, side windows shattering, bullets ripping into fender and hood and top.

I didn't see us hit him but I *felt* us hit him, the car traveling that fast, the creep so intent on killing us he hadn't bothered to get out of the way in time.

The front of the car picked him up and hurled him into a garage near the head of the alley.

We both sat up, watched as his entire body was broken against the edge of the garage, and he then fell smashed and unmoving to the grass.

"Kill the lights," I said.

"What?"

"Kill the lights and let's go look at him."

Neil punched off the headlights.

We left the car and ran over to him.

A white rib stuck bloody and brazen from his side. Blood poured from his ears, nose, mouth. One leg had been crushed and also showed white bone. His arms had been broken, too.

I played my flashlight beam over him.

He was dead, all right.

"Looks like we can save our money," I said. "It's all over now."

"I want to get the hell out of here."

"Yeah," I said. "So do I."

We got the hell out of there.

7.

A month later, just as you could smell autumn on the summer winds, Jan and I celebrated our twelfth wedding anniversary. We drove up to Lake Geneva, in Wisconsin, and stayed at a very nice hotel and rented a Chris-Craft for a couple of days. This was the first time I'd been able to relax since the thing with the burglar had started.

The funny thing was, I didn't see Neil much anymore. It was as if the sight of each other brought back a lot of bad memories.

Not that I made any new friends. The notion of a mid-week poker game had lost all its appeal. There was work and my family and little else.

Then one sunny Indian Summer afternoon, Neil called and said, "Maybe we should get together again."

"Maybe."

"It's over, Aaron. It really is."

"I know."

"Will you at least think about it?"

I felt embarrassed. "Oh, hell, Neil. Is that swimming pool of yours open Saturday afternoon?"

"As a matter of fact, it is. And as a matter of fact, Sarah and the girls are going to be gone to a fashion show at the club."

"Perfect. We'll have a couple of beers."

"You know how to swim?"

"No," I said, laughing. "And from what Sarah says, you don't, either."

I got there about three, pulled into the drive, walked to the back where the gate in the wooden fence led to the swimming pool. It was eighty degrees and even from here I could smell the chlorine.

I opened the gate and went inside and saw him right away. The funny thing was, I didn't have much of a reaction at all. I just watched him. He was floating. Face down. He looked pale in his red trunks. This, like the others, would be judged an accidental death. Of that I had no doubt at all.

I used the cellular phone in my car to call 911.

I didn't want Sarah and the girls coming back to see an ambulance and police cars in the drive and them not knowing what was going on. I called the club and had her paged.

I told her what I'd found. I let her cry. I didn't know what to say. I never do.

In the distance, I could hear the ambulance working its way toward the Neil Solomon residence.

I was about to get out of the car when my cellular phone rang.

I picked up. "Hello?"

"There were three of us that night at your house, Mr. Bellini. You killed two of us. I recovered from when your friend stabbed me, remember? Now I'm ready for action. I really am, Mr. Bellini."

Then the emergency people were there, and neighbors, too, and then wan, trembling Sarah. I just let her cry some more. Gave her whiskey and let her cry.

8.

He knows how to do it, whoever he is.

He lets a long time go between late-night calls. He lets me start to think that maybe he changed his mind and left town. And then he calls.

Oh yes, he knows just how to play this little game.

He never says anything, of course. He doesn't need to. He just listens. And then hangs up.

I've considered going to the police, of course, but it's way too late for that. Way too late.

Or I could ask Jan and the kids to move away to a different city with me. But he knows who I am and he'd find me again.

So all I can do is wait and hope that I get lucky, the way Neil and I got lucky the night we killed the second of them.

Tonight I can't sleep.

It's after midnight.

Jan and I wrapped presents until well after eleven. She asked me again if anything was wrong. We don't make love as much as we used to, she said; and then there are the nightmares. Please tell me if something's wrong, Aaron. Please.

I stand at the window watching the snow come down. Soft and beautiful snow. In the morning, a Saturday, the kids will make a snowman and then go sledding and then have themselves a good old-fashioned snowball fight, which invariably means that one of them will come rushing in at some point and accuse the other of some terrible misdeed.

I see all this from the attic window.

Then I turn back and look around the poker table. Four empty chairs. Three of them belong to dead men.

I look at the empty chairs and think back to summer.

I look at the empty chairs and wait for the phone to ring.

I wait for the phone to ring.